FILTHY SINNER

THE SINNERS & FIVE POINTS' MOB CROSSOVER
NOVEL

SERENA AKEROYD

FOREWORD & TRIGGER WARNINGS

DEAR READER,

Some books are healing.

You might be reading this author's note years after the book's release, so I'll give you some context.

It's January 2023.

I've just released *Filthy Lies* and *Filthy Truth*, the final books in *The Five Points' Mob Collection.*

It's funny to think that, years down the line, people will be reading this book *before* those two—the advantage, I suppose, of binge-reading once a series is complete. ;)

However, this book… these characters… something about them has healed me. I think it's the hopefulness written within the story. A chance taken, an opportunity snatched, and the rewards go to those who dared to *try*.

I hope you enjoy this story as much as I enjoyed writing it.

You should know that there is mention of rape and sexual abuse against women as a means of forcing marriage. There are also scenes of violence and references to bullying as well as memories of violent parental abuse.

NONE OF THIS OCCURS BETWEEN THE MAIN CHARACTERS.

May this make the book hangover from *Filthy Lies* and *Filthy Truth* that much easier to bear. <3

Much love to you all,

Serena

xo

PLAYLIST

If you'd like to hear a curated soundtrack, with songs that are featured in the book, as well as songs that inspired it, then here's the link:

https://open.spotify.com/playlist/3XRCAZfgmq5RfwSnW9fl8E?si=6f9a54a0ca3c4944

THE CROSSOVER READING ORDER
WITH THE SINNERS & VALENTINIS

FILTHY
FILTHY SINNER
NYX
LINK
FILTHY RICH
SIN
STEEL
FILTHY DARK
CRUZ
MAVERICK
FILTHY SEX
HAWK
FILTHY HOT
STORM
THE DON
THE LADY
FILTHY SECRET
REX
RACHEL

FILTHY KING
REVELATION BOOK ONE
REVELATION BOOK TWO
FILTHY LIES
FILTHY TRUTH

Please be advised that the first half of the book has been **HEAVILY EXTENDED** since its original inclusion in *A Naughty MC Christmas Anthology*. **So,** *please*, **do NOT skip the first half.**

MARY CATHERINE

MARY CATHERINE

I WAS sixteen when I first saw the bikers.

Primarily, I noticed their rides outside our house in Westchester, where Daddy never stayed anymore and I had to hole up with Mother in suburban hell until he hauled us into the city for our 'family duties.' I.e., church with Father Doyle and his endless sermons.

Bleugh.

It was a surreal sight to behold, though.

Amid the pristine prettiness of 'Stepford Wife Lane,' the royal blue bike was riderless, but the owner had dared to drive over our lawn, leaving tire tracks behind that showed the earth beneath.

Mother was going to have a literal cow over that.

As for the other bike, it was a stark, bright red with a fire pattern on its body. The rider had been considerate, however. He was currently parked on the driveway, his head tilted down as he stared at his cell phone.

With that tousled mop of hair, he should've looked dirty, but he didn't. Oh, his hair was definitely tangled and in need of a brush, and combined with the bushy beard, he certainly wasn't as elegantly attired as I was used to guys appearing.

Perhaps that was why he caught my eye and why I couldn't stop staring as I walked toward my house.

With every step I took, the more I could see of him.

That mop on his head, which should have been a deterrent, doubled his appeal, and the massive biceps and how he filled out a Henley helped matters too. Enough that my curiosity at the reason behind the bikers' presence in my driveway was minimal.

More focused on trying to catch as many glimpses of the stranger's face as possible, I didn't think about things like security or my mother's safety...

That was when my BFF reminded me that we were on the phone together.

"Why are you ignoring me when *you* called *me*?"

"I'm not ignoring you, Sarah," I breathed. "There's the hottest guy in the world sitting in my driveway."

"Sitting *in* your driveway," she repeated. "What is he? A traveling salesman?"

My lips twitched as I studied the bike. "I don't know what he'd be selling if he were."

"How hot is he? Jensen-hot or Harry Styles-hot?"

I mock-gagged. "Jensen isn't hot. I don't care if he's the star QB or not."

"His ass is beautiful."

"Asses aren't beautiful."

"I swear you're asexual."

"Not a crime, is it?" I snapped, even though I'd often thought the same thing about myself.

Well, until today.

Until this gorgeous specimen crossed my path.

"He's Charlie Hunnam-hot," I muttered, not letting her answer me.

She whistled. "Take a picture?"

The tapping of my heels against the sidewalk finally drew the man's attention, and when our eyes clashed and held, I was sure I felt that connection in my soul.

God, had there ever been browner eyes?

They were both hard and soft, piercing yet uber aware.

"I can't take a picture," I gasped, trying to catch my breath. "He can see me."

"Are you having an asthma attack?"

I didn't think so, but it was only because she was marring the moment with her commentary.

For a second, with his gaze locked on mine, the link between us burned brightly, a solid connection that settled inside me.

That made something burn to life in my belly.

That made my nipples tighten.

Then his glance drifted, flying over my prep-school uniform, and I felt his dismissal to my bones.

Interest averted now that he saw I was jailbait, the stranger returned his focus to his cell phone.

Though disappointed, I appreciated the fact that he wasn't a pervert. Plus, it gave me the chance to take in the ink on his throat and how his fingers were loaded with more tattoos. It let me absorb just how massive he was, those muscles in his shoulders bulging in a way that made me want to melt. Then, there was his size.

He was a giant.

He'd probably be able to lift me up with one hand.

Swoon.

"He has muscles on top of muscles on top of muscles, Sarah," I keened.

"Picture or it didn't happen."

I heaved a sigh. "Then it didn't happen."

"Share the spoils."

"Nope."

That was when the front door burst open.

Another biker, this one with a buzz cut, stormed out of the house, slamming the door closed behind him with such force that I thought the front windows shuddered in response to his wrath.

"Jesus Christ! What was that?" Sarah demanded.

The stranger's rage simmered along the airwaves, a visceral force that replaced my curiosity with fear. That cooled my budding arousal instantly.

What the hell had I been thinking by walking toward the unfamiliar, scary biker and not running far, far away?

Daddy wasn't here to protect us anymore.

It wasn't like he could come racing after this stranger to defend us all the way from Hell's Kitchen. Heck, he might not have cared if I *did* contact him.

Mother had a guard, but because she spent most of her time at home drinking, he usually went off and did his own thing, and she never said a word because it meant she could bang the pool guy without it coming to Daddy's attention. That mattered since he'd moved out and her allowance was under threat.

As for the neighbors, sure, they'd see what was happening, but would they care? Mother wasn't popular and, by extension, neither was I.

Should I call the cops?

The bikers didn't seem to have done anything wrong, but they'd...

Why was he in my house?

Why was the second one waiting outside?

"MARY CATHERINE! What was that noise?"

"My front door. I-I, someone, I, he—"

"Speak English."

"Stop being a bitch," I retorted, but, much as always, she calmed me down.

The new guy didn't notice me, but I couldn't avoid noticing him. He sucked the oxygen from the air itself, much as my mother did when she was in one of her tempers.

As terrifying as his wrath was, what stole the breath from my lungs were the similarities between the biker and my grandfather.

"What the hell?" I whispered with a shaky exhalation.

"What is it?"

"This guy just came out of my house. He's the one who slammed the front door closed. He's an exact replica of my grandad."

"The Vietnam veteran?"

"Yeah."

We had pictures of Grandad fresh from 'Nam: head shaved, eyes haunted, body rippling with muscles but somehow gaunt too. As if something were eating him alive.

This guy was the same.

It was even stranger because his current facial expression, as well as his features, were all my mother's. Which, to be frank, would explain the matching tempers if nothing else.

Finally, he glanced at me, but there was zero acknowledgment there. His dismissal was more abrupt than his friend's.

Unlike the other guy, I didn't mind escaping his attention.

Yet, as I wondered who the hell he was and why he was storming out of my house like he'd left a fire in his wake, he was jumping onto his bike, kicking his foot against the stand, and a second later, the engine was roaring to life with the iconic rumble that could only be...

"Was that a Harley?" Sarah blurted in my ear.

"Let's get the fuck out of here," the guy shouted, riding off.

That was when I saw the back of his leather vest which declared *Satan's Sinners' MC, Mother Chapter, West Orange* to the world.

The other guy tucked his cell phone away and, without a single glance at me, took off as well.

With faint wistfulness, aware I'd never see him again, I watched the guy go, noticing that his vest sported the Sinners' patch too.

West Orange? I knew that town.

"When you said he looked like Charlie Hunnam, what you really meant was that he's Jax Teller in the flesh," she teased.

"A brown-haired one," I muttered as the world returned to normal around me.

"Can't believe you didn't send me a picture," she said with a pout, but I ignored her.

In under five minutes, the boring 'burbs had been stirred to life before the vibrancy of the unusual faded away, shifting it back to the perpetual state of deadly dullness.

Of course, when I thought about that biker's wrathful expression, *deadly* might be more apt than I realized.

"He was so angry," I murmured in a daze. "So like Mother."

"Could they be related? A cousin or something?"

"I don't think so. But, maybe?"

"If they have matching tempers, can you imagine the argument you missed?" She released a heavy exhalation. "Didn't she throw a vase at your dad the last time they argued?"

I nodded, though she couldn't see it. "He moved out the next day."

Mother hadn't hurt the biker—I'd seen no sign of injury on his person.

Had the stranger who shared my features hurt *her*?

"Your mom could piss off a Buddhist monk."

I had to snort. "And make a saint pull out their hair."

My brain whirred as Sarah demanded, "It's one thing for someone who looks *and* acts like Miss American Bitchface to come racing out of your house, but bikers? And, why were the Charlie Hunnam and Grandad impostors at your place?"

"How should I know?"

"Are you safe, Mary Catherine? Should I call the cops?"

I rubbed my forehead. "No! They've gone now. You heard their bikes."

I wasn't sure why I did it, had no real idea what made me retrace my steps to the bus stop, but my body took control of the situation for me.

"It's taking you a while to get to the house," Sarah said dubiously. "What's going on?"

"I'm not going inside. Yet."

"Huh. Why not?"

Could I tell her?

Should I?

"You know I hate her."

"She's a bitch. Everyone hates her," was Sarah's dismissive retort. "I bet God hates her too."

I ignored that. "What if he killed her?" Sarah fell silent so I continued, "You didn't see his face—"

"Because you didn't take a picture."

"No, it was Grandad, not Charlie. Grandad-guy was furious, Sarah. Honestly, just like how Mother gets."

"What are you thinking?"

"Maybe he killed her," I said in a rush.

"I think that's wishful thinking, Mary Catherine," was my best friend's dubious yet judgment-free response. "Everyone wants our bullies to drop dead, but no matter how hard we pray, it never comes true. Elizabeth Ferrier would have died five years ago if that were the case."

I grimaced because she was right, but how often did anyone from a group called the 'Satan's Sinners' come to Westchester?

Maybe it was my lucky day.

"So, what? You're taking the long route home so that if she's in the middle of croaking it, you can't fuck things up by saving her?"

My cheeks tinged bright red—the curse of being auburn. "When you put it like that, it sounds bad."

She snorted. "Because it is?" Still no judgment, though.

It let me whisper, "I'd be free of her."

"Ugh. True. She's such a bitch. She has everyone but me hating you in school."

Hurt washed through me as I started back toward the house. "I know."

"And at church, they all avoid you like you have leprosy."

"I'm well aware," I grumbled. "You don't need to rub salt in the wound."

"Just keeping it real." She hummed. "Hey, if the bitch *is* dead, you'd be able to move in with your dad. And we'd be closer. His house is only two blocks away from mine."

The hurt faded and was replaced with hope. "That would be awesome."

"On the other hand, if the biker *did* kill her, then you're fucked because you're a loose end."

"That's tomorrow's problem."

She snickered. "It's a pretty big problem but I'll hide you under my bed. Don't worry."

My smile was feeble. "Either way, if she's dead or not, it's best if she doesn't know that I saw what I saw."

"I don't know what you saw."

"Me either, but she wouldn't have wanted me to see it. Whatever it was."

"Confusing."

"Definitely. But you know what she's like."

"Spiteful? Cruel? Vindictive? Makes the Wicked Witch of the West look warm and cuddly?"

"Yeah. All that. But she's secretive as heck too." I sucked in a breath as I walked along the garden path toward the front door. "I'm here," I mumbled. "I'd better go."

"Keep me on the line. If she's dead and you have to find her body, you'll need moral support."

I had to reason that both of us were so blasé about my mother's potential murder because we were the spawn of the Irish Mob—the Five Points.

Well, that, and Mother truly was horrible.

I didn't think Father Doyle liked her and he was a priest—he had to treat everyone with the same amount of disdain apart from Uncle Aidan, the head of the Five Points, of course.

"Okay, I'm going in."

"One small step for man," Sarah teased, "one giant step for Mary Catherine."

Ignoring her, I opened the door then called out, "I'm home!"

There was silence.

My heart started pounding.

Hope spilled inside me.

"Maybe she *is* dead?" Sarah whispered. "Just think, with her gone, you might make up with your dad?"

Grief splintered inside me.

Sarah had a habit of hitting the nail on the head. If I didn't love her, I'd probably hate her for her candor.

"He sees her when he looks at me," I whispered miserably. "All the stunts she's pulled and everything she's done to hurt him... I-I remind him of all that. The affairs and the arguments and the harsh words. The spite and the laziness and the bitterness." I bit my lip. "She's hell to live with. I never blamed him for moving out."

"I mean, I didn't either, but it sucks that he ignores you like he does. It's so irrational to pin her shit on you just because you inherited her DNA."

I didn't disagree, but Sarah had only heard about everything Mother had done secondhand. She hadn't witnessed it for herself.

When I heard Mother's stiletto heels clattering against the marble tiles, my heart sank. That noise came first as those spindly shoes clacked down the hall.

"Ah, shit. I hear her shoes. Fuck." Sarah sighed noisily in my ear. "Maybe next time?"

I swallowed. "Maybe. I gotta go."

"Call me later?"

"Will do."

By the time I was shoving my phone in my pocket, she was there.

Mother was always dressed to impress even though I was the only one who saw her some days.

She kept herself too thin and encouraged me to be the same. Size 0 was too fat for her, but it was starting to weather badly. Her features were looking haggard, and the amount of wine she drank was beginning to creep up on her.

I'd tried to love her, but she wasn't particularly lovable, so I'd stopped when I was five.

Something she reminded me of as she hissed, "You're late!"

My brow furrowed. "Barely. Is it my fault the bus was five minutes behind schedule?"

She narrowed her eyes at me. "What happened? Why was it late?"

"Jeez, I don't know. It just was. There was traffic." I stared at her. "Is everything okay?" She was riled up, and I knew why. Not that she was going to share that with me.

When she hissed some bullshit at me about always being tardy, I knew I'd been wise to play innocent about the bikers in our front yard.

I didn't know why it was a secret, just knew that it was.

She didn't normally give a damn about what time I got home, but today was clearly different thanks to those bikers...

Two days later, when I checked the letters on the stand that Mary, our maid, had placed there when she collected the mail that morning, I saw a bubble-wrapped envelope with my name on it, and I got a 'sort of' answer and a 'sort of' confirmation about why she was worried.

Tucked around a cheap cell phone, there was a slip of paper with a note inscribed on it that read:

You don't know me, but I know you, Mary Catherine.

I'm Padraig. Your half-brother. We've met before, but I doubt you remember.

Anyway, we both know she's insane. You can reach me on the cell phone if you ever need me, but I hope for your sake you never do.

Good luck.

Sin (Padraig)

As much as his letter and his existence rocked my world, he'd never know that that phone would become my lifeline.

That it would be the light at the end of the tunnel...

2

MARY CATHERINE
HYSTERIA - MUSE

MARY CATHERINE

HELL'S KITCHEN, NEW YORK

PRESENT DAY

"IT'S time for you to get married, Mary Catherine."

As crazy as he sounded, and as crazy as I was for not reacting, I knew the rest of my life hinged on this moment.

My reaction to his statement was pivotal.

Over the last few years, Daddy had morphed into Dad then into Father as his bitterness grew, his hatred for my mother alongside it.

As a result, while his declaration should have had me bursting into tears, I remained calm.

Losing my shit would get me nowhere.

So, instead of rushing to the bathroom to puke, and rather than hurling my plate at the wall in a tantrum, I scooped up some chicken noodle soup and raised the spoon to my mouth.

His tone brokered no argument—defiance wouldn't serve a purpose in this interaction. But that didn't mean I was about to roll over and take whatever bullshit he was handing out.

Not this time.

Him dictating what I wore and which college I went to was different than him deciding my future husband.

Swallowing the small puddle of broth on my spoon was like asking me to chug down Niagara Falls, but I managed it then asked, "When?"

He arched a brow at me. "That's your only question?"

"What else is there to ask?" I queried, shooting him a calm, polite smile while trying to exude the elegance he demanded from me.

Elegance he insisted my mother didn't have.

Elegance that appeased him and made him a tolerable dinner partner.

"Who your groom is, of course." When I didn't leap to ask him, he stated, "Bill Murphy."

Inside, I felt everything youthful in me shrivel up as if I were on the brink of death.

He eyed me, a challenge in his expression as if he knew what I was thinking, as if he longed for my reaction.

As if he wanted to punish me for it.

Bill Murphy was closer to sixty than fifty, older than my father by a good ten years, and had six dead wives to his name.

Aside from the rumors of him being a very merry widower, rumors that were pretty goddamn bad on their own, I didn't think he had a reputation for being cruel.

He'd always been pleasant to me when he came over for dinner. By comparison to my father, he'd probably be the lesser evil.

Jesus.

What had I ever done to deserve the *lesser evil?*

I wanted to ask him why he hated me so much, enough to tie me to a man that old, to a man who had married six times already, but he wouldn't answer.

The past taught me that much.

My fate had been sealed a long time ago.

I was a broodmare.

I'd learned that the hard way, but I'd hoped it would be with somebody I knew and who was of my generation, not my grandfather's. Somebody I could at least tolerate.

There were young Five Pointers. Not all of them had a marital history worthy of *The Oprah Winfrey Show*. He could have married me off to Jonny Kendall or Cade Frasier. Men I'd been raised with. Both jackasses and loyal to the Five Points but, because of their ages, due to marry.

That he hadn't chosen them was a punishment in itself.

But the punishment wasn't mine.

Like always, it was aimed at my mother, then at me for daring to share her genes, but she wasn't the one who would be dealing with the aftermath of this.

I was.

This was my future.

She'd already ruined hers by screwing around on my father and now was a prisoner in her own home. By passing on her DNA to me, she might have destroyed my life too...

But I wasn't going to take this lying down.

I refused to.

Carefully, I placed the spoon between my lips and carried on eating the chicken broth.

"Aren't you excited?" he derided, his satisfaction clear even though my lack of reaction appeared to annoy him. "Isn't this what every girl wants? Bill is quite a catch. He's high up in the ranks. You'll be able to rub shoulders with the O'Donnellys as his bride."

"We're related to them. If it hasn't happened by now—" I almost wanted to slap myself for the retort because reminding him of our low status was a recipe for disaster.

Shit.

We *were* related to the leaders of the Five Points—through Mother.

That link should have been enough to have them invite us to all the big events including Finn and Aoife O'Grady's wedding, but we hadn't been because of two or ten fuckups on his part.

He'd been complaining about that ever since. It didn't matter that the day had ended in a bloodbath. He'd just resented the lack of an invitation.

Seeing his ears turn red with rage, quickly, I added, "But of course, you're right. I hope that my marriage will be... I hope..." *Finish the sentence, Mary Catherine. Finish it! Now! Before he gets even more suspicious than he already is.* "I hope it serves our family well."

His eyes widened, and his shoulders straightened. But his mouth didn't pinch, and the usual sight of his anger didn't blast me like flames from a dragon's maw. No, if anything, he stunned me by actually smiling.

It had been so long since I saw that smile that I almost expected him to leap from the table, hand raised to slap me.

But he didn't.

He smiled at me, and it was genuine.

Which was terrifying.

I felt my stomach start churning with nausea as I recognized the precariousness of my situation.

I'd pleased him. Pleasing him was always short-lived.

My 4.0 GPA, the scholarship to NYU, the high grades, and the accolades I'd already started to accrue in my Urban Design and Architecture Studies course—none of those things had earned me a smile.

This did.

Our family's future rested on my ovaries. Ovaries he was going to tie to Bill Murphy.

God help me.

"I'm so pleased you agree," Father drawled, but his tone was content, cordial, and he picked up his spoon and continued eating.

A good sign. The best, actually.

He'd come prepared for an argument, I registered. But I was smarter than him. An argument would get me locked in my bedroom again.

Like the last time.

Being locked in there wouldn't do me any good.

If I wanted out of this, I had to save myself.

"I'll arrange an official meeting between you two," Father intoned.

That he hadn't arranged it already was further proof that he'd expected me to put up a fight that would see me caged in my bedroom for days on end.

The back of my neck turned clammy; my palms grew slick too. I wasn't sure what was going on with my face, but I could only hope that I appeared relatively normal. That I was managing to hide the growing horror at what he was saying, what he was admitting to without words —*he was going to force my compliance.*

My wishes didn't matter to him. My safety didn't either.

God, how I wished I weren't his daughter.

Or Mother's.

Before I'd moved in with him, I thought things would be better than with her. I could never have imagined how cruel he could be, would never have believed that he could be even more vicious than her, but he was.

How perfect they were for each other, and they didn't even know it.

I dropped my hand into my lap and clenched it into a fist so tight that I felt the joints ache as he told me how the next few weeks would go.

First, a meeting between my future groom and me, he shared, followed by an engagement announcement and a party that the O'Donnellys would likely attend.

Then, the banns would be read in church, and as soon as Father Doyle was content this marriage wasn't being rushed along because I was pregnant—God forbid—we'd wed in Saint Patrick's, where all Five Pointers were wed.

I had six weeks at the most to escape.

Six weeks.

As he talked, my mind whirred because I knew I didn't *actually* have six weeks. Six weeks was a luxury that wasn't going to be afforded to me.

Bill Murphy wouldn't wait for the wedding night.

He'd seal the deal before then, compromising me, tying me to him even if I didn't want that, even if...

I sucked in a breath.

No, my consent wasn't required.

Not where this marriage was concerned, nor where my body was.

I sailed through the rest of the evening like I was high. I wished I were. I wished this were the worst downer ever, but it wasn't.

Somehow, despite my internalized distress, I managed to fool him into believing that I wanted what was best for the family.

I'd never known I was that good an actress.

Padraig's cell phone called to me like a siren song that I was pretty sure stopped me from going insane as I ate my dinner.

I finished the bowl of soup, then my main course, leaving behind only the vegetables he knew I loathed—carrots. I even devoured the peach cobbler for dessert and enjoyed a glass of wine with him as I talked about a challenging yet enjoyable lecture I'd had today.

"I'll speak with Bill. You only have a year left. It would be a waste not to complete your degree."

That he believed Bill could stop me from finishing my education was a death knell I heard chiming in my ears.

I felt my entire being freeze and I forced myself to defrost, to drink the last few sips of my wine.

Somehow, I managed to intone, "I'd appreciate that. Thank you."

He smiled at me.

Again.

Evidently, he was appreciative of my gratitude.

Ha.

How I maintained the charade by that point was beyond me. Sweat kept beading on my top lip, and every single one of my flight/fight responses was kicking into high gear when, finally, he dismissed me.

As always, I got to my feet and kissed his cheek. This time more than most, I'd have preferred to slap him.

Like a good little girl, I went upstairs, and even then, I carried on as if I were content with my situation because I was ninety-nine percent sure that he had cameras in there.

The only room that was safe was the bathroom. I didn't think he was that perverted, and he'd yet to call my bluff because I stored some things in the toilet tank.

I was, however, sure he'd had the bookshelves on either side of the bathroom door bugged, which meant that I couldn't have secret phone calls anymore.

All this because I dared to have a boyfriend.

All this because senior year, I started dating a non-Five Pointer.

My life had been a nightmare ever since.

Remembering how the doctor had checked my hymen, shame and revulsion crawled over me as I knew that would be expected of me again.

But Bill would've broken that sliver of tissue by that point and would use that to tie me to him.

I knew how this worked.

Knew it because Sarah had gone through it last year. Which took her out of the running for helping me. She was as stuck in this game as I was—we were pawns in a chess match that we should've dominated as queens.

But I refused to be a pawn.

I'd take rook or knight over queen, and I'd save my own damn ass if Padraig wouldn't help me.

It was just a matter of planning.

As always, after dinner, I worked on my homework. I gave the cameras a show just in case he was watching, and then, as usual, I headed into the bathroom and changed into workout gear.

I longed to reach for the cell in the toilet tank, but I didn't.

That would break my routine.

After forty minutes of yoga, sweaty and in need of a shower, I did as I'd been longing to since his initial declaration.

Once the bathroom door was locked behind me, I took off the lid to the toilet and found the Ziploc bag in there which housed the cell phone Padraig had given me all those years ago.

Carefully placing it on the toilet seat, I returned the lid to the tank and then let the bag dry off as I darted into the shower for a quick wash.

I knew it was crazy, but I headed over to the door with my toothbrush in my mouth and almost made my gums bleed as I brushed them hard enough to be audible to the mics.

Then, I let the water run as I gargled to further cover the noise of me opening the bag, and only when the cell phone was tucked into the pocket of my pajama pants did I breathe a sigh of relief.

I finished up in the bathroom, feeling the comforting presence of the cell phone against my side as I got into bed.

It would need charging, and between now and then, I'd have to develop a strategy to escape my guards' attention while I was in class, but that was for tonight when I was supposed to be sleeping.

Tomorrow, I'd rewrite my fate.

Tomorrow, I'd take back what was rightfully mine—my future.

3

DIGGER

DIGGER

"I THOUGHT the whole point of getting high was to be high," I grumbled at Sin, who shrugged.

A shrug was pretty much the only answer any of us had right now when it came to Storm, who was the club's VP and pretty much the daddy of the council if daddies thought tough love was how discipline worked...

Which made this current fuckfest even more interesting.

'Daddies' had their shit together. Storm was currently on a downer. In the worst way.

Take now.

The VP was plunked on the floor, his back to the corner of the wall, shoulders hunched, gaze trained on his phone. If he'd started sobbing, I wouldn't have been fucking surprised.

I didn't need to walk over there to see that he was looking at pictures of his family. A family that, well, nobody knew what the hell was going on with.

These were the facts:

Storm was head over fucking heels for his Old Lady, to the point of obsession—and I'd know more than most seeing as I'd officiated their wedding.

Yet for some reason, Storm was staying here and not at his home with his beautiful wife and daughter.

The deflated whoopee cushion that was shaped like our VP spent most of his day mooning over his camera roll like he couldn't go home, but I knew for a fact he could because Keira hadn't tossed him out. At least, not yet. If he carried on like this, getting high and wasting away on the clubhouse floor, shit wasn't going to last.

Storm's breakdown wasn't just causing problems with his wife, either.

The clubhouse was in disarray because a lot of the tasks he handled had been shuffled around the MC. As a result, we were all grumbling and groaning about the extra work while trying not to drop the ball.

Bitching was one thing; letting the club down was another.

We were family. One of our own was fucked in the head, so we had to make things right as best we could.

You rallied around loved ones when they were at their lowest, and for all that Storm was drifting from one high to another, I'd never seen him lower than this.

Letting my gaze dart away from the VP, I saw Sin was watching him too as he muttered, "Can you take my shift at the gate so that I can handle the shit in town for him?"

I nodded. "No worries. Why's Rex got you on the gate, anyway?"

"That Prospect, Cruz, has got gut rot."

Pulling a face, I asked, "Your business in town have anything to do with those guns being trucked into the city?"

Sin shot me a smirk. "That would be telling, wouldn't it?"

I snorted, but accustomed to the secrecy, especially when jobs were assigned by the council, I didn't give him any crap. There wasn't much point.

Sure, I'd have preferred to be more involved and to take a deeper cut, but there was time for that.

Considering the setbacks I'd had, I figured I was advancing nicely in the Satan's Sinners' MC hierarchy.

Both of us finished off our beers, and we parted ways at the bar's entrance, him going to the main office—the place where Rex, our Prez, reigned supreme—and me heading to the gatehouse. That was when I noticed the bike of our Enforcer—Nyx—was out and the saddlebags were stuffed full.

Eyes narrowed at the sight, I stretched, letting some of the meager sunlight from the chilly day beat into my bones.

After a short stroll down the driveway, I clapped Jackson on the back in greeting. He'd heard my booted feet against the gravel and had come out to meet me, eager to hand over the tedious as fuck duty.

"It's okay, brother, you can go and get some rest now."

Wearily, Jackson complained, "Jesus, it's been a long morning."

That was the boredom.

Anyone who had guarded these gates, which was pretty much everyone as it was a basic job that each brother was tasked with at some point, knew how fucking soul-sucking it was to just hover beside them, waiting for somebody or nobody to show up.

It was an important duty but boring all the same. We had alarms and other kinds of security systems in place, but it was tradition to have somebody standing at the gate, waiting to let brothers in and to keep enemies out.

Jackson wasn't in a talking mood, mostly he just yawned as he trudged toward the clubhouse, leaving me to shuffle inside the gatehouse, where I perched my ass on the uncomfortable armchair that had more springs sprung than were held in place.

Kicking my feet up against the wall, I crossed them at the ankle and decided that wasting time on my phone was the only way to go.

I'd have preferred to have been in on whatever business Sin was handling for the council, but I got it. Not only was he older than me, he had an in with the council even though he wasn't a part of it.

His father, though a son of a bitch, was MC royalty. Grizzly might have been a fucker, but Rex and Bear, Rex's dad, were all about family loyalty.

Kendra: Where are you? Wanna hang out?

When the clubwhore sent a picture of her pussy to me, I rolled my eyes, deleted the shot of her cunt, and ignored her.

Wishing that I'd grabbed my iPad before I'd come down to the gatehouse, instead, I went through the photos on my camera, deciding which one I'd be replicating in a few hours' time.

Nobody knew that I was into art, and I wanted to keep it that way. My brothers already gave me crap about being a nosy bastard—like I could help ferreting out the truth—but adding on the art stuff was more than I wanted to deal with on the regular.

My brothers—Rex, in particular—weren't dumb fucks, but we led simple lives. Sure, there was a lot of violence and crime tucked away in our schedules, but we existed for our hogs. Lived for the freedom of flying down the highway, no one yanking our chains other than the council we entrusted our futures to and the men we chose to be our kin.

Art wasn't simple. Art wasn't about riding down Route 66 just for the sheer fuck of it.

And my stuff wasn't technically necessary. I knew what people would ask. Why replicate a photo when the photo was enough?

I had no answer, but I liked doing it. Storm liked getting high, Nyx liked killing pedophiles, and me? Well, I just liked duplicating a photograph with a number two pencil.

It wasn't as if my hobby were illegal. It didn't hurt anybody and didn't ruin lives—even if some lives deserved to be ruined.

A few hours later, I'd welcomed five brothers back home and had watched Sin join a small run as they left for 'town.'

Fucking bullshitter.

No way they were just heading into West Orange. Not with their saddlebags bulging so much. And not with Link, our Road Captain, and Steel, our Secretary, tucked into Nyx's mix.

Did Sin think I was an idiot?

Whatever.

"Sorting out shit in town, my ass," I muttered to myself.

Still, it got me thinking about how hush-hush the council had been recently.

Me: Something going on that I should know about?

It was a risky move, as the Prez didn't owe me jack.

Rex: No? You talking about anything in particular?

Me: Dunno. Just making sure everything's copacetic.

Rex: You're a fucking worrier.

Me: Storm's high, and Nyx, Link, Steel, and Sin just headed off to play hunt the monster under the bed...

Me: Just saying, that's a big chunk of the council on the road or compromised.

Rex: Is it your job to worry about this?

Me: No.

Rex: So, don't.

Rex: If you need something to worry about, I can always dump extra work on your shoulders...

Me: Whatever you need.

Rex: You always fucking surprise me, Digger.

Me: What can I say? It's a talent.

Rex: Where are you?

Me: Guarding the gates.

Rex: Ahhh. So you're bored shitless, lol. No need to question where this is coming from. I wondered who Sin dumped that job on.

> Me: Dumbfuck me.

> Rex: Wouldn't say you were a dumbfuck. Too trusting… sure.

> Me: ME? ROFL.

> Rex: Hehe. Yeah, you.

> Rex: Fuck off, anyway. I'm busy.

> Rex: All is right with the world and you don't have to worry your pretty little head about nothing.

> Me: You say the sweetest shit.

> Rex: Don't I fucking know it. And it's wasted on you motherfuckers.

> Me: :P

It was second nature for me to dig—it was how I'd earned my road name. But Rex's assurance did offset some of my curiosity.

By not saying anything, he'd pretty much confirmed what I thought. Nyx *was* on a pedo hunt, and I wasn't sorry about not being invited.

Even if the bastards deserved to be tortured, that wasn't how I got my kicks.

Sin had anger issues and had even… Well, beating men to death wasn't outside of his capabilities, that was all I would say about that.

And still, it would make sense why Sin had to keep quiet. Storm was one of the guys who usually accompanied Nyx, but with him being so down and out of it, it would make sense for Nyx to drag Sin into this sorry business of his.

No longer wishing that I'd been called up to help and preferring this dry as a desert task, seeing as this wouldn't get my ass hauled back in jail, I finally settled on a picture of a snake that I found in the yard two days ago.

I was going to graft two photographs together. The snake had been hidden among wet leaves under a bush in the yard, but I was going to have it lying somewhere a lot more interesting... I just wasn't sure where. Somewhere a lot more atmospheric than under a bush, that was for sure. I just didn't have a suitable picture yet.

No one else came or went over the next couple hours, so I switched from how I'd been passing the time when I was free to do whatever I wanted and had moved on to a game. It was then that I heard the engine, one that was definitely not a hog.

There was very little traffic in this part of West Orange because we owned most of this hill, and there was only one property above us which belonged to the MC's lawyer, Rachel Laker.

She had a house there where she lived with her brother, Rain, and part of her law practice was on that compound. But I recognized her SUV, knew her engine, and was well aware that this vehicle wasn't hers.

People didn't get lost up here, so I knew we had a visitor.

Getting to my feet, I left the gatehouse behind. Tucking my cell phone into my pocket, I shuffled outside, finding a run-of-the-mill yellow cab from the city idling beyond the gates.

When a young woman climbed out of the back, I knew immediately who it was.

Maybe it was the artist in me, maybe it was the man who recognized a beautiful woman, or maybe it was simply somebody who recognized jailbait when they saw it...

Although Mary Catherine wasn't jailbait anymore.

That wouldn't stop Sin from beating the fuck out of me if he knew I thought his sister was hot, though.

I'd only seen her once, but there was something about her features that was worthy of a third, *fourth* glance, even.

Cheekbones carved from ice, skin as pale as cream. Those eyes of hers glinted like peridots, seeing more than they should, looking ancient and brand new, like fresh leaves, all at the same time.

Everything about her was rich.

Everything.

And I wasn't even talking about the designer clothes she wore that put her out of my price range by a good couple thousand dollars.

I just meant how her hair gleamed like velvet in the miserable sunlight, strawberry blonde and silky with it. It made my palms and fingers tingle with the need to touch it.

No, bikers shouldn't get fucking tingles, but the need to stroke this woman's hair was a craving, and I knew all about those. She was like nicotine or junk food. Both were really bad for you, but the first puff of a cig, the first chew of a double cheeseburger—heaven.

Those peridot eyes sparked with life as she watched me take her in. Layers within layers. Deep green striations and gold highlights that would make them impossible to replicate if I were drawing her.

She had a heart-shaped face that gave her a pointed chin with a tiny divot my thumb ached to slot into.

I had the strangest feeling that my thumb alone was made to sit there.

Stupid, right?

This wasn't a Nicholas Sparks' novel.

Not that I'd read any of those.

Nope.

Never.

Not me.

As I processed exactly how badly I wanted my hands all over her, I also processed how out of reach she was to me.

My brother's sister? Definitely hands off before he sliced them off.

So why did my fingers curl in at the thought? Why did I ache to smooth back her hair from her furrowed brow?

Upon approaching the gates, her fear hit me like a sucker punch, and I reasoned that was why everything about her got to me. My Robin Hood complex pinged to life in her company.

A quick scan behind her revealed nothing, but then, West Orange wasn't exactly her stomping ground.

"What do you want?"

If my voice wasn't welcoming, then so be it. She *wasn't* welcome here.

I knew Sin kept an eye on her from time to time; I had even helped him out with that when he'd been deployed.

Much as Storm had done with his missus, I'd been tasked with guard duty on a few occasions.

Especially when shit in Manhattan was getting interesting, and where those Irish were concerned, it was rare that some mischief wasn't afoot.

For all that I'd collected bits and pieces about her, one thing I did know—Sin was a stranger to her.

So why the fuck had she come to the compound?

"I need Padraig. Is he here?"

It was ridiculous. But my temper was pricked at her saying she needed Sin.

"His name's Sin," I corrected. "Why do you ask?"

"I've been trying to call *Sin* but there's no answer."

"How do you have his number?" I demanded.

She didn't reply, just raised her hand and there was a cell phone in it. Nothing swanky, definitely a burner cell and not a device that a society princess like her would be carrying.

Well, not one from this year, at any rate.

Sin must have given it to her.

Letting that be the answer to my question, I asked, "Why do you want to speak with him?"

She gnawed on her bottom lip. "He's… I am… He's my half-brother," she managed to blurt out, still standing behind the door to the back seat.

Was it a shield?

Was she getting ready to dive back in?

I knew that the situation had to be bad for her to come here.

She was the daughter of a Five Pointer, and Five Pointers tended to think that they were infallible or untouchable even though they were *very* fallible and touchable.

Bikers and the mob weren't exactly on friendly terms. We'd been used by them a couple of times for transportation, but it was always quite clear that we weren't respected.

Jackasses.

But hey, I didn't respect them either. I knew the stunts they pulled and had seen them for myself.

Either way, I knew the situation in the city had calmed down since the Colombians had been taken out in Manhattan.

There'd been a couple drive-by shootings targeting the Five Points, and ever since, shit had been touch and go for a while, but as calm as NYC could ever be, it was.

Ergo, there was no real reason for her to be here. Otherwise, Sin would have had me or another brother guarding her while he was out on this run—last minute or not.

She wasn't my problem.

My dick said it really wanted her to be.

"He left. Is there something that I can do?"

Initially, she sagged, then, clinging to the offer I made, she straightened, questioning, "So you know who I am?"

"Yeah."

She stared at me with a wide-eyed desperation that ate at me. I'd sensed her fear, but this was new.

This woman was not born to appear desperate.

Maybe for dick in the sack, but not where real-life shit was concerned.

"I need his help," she muttered bleakly.

"I told you—he ain't here. He's on a run. But if you need help or are in danger, then I'll do my best to fix things for you."

"Why would you do that? I'm nothing to you."

Rolling my eyes, I pushed my hands into my pockets and slouched closer to the gate. "Do you want my help or not?"

I flicked a glance at the car and saw the driver was starting to get nervous—I could see the sweat on his brow from here and it was a cold ass fucking day.

"Dude is looking antsy. I'd make my mind up if I were you, Mary Catherine."

She gasped. "You know my name."

"Why are you so surprised? The MC knows who you are."

"What? Really? Why would Sin talk about me?"

"Your mother is… Well, let's just say she ain't popular around here. Sin knew that a day would come when you would need his help, and when he was deployed and didn't know if he was going to come back, he called in a favor."

Several favors.

For a half-sister he didn't know and didn't want but who had the misfortune of being his mother's spawn too.

She released a soft breath. "I knew he was a soldier. I just knew it."

I wasn't sure why that of all the things I said had piqued her interest, but to each their own.

For whatever reason, it had her dipping down and retrieving a satchel from the back seat. She murmured, "Thanks for the ride," to the driver before dragging the satchel onto her shoulder and tucking the phone Sin gave her into her pocket.

She slammed the door closed and then took a few steps toward me as the driver instantly took off, recognizing that this was not a safe place for weary travelers.

It wasn't like we had the devil's stamp etched into the sky above us, and the clubhouse itself was pretty respectable truth be told, but he was smart to get the hell out of here.

"He cared enough about me to ask for his club's help?" she questioned as I watched the car fade into the distance as it raced down the road.

Giving her my full attention, I saw that there were stars in her eyes, and call me a sap, but I didn't feel like erasing them. Sin wasn't a saint. He earned his road name naturally, but she didn't need to know that. Not when she'd looked so scared and those stars had replaced the fear.

I didn't answer her, just demanded, "What's going on?"

She moved closer to the bars separating us. "Aren't you going to let me in?"

"It depends." I studied her. "You might be better off staying outside the compound's territory."

She scowled at me. "Why did you let my taxi drive off if you don't think I should come inside?"

"Because it's not as if you could discuss whatever the hell is going on with him listening in... Taxi drivers don't come with plausible deniability as a part of the service." I scowled right back at her. "So, come on, tell me. What's going on?"

"I'd prefer to tell Sin," she rattled off.

"Well, preferences don't mean jack. Sin ain't here." I grimaced at her. "I have no idea when he'll be back either." I wasn't lying. Runs took however long they took. It wasn't as if we had a timetable. "He could be gone for days."

With Nyx a part of that run, and some sick fuck potentially on the hook and about to lose his balls to the Sinners' Enforcer, days was an understatement.

She sucked in a sharp breath. "I don't have days."

I frowned at her. "Why not?"

Her panic was a real and visceral thing and, like it or not, it put me on edge.

If she cried, I'd lose my shit.

"I'm not even sure if you can help," she whispered, taking a step backward, her eyes massive in her face.

It was then I realized that if I didn't soften up and coddle her, she'd flee.

When Ma had gotten sick the first time, Sin had helped us with the co-pay for her prescriptions—he deserved better than for me to run off his sister.

"We're the Sinners. Ain't nothing we can't do." I asked her something to get her out of her head: "How did you know to come here anyway?"

She blinked. Took a step closer to the gate. "One day, he came to our house. I saw his patch. The internet told me the rest."

I knew she wasn't lying because I'd seen her with my own two eyes that day in Westchester, but I knew Maverick, our resident tech genius, would be scrubbing Google for references to us if that was how she'd located our clubhouse.

"Where did you get the address?"

"There's a blog about you."

My eyes widened. "A blog?"

"Yeah." She nodded to compound her admission. "I was surprised."

Jesus. *A blog?*

"I'll need the website's address."

"Sure. Whatever. I thought it was weird… but I was desperate enough to give it a shot. I thought it was a hoax at first."

"So, you mean to tell me that you got a taxi to an address that could've been wrong and that could have led to some kind of serial killer's lair? Is that what you're saying?"

I shouldn't have been angry with her.

But I really fucking was.

Those stars had faded by now, and the fear was back. She reached out, her dainty hands curling about the bars, French tip nails, so clean, elegant just like her, peeping at me as she clenched down, whispering, "That tells you how desperate I am."

Desperate? More like stupid.

Sin had done due diligence on her, and I'd been along for the ride, so I knew it was grades, not her daddy's money, that got her into NYU.

Pulling stupid moves was not something a woman this smart should do.

I could fucking smell the trouble brewing in the air.

Living up to my road name, I pinned her with a stare. "Why are you desperate?"

4

MARY CATHERINE
WITH EVERY HEARTBEAT - ROBYN, KLEERUP

MARY CATHERINE

WHY WAS I DESPERATE?

What a question.

I recognized him. How couldn't I? The guy had been the star of my first fumbles beneath the comforter as I shrugged off Catholic guilt and decided to touch myself.

He looked different now.

He'd had a haircut and it was brushed. He appeared well-kept.

If anything, he looked better than he had before, confirming my initial suspicion that he was pretty-boy handsome.

That level of masculine beauty couldn't be hidden away by a mop of hair.

His cheekbones made him seem gaunt, but he was too bulky for that. His eyebrows were thick and with a high arch, but not bushy, strong enough to frame his face. They shielded velvet brown eyes that I felt certain could see deep into my soul.

A stupid, unnecessary thought.

But damn, if he didn't make me think stupid, unnecessary things.

Even in the middle of a crisis, apparently.

Still, he didn't recognize me from that day in Westchester. Even if he *did* know my name. His interest was purely because of Padraig, *Sin*, who wasn't goddamn here.

With all my efforts to escape, and the sheer amount of sweat I'd perspired as I fled the college campus without my guards finding me, I could feel the clock ticking. It was only a matter of time before they showed up.

They always showed up.

I knew that from Mother.

How many times had she tried to run away but had been hauled back to the house in Westchester like she was a missing cat?

But this morning's terror was for nothing if Sin wasn't here and this guy wouldn't help me.

"If my guards find me, they'll…" The words were choked in my throat because how could this guy understand what it possibly felt like to be forced into marriage? To have no choice? To have no say?

He lived his life on the road.

He was an outlaw.

He was a rebel.

I was a monster's daughter.

I had no freedom.

"Mary Catherine," he rasped. "It's okay. Whatever you're running from, we… I won't let them get to you."

His correction had me blinking at him. "You won't?" I clung to that.

He shook his head. "I won't."

"Why do you care?" I breathed.

"Because Sin's a brother. He's family. And when my mom got sick and I couldn't pay her bills, Sin helped me out. He's a good man."

I pressed closer to the bars. "He is?"

"He is."

"I don't know him. I don't know anything about him. I'm glad he's a good person."

The guy's lips quirked. "I never said that. There's a difference."

I blinked. "I guess there is."

Disappointment settled inside me. Sin might not be a mobster, but he was a biker. I didn't know much about the business aside from what I read on the internet, but I knew mobsters looked down on bikers.

If there was an organized crime hierarchy, mobsters were on the top tiers and bikers were on the bottom. But hey, for all that they were on the bottom, I didn't think *they* would be into forcing their daughters to get married to old men.

"Either way, Sin reached out to you, didn't he? That phone he gave you means he offered to help. He might not be here, but I can stand in until he gets back. I'm pretty sure that the rest of the MC will feel the same. You're blood, and that matters to us."

His words resonated, and I needed so badly to believe they were true.

My palms ached, burning with the cold metal pressed against them, making me regret that my gloves were in my satchel.

Discomfort gnawed at my joints as I clenched down harder, whispering, "My father's going to make me get married."

He pinpointed me with a laser-like stare that I really should have been too flustered to feel, but a wave of butterflies seemed to settle in my belly regardless.

"*Make* you get married? Doesn't he need your consent?"

Didn't he believe me?

"If I don't say yes, he'll just lock me in my room until I agree to it."

"What?" His brow furrowed. "You're an adult, not a little girl."

"You shouldn't lock people in their rooms no matter their age," I said with a huff.

"Well, that's a given." He rolled his eyes. "You say no, then you get locked in your room?"

I nodded slowly. "It happened a couple years ago."

When I'd grown sick of jilling off to the fading memory of a rough biker who had stirred something in me that had made me want to touch myself.

Perhaps he should have been the antithesis of what a woman like me fantasized about, but my life was so pristine, so clean... the fact that he hadn't brushed his hair, that he was dangerous and that it was so outwardly visible… He'd been attractive to me then.

Now, with this more presentable look, he was even more handsome.

Stupid, Mary Catherine. What are you even thinking about that for?

God, men were the problem in my life. I didn't need to add to the list.

"Why the hell did he do that?"

It took me a second to catch up. "He did it when I got a boyfriend. To stop me from seeing him." My mouth trembled. "Father still killed him, though. To punish me."

Poor Kris.

He'd done nothing wrong apart from hold my hand and kiss me badly.

Gulping down my sorrow, I rasped, "Father kept me imprisoned in my room until I was ready to apologize to him, and then he let me go back to school. He told everyone I was sick."

"What about the kid? Didn't they ask about him?"

He didn't even cock a brow. How fucked up was our world that he believed me?

"Kris had gone 'missing.' He'd run away from home, apparently." It hurt my heart that his parents believed he was out there somewhere. That they were waiting for him to come home one day. "Everyone seemed to believe the ruse. Father can be quite thorough when he wants to be." I licked my lips. "What's your name?"

He tipped his head to the side. "Why?"

"Because you know mine and I don't know yours. Anyway, isn't that a standard question?"

"There's power in a name."

"Is that why bikers use road names?"

His smile grew. "No."

His silence told me he wasn't going to share it with me, then I noticed he straightened his shoulders, which made his leather vest shift.

For the first time, I looked at the patches on his cut. "You're Digger?"

"Yeah."

I stared into his eyes. "Do you bury bodies?"

"In the past," he said, no shame in his voice. Not that he needed to be ashamed. Death was as much of a part of life as birth. Especially to a daughter of the Five Points. "But I got my name because I don't stop digging until I find out what I want."

"Information?"

He nodded. "Secrets are my stock-in-trade."

"Interesting." I bit my lip. "Are you going to let me inside now?"

"Who does your father want you to marry?"

"You won't have heard of him."

"I'm a keeper of secrets, Mary Catherine. As well as an unearther of them. Who?"

"A man named Bill Murphy."

His shoulders straightened. "The Five Pointer?"

Did he know Bill? Something about his expression made me think he did.

"Of course. Like he'd marry me off to someone outside of the Firm."

"'More wives than Henry VIII Bill?'"

"Six." I frowned. "You know him?"

"Heard of him." He stepped back and then pulled open the gates. "Come inside."

Bill Murphy was my passcode to getting in?

A shiver rushed down my spine, but I didn't cross the threshold. "How do you recognize his name?"

"You don't want to know."

"I do," I snapped. "If I don't figure out a way..." I took a deep breath, my temper dispersing as fear rammed me in the stomach. "If I don't run away, I'll end up married to him."

Digger's gaze was calm, measured as he stared at me. "Let's just say I know where he's buried a couple of his missing wives. The guy's got more in common with Henry VIII than obesity."

My eyes closed of their own volition, and I stood there, feeling as frail as a sapling in a tornado when I knew I had to be as strong as a sequoia. Only, I wasn't. I wasn't that strong. I never had been.

Women in my world weren't bred to be.

I'd already accomplished more than most in my social circle by going to college. But knowing my father wanted to marry me off to a man who'd murdered his wives told me I'd been right to grow some balls and attempt an escape.

A hand dropped onto my shoulder, and it smoothed down my arm. "Hey, it's okay. We'll figure it out."

Fear throbbed through my being. "There's no escaping death."

His brow puckered, then he did the craziest thing—he moved his hand higher so that he could cup my chin. I tensed, unsure of what he was going to do next, but he just let his warmth fill me.

In the quiet that followed, his scent reached out like a hug, and I sucked it in.

He smelled nothing like the men I knew. No expensive aftershaves or colognes. No fancy starch for his suits. He just smelled like soap.

I had no idea why that was comforting, but it was.

He smelled clean. No frills, nothing fancy.

I liked that. It was reassuring because it was so different than what I was used to. And what I was used to was toxic and sullied.

As our gazes tangled, held, *linked*, much like what had happened at the house in Westchester so many years ago, it felt as if someone hit pause on life.

As if everything came to a halt.

The whirl of the wind around us, the noise of traffic in the distance, the loud music from the clubhouse—it all came to a stop.

Then, he murmured, "There's no escaping death, but you gotta live your life to the fullest before your time is up."

And somehow, I knew he'd help me do exactly that.

5

DIGGER

HOW TO SAVE A LIFE - THE FRAY

DIGGER

WHEN SHE STOOD THERE, eyes closed in front of a man with more blood on his hands than a butcher, as vulnerable as a woman could be, something twinged inside me.

At that moment, her fear was such that she was more scared of what she was running from than the threats in front of her.

That was a dangerous position to be in.

I wasn't a sexual predator, and though I trusted my brothers implicitly, some'd proven themselves unworthy of a Sinner's patch.

Dog, a mean motherfucker, was one of them.

If he'd been on the gates, if she'd just exposed her vulnerabilities to him, he'd have taken advantage of her.

He wouldn't care that she was Sin's sister. He wouldn't give a damn that she was family—he'd have hurt her.

And if she hadn't come here, many other men could've hurt her too. Her father included if he was going to tie her to a fucker like Bill Murphy.

As I tugged her onto Sinners' property, I felt like I was signing a warrant on my destiny.

Death?

Maybe.

I'd been outrunning death since I was a kid, though, so that was nothing new.

Arrest?

Same thing.

I'd wasted too many years inside a jail cell.

I wasn't a good man. No Sinner was. But that didn't mean we didn't have our own code of ethics that we lived by. I couldn't leave her out here, as vulnerable as a chicken who'd found herself in a fox's den.

Not just because she was Sin's sister, either.

"Where are we going?" she rasped as I hurried her over to the gatehouse.

"I need to get you out of sight from the clubhouse."

She peered at me but had the smarts not to argue.

Still, did Five Pointers send their women out into the world with no street smarts whatsoever?

Jesus Christ.

When we were in the tiny shelter, she asked, "What's going on?"

Did she know her lashes were ridiculously long?

I was used to seeing those false spikes, but these weren't. They were all natural. Everything about her was. She didn't even use that much makeup, but makeup on her skin would have been a crime against nature anyway.

My jaw clenched as I shoved those inappropriate thoughts away. "I don't want them to see you up at the clubhouse."

"Why not?"

I didn't answer her.

The Five Points were business associates. We were *not* allies. And though she was related to Sin, she wasn't related to anyone on the council that led the MC, which was a problem.

Sin had Rex's ear, but Sin wasn't fucking here, so he couldn't help. Seeing as he'd just taken off, he wouldn't be able to answer his phone yet, and with her guards on the hunt, time was running out for her. She didn't have time to wait for Sin to deign to answer my call.

If a barrage of Five Pointers were currently ramming their way down the Jersey turnpike to find Mary Catherine, the council might throw her back to them to avoid a war if I didn't get involved.

I scrubbed my hand over my jaw. "What was the game plan?"

She swallowed as she shuffled over to perch on the armrest of the armchair. As she did, I took in her poise, how straight her spine was, how daintily she tucked her feet together.

So, they gave daughters of the Irish Mob lessons on grace but not on self-defense—*got it*.

"The game plan?" She released a shaky breath. "When Father told me—" Father, not Dad—*got it*. "I knew I couldn't react. If I reacted, he'd throw me in my room. If I was in my room, I couldn't escape. I knew I had to get to Sin."

"So, Sin was the game plan?" I queried, hoping that she wasn't about to say yes.

She bit her lip and gave me a wordless answer.

Shit.

"I-I, you don't understand how much patience and work it took to get here. He upped my guards, Digger. *Overnight*. I had two; now I have four. I had to evade *four* men's notice as I escaped my college campus. All while trying to behave like nothing was happening when my world was collapsing.

"Father even expected me to be excited." She shuddered. "Can you imagine? Even worse, he was going to arrange our first meeting and I know exactly what that means—"

I was okay with letting her ramble, but the way she paled had me growing tense. "What does it mean?"

A shiver whispered along her spine, breaking that straight-as-a-ruler stance of hers. "The m-meeting should be when Bill proposes..." Her mouth trembled. "It's not as simple as that."

Crouching down in front of her, I asked, "What happens at the meeting, Mary Catherine?"

"My friend got married last year. When her now-husband proposed..." She swallowed. "He didn't listen when she said no. H-He made it so that she had to say yes."

My brows lowered. "He raped her?"

"He did. Used it as leverage against her so she couldn't run away from him." Her mouth wobbled. "She was a virgin."

Temper stirred, I demanded, "Because without her hymen, she had no value?"

Mary Catherine nodded, but her eyes—Jesus fuck, they were loaded with terror and horror. Who could blame her?

I knew the Five Points had their ways of doing business, but this was on a whole other level.

"You know it's only a piece of skin, don't you?" I asked her gently.

"Of course I do," she snapped heatedly, "but it isn't to those men."

"Those men?"

"The pretenders."

I arched a brow. "What does that mean?"

"It means the men who *wish* they were in higher positions of power. Who *pretend* to be something they're not because they'll never be more than where they are.

"It turbocharges things. Makes them demand perfection because, to the outside world, they have to be perfect or the house of cards will tumble down." Her nostrils flared. "I'm related to the O'Donnellys, so I should be treated better, but that connection might just—"

She was related to the O'Donnellys?

The Five Points' ruling family?

Fucking hell.

Then war really was barreling toward us if her father figured out where she was.

"Might just what?" I asked her when her words faltered.

She was staring down at her lap.

Her lap where my hand was.

Not creepily, but my fingers were clasped around hers in reassurance.

I blinked.

When the fuck did that happen?

I made to pull back, but she tightened hers around mine, saying, "My value is higher because of that connection. All the more reason for Bill to want to seal the deal."

Hearing her talk about herself as if she were a baggy of coke had rage hitting me. "You're not a business deal."

"That's precisely what I am," she muttered miserably.

"Do the O'Donnellys know that their fucking men treat women like this?"

She shrugged. "Probably not, but we're chattel."

"Women stopped being that—"

"No, you misunderstand me. *We*. Men and women alike. They're just the same. Didn't you hear that Eoghan O'Donnelly is going to have to marry a daughter of the Bratva?"

"I had heard that," I confirmed.

"Eoghan won't like that," she said wryly. "He won't want that. But he'll do it. Because that's what we do. We get married and we have kids and we keep the Five Points alive." Her teeth bit down on her bottom lip again. "Truly, I knew it was coming. I could have accepted it if it were someone my age, someone I knew and liked, but..." She shook her head. "He did this to hurt me."

"Who did? Your father?"

She nodded. "He hates Mother, and because I look just like her, he hates me."

"That's illogical."

Her smile was timid. "Hatred tends to be illogical."

I conceded that with a grimace.

She tugged on my fingers. "I'm sorry for bringing this trouble to your door. I was just... I was hoping Sin would be able to help me run away."

"You can't go to your mother for help?"

That was wishful thinking because I knew what a piece of work Sin's egg donor was.

"She'd throw me to the wolves as soon as she looked at me," she disregarded instantly. "She had this fate. She even tried to run. That Sin exists at all says she succeeded for a time, but the life still caught up to her. It always does." Her eyes clenched closed. "God, I'm going to *become* her, aren't I?"

If she cried, I didn't have a fucking clue what I'd do. I hated when women cried. It made me angry and sad and all kinds of agitated.

Only, she didn't.

Her eyes opened. They were glossy with emotion, but no tears began to fall, and somehow, that packed more power than a Category Four hurricane, and it shook me in my boots.

"I should go back, shouldn't I?" Her distress acute, she rubbed her brow. "I should go home before he realizes I tried to run." Those peridot irises were wild, the pupils tiny as fear ate at her. "There might still be time. Class only got out forty minutes ago. Going back would be the best thing to do—"

A half hour ago, I'd have said yes.

Now?

With her manicured fingers digging into my palm, her never-seen-a-day's-work-in-her-life hands tucked in mine, I couldn't do that.

I just fucking couldn't.

"There's another way," I countered.

"I've already wasted your time. I'm so sorry—"

I squeezed her fingers. "No. A trapped animal will always try to escape, but you're not an animal, Mary Catherine. You're a person, with choices and goals and desires of your own. Let me help you."

"Why would you want to? I'm nothing to you."

"Sin isn't. I meant it when I said he's helped me out over the years. I have an idea, and you might not like it, but it'll work."

Her gaze caught mine, distraught and scared but… now, there was a tiny glimmer of hope.

I saw it.

I felt it.

It was like seeing a ten-carat diamond peeking out from amid a lava field.

It stirred something in me, something that had died when Mom had. Something that I couldn't afford to feel, but that I did all the same.

"What's your idea?"

"Well, it goes like this…"

6

MARY CATHERINE

MARY CATHERINE

MARY CATHERINE

I WAS INSANE.

I knew it.

Impending marriage had turned me crazy, but I'd accept it; I'd accept *anything* other than Bill Murphy's slimy hands clasping mine and thrusting a ring onto my finger.

I'd accept anything other than his heaving form on top of mine as he robbed me of my choices.

Digger was right.

This *was* my choice.

My body, my life.

But those things were infringing on *his*. That was what I didn't understand.

As we stood in the gas station, Digger filling up his gas tank for the long ride ahead, I stared at him.

My things were back at the clubhouse, including the phone Sin had given me so someone called Maverick couldn't trace my whereabouts. I felt oddly vulnerable without it, but I was desperate enough that I didn't care.

If this Maverick guy obstructed Digger's game plan, if it led to me ending up locked in my room for daring to choose my fate and being forced to become Mrs. Murphy, then that cell phone could rot.

That meant putting a hell of a lot of trust in a man I didn't know.

A man who, crazy or not, I had more faith in than I did my father.

Drowning in a massive Sinners' leather jacket and hoodie he'd given me to wear, I shoved my glove-covered hands into the pockets as I peered into Digger's eyes. "Why?"

Around me, the stench of gas was prominent, and car engines blasted over the noise of the carols on the speakers, but *he* was all I saw.

An unlikely savior in a leather cut.

He shot me a cocky smile. "Why not?"

The cockiness had me grunting. "This marriage isn't going to last long if I hit you over the head with a frying pan, is it?"

The smirk morphed into a genuine grin. "So, you do have some bite."

"Of course I do," I said with a huff. "I don't whine and moan all the time. But these were extenuating circumstances, and I can't help but feel like I'm doing to you what was being done to me. If that makes sense."

He shrugged. "I suggested this."

"You did," I agreed. "But no one gets married to a stranger because they're close friends with that stranger's brother."

"I'm special."

"If it sounds too good to be true, then that's because it usually is," I retorted, not appreciating his mockery as I folded my arms across my chest.

We'd only traveled into West Orange to get gas for his bike, so before this could derail further, I needed to make sure he was okay with this.

I needed to understand his motivations.

It had made sense when we were sitting in that tiny gatehouse, his hand tight around my fingers, his gaze and mine colliding in a way that made me feel like he could see into my very soul.

But throw in a dash of fresh air and I was starting to wonder if he'd been smoking pot—which was something I also needed to know—before we embarked on an epic road trip that'd span the country.

"I've never sounded too good to be true in my life," Digger murmured. "I think I like it."

"You've always been trouble?"

"Yes." He arched a brow at me. "Ever heard of that little thing called divorce?"

"I have, but it doesn't happen a lot in my world," I said dryly. "I mean, why would it? We're Catholic."

"Are you?" He turned his focus on me.

I knew what he meant. Was I devout or did I go through the motions?

"I'm not devout."

"Well, then, what's the problem?"

I wriggled my shoulders. "I don't think you understand the situation." I let the fear get to me, and it would be irresponsible if I didn't spell it out. "My father's a dangerous man, Digger."

As I stepped closer to him, his head tilted to the side. "Let me get this straight. You're trying to protect me from your father?"

"Yes. He's scary." I shivered. "He's a bad man."

"I'm sure he is. I'm not exactly Tinkerbell, Mary Catherine. You're getting out of one dicey situation and diving headfirst into another." I flinched at that. "I'm not going to lie to you. I'm telling you that you won't get hurt. This is like a knife to the heart rather than a GSW to the gut. You get me?"

My brow puckered. "Not exactly."

He grunted. "You started something when you left campus. The minute those guards of yours registered that you weren't where you were supposed to be, the minute they stirred their panic mode into motion, you changed the course of your life.

"Whether or not your father knows about your connection with Sin is another matter entirely. But, as it stands, you've got a good chunk of the Five Points out on the hunt for you. It's only a matter of time before they ask your mom where they think you might be—"

"As if she'd know," I grumbled.

SERENA AKEROYD

"Doesn't matter. They could ask her. They know that she's got a kid with the Sinners. It takes a phone call to find out the truth. And if no one answers the phone, then a visit—"

"That's why you didn't want anyone to see me," I rasped. My arms were folded across my chest, and I began rubbing my hands up and down my biceps, trying not to feel nervous and failing.

"Partly," he confirmed. "The second someone saw you, shit would have changed."

"Why?"

"Rex is our Prez. I love him like a brother, but I'm not that close to him. Not like I am Sin and Storm, the VP. And while Storm would help you in an instant because he's a sucker for damsels in distress, he's currently wired out of his skull on coke." He ground his teeth, but I didn't think it was from annoyance with me, but at Storm. "So, with that in mind, both Sin and Storm are AWOL, and they won't be able to help you.

"If we've got Five Pointers about to beat a path into West Orange to find you, then what do you think is going to happen?"

"Rex will hand me over to allay a war."

"Exactly."

He'd warned me about that already, but I still shivered. "I'm so sorry, Digger. I forced your hand." If he'd been trying to make me feel better, he'd failed.

"You didn't," he countered, his tone as measured as his gaze when it settled on mine.

"I did!"

"No, you didn't," he snapped, for the first time losing his temper with me. "Ask me about my father, Mary Catherine."

I straightened up at that, surprise making me gape a second before I sputtered, "Who's your father?"

His gaze drifted onto passing traffic a second when a truck hooted as it raced down the street. "I don't have one, Mary Catherine. Back in college, Mom was raped, and instead of getting rid of the baby that that fucker implanted in her belly, she had me.

"When you told me what Bill Murphy was going to do to you, I knew what *I* had to do to stop that from happening to someone else.

"The Sinners will back you as my wife. With war a potential repercussion of us supporting you, there's a chance the council might not help if your only tie to the club is being Sin's sister... one he doesn't even know."

Unease hit me, not just because he was right, but because I didn't want him to think I'd misrepresented what could happen between Bill and me.

"He might have been different. I just know what my friend went through—"

"You're really bad at accepting help, aren't you?" he drawled.

"No, I wouldn't have sought Sin out if that were the case," I argued. "But I don't like feeling as if I've coerced you into this."

"Baby, no one coerces me into shit." His smile was genuine, and it made the light in his eyes flare into being.

I liked him when he was grumpy.

I liked him when he had bedhead hair.

I *loved* him when he smiled.

And I *freakin'* loved it when he called me 'baby.'

Hesitantly, I warbled, "If you're sure—"

"In your words, you thought Bill was going to 'seal the deal' before you decided to run off. What the fuck do you think he's going to do now that he knows you're a runner?"

I shuddered. But not because of Bill. Because of my father.

He pointed at me. "That, Mary Catherine, is why I'm sure."

I stared at him, and he stared at me.

"Thank you," I breathed.

"You're welcome. We've got a long ride ahead of us and you ain't exactly used to riding bitch. We'll go as long as we can before we get a room, okay?"

Riding bitch?

My nose crinkled at the term, but I didn't argue. I was in no position to.

This man had admitted to me that he'd buried several bodies, and yet he was being chivalrous by protecting me from a fate that had befallen his mom.

I didn't know him. Didn't know who he was or what he stood for, but I already knew that he'd done more for a stranger than anyone in my circle would have.

I straightened my shoulders. "I'll be fine." And I vowed I would be.

Digger's grin made another appearance, and he laughed as he pushed the nozzle back on the gas pump. "You say that now, MaryCat, but you won't be saying that after ten hours on the road."

I arched a brow at him. "MaryCat?"

He winked. "Mary Catherine's too big of a mouthful between husband and wife."

And with that, he left me to go and pay.

7

DIGGER

DIGGER

WAS I the Grinch in thinking it was too early for "Jingle Bells" to be playing as I walked toward the desk?

"Fucking Christmas," I muttered to myself.

I hated this time of the year.

Blowing out a breath as "Deck the Halls" graced my ears next, I was grateful the line wasn't that long. But it was long enough that I figured it gave her sufficient time for my words to resonate, and for me to ask myself if I was a goddamn lunatic or not.

Anyone who knew me would probably say they already had the answer to that without this attempt at playing knight in shining armor, but even though I was only getting myself into a whole world of shit, I didn't feel that cut up about it.

What was marriage nowadays? Not worth more than the piece of fucking paper that we'd sign our names to after the ceremony, that was what.

We'd get married, her father would lose his shit, we could avert a war or trigger one, and then we could get divorced.

Simple.

Either way, it'd end up without her getting raped and trapped into marrying her rapist.

My temper surged at the thought, and Marley Sue, a girl I'd gone to school with, winced. "Jeez, Digger, you look mean."

I blinked at her. "Sorry."

She sniffed and her head bobbed, making the dancing Santas on her earrings sway with the move. "Not like you to say sorry. Is this the day of the rapture and no one told me?"

"Like I'd be the one in the know about that," I retorted with a snort. "I'm four."

"A four? More like a ten."

I jerked my thumb at the pump. "Four."

Her cheeks burned with heat. "Oh. Four. Understood."

She rang up the bill, and I tossed a pack of gum on the counter and dragged out a stick for me to start chewing.

After paying my tab, I snagged my cell phone, saw I had a couple messages, and calculated the likelihood that my absence would be noticed by Rex. With Storm out of it, the likelihood was high.

A quick scan of Google Maps confirmed what I already knew—a forty-hour, one-way trip to Las Vegas was in my future. That prissy little cat out there's future as well.

My lips quirked as I thought about how her ass was about to ache from a ride that long before I accepted that *my* ass was definitely about to be missed if I was away for ten days.

Deciding that it was easier to say sorry than to ask for permission that could be denied, I headed onto the forecourt, which was when I saw the bastard.

He came running off Main Street like he had an enraged German Shepherd chasing him, and he collided with an old woman who shrieked at the point of collision and cried out as she went down.

"Digger!" MaryCat screamed.

Recognizing the victim and noticing that MaryCat was already heading over to Mrs. K, I urged her to: "Call 911."

Then I took off after the asshole who thought it was okay to steal an old woman's purse that probably had nothing more than a tin of Altoids and a couple bucks in it.

Eyes narrowed, I hurtled down the street, seeing the douchebag's blond head tunneling toward St. John's Evangelist, and sped up. Running with boots was a fucking nightmare, but I'd dealt with worse pain.

When I made it around the bend in the road, I saw him edging toward a park. The second he went in there, I knew I had him. He raced across the road, nearly causing a fucking car crash, but karma served him some justice—he got clipped by a fender.

His speed dropped dramatically.

I maneuvered through the mess he'd made and leaped at him the second I saw he was running downhill. It was a calculated risk—I could have face-planted, but he was slower now, hobbling.

When I landed on him, he went down like a pile of bricks, and when my fist collided with his face, well, he wished he were a pile of goddamn bricks.

I beat the fuck out of him, purging every ounce of my temper on this trash bag of bones that represented everything that was wrong with our society.

When I was done, and my knees were killing me from the run and the landing, I snatched the purse and shoved it under my arm. Then, with him a splatter, I grabbed his collar and used it to haul him through the park and back to the gas station.

Sporadic moans escaped him, and I figured that was because friction between his jeans and the concrete fucked up his ass—more karma —but I didn't stop until we made it to the gas station where the police and an ambulance were waiting.

"Digger!" MaryCat hollered, her relief clear as she rushed over to me. Then, she stopped, and she eyed the guy caterwauling on the ground. "Oh."

The cops had turned at her holler, but when they saw me and the guy in my hold, Officer Newton merely snorted.

"You and your goddamn white-knight syndrome."

I shot a smug smile at another kid I'd gone to school with who'd made the foolish choice of becoming a cop. "You know me too well, Gary."

I dumped the piece of shit on the ground then hobbled over to the ambulance, leaving them to deal with the fucker.

As I approached the vehicle, I saw Mrs. Ketteridge was huddled beneath one of those aluminum blankets. Though she was sniffling, she glanced at me intently. "You get my purse, James?"

"Like you'd expect anything less, Mrs. K."

She rubbed at her tear-slick cheeks. "You always could run."

"I always could." I passed her the purse. "Beat him up some too."

"Good," she mumbled. "Not that you'll tell anyone I said that."

I smirked. "Nope." Bending down, I studied her face. "You okay?"

"No. He clipped me on the hip I had replaced last year."

Wincing, I asked, "Maybe it's just a bruise?"

"I hope so. They're taking me in."

"You need me to get your family together?"

She shook her head. "No, it's okay. Not now that you got my purse back for me." Mrs. K patted my cheek. "You always were a good boy beneath all that hair."

Snorting, I told her, "You're messing with my rep."

"Some reps were made to be messed with."

I stepped back so the EMTs could do their thing and told her, "You watch out for yourself, Mrs. K."

"Will do." She hugged her purse. "Thank you."

"My pleasure."

I turned away and almost collided with MaryCat, who asked, "You know her?"

"She was the principal's secretary."

"Spent a lot of time together?"

I tapped my nose. "I'm a bloodhound for trouble."

"I'll bet." She stared at the older woman. "Will she be okay?"

"She says her hip's hurting."

"That sucks," she breathed miserably.

It did.

I'd beaten the fuck out of the mugger, and he'd gotten clipped by a car, but that didn't take away Mrs. K's suffering—karma was good, but not that good.

I let loose an annoyed breath as the pain in my knees made itself known to me. "Wait by the bike? I just gotta grab something else from the gas station."

"Oh, okay."

"You want anything?"

"You have some gum?" I handed the pack to her, and she smiled. "Thanks."

As I returned to the store, I heard her footsteps as she rushed behind me. "What is it?" I grumbled as I looked down at her. A *long* way down. Christ, she was tiny.

"You're limping."

I scowled. "I know I am."

"Why? Did he hurt you?"

"That fucker?" I scoffed. "He was 100% donut."

"He wasn't. He was fast like a whippet."

"Like a whippet? Nah. My knees are fucked from track. Leather boots don't help them."

"Go and sit on the bike. I'll get you some Tylenol."

"You have any money?"

"I have some," she said with a sniff.

"I'm surprised. Thought you'd been weaned on Daddy's credit card."

"I was, but ever heard of cash back? Cash can't be traced. And he *isn't* my daddy."

I hummed, then I took a look around and, spying that I was nearer to my bike than the front door of the store, muttered, "You okay doing that?"

"Wouldn't have said I was if I wasn't," she groused back, but a smile curved her lips.

As she took off, I snagged her arm and gave her a twenty. "Don't eat into your slush fund."

"Thank you." Her smile quivered some before she turned away and headed into the small store where Marley Sue was more interested in watching the 'cops and robbers' show on her forecourt than serving customers.

I didn't immediately hobble over to my bike, just watched her go and had to admit that she was as fine going as she was coming.

My dick twitched because I thought about her coming in a different way as well...

There was something about her.

Sweet but strong.

I loved fighters, but I liked a woman to be a woman too.

Figured that was my insecurities at work though.

MaryCat was quick to smile, even though her situation wasn't the best, and her features were expressive enough that I knew she'd look fucking beautiful as she climaxed.

Scratching my chin at the thought, I twisted away to limp over to my hog. Clambering onto it with less grace than usual, and though I kept an eye on the situation with the cops and the ambulance, mostly, I watched her.

She was easy to watch.

Graceful, elegant, even in a pair of jeans and an old leather jacket and hoodie of mine that were about five sizes too large.

She didn't fit in around here, I thought.

Maybe at the gas station on the other side of town that served the rich assfucks who went to the country clubs around these parts, but not here.

This was regular.

Mary Catherine was not regular.

I pursed my lips, wondering if *MaryCat* could be.

8

MARYCAT

MARYCAT

THE NEXT TIME WE STOPPED, I was going to down the whole bottle of acetaminophen I'd bought Digger back in West Orange.

Sweet. Lord. On. A. Cracker. With. Peanut. Butter.

Ouch.

Just, ouch.

This hurt worse than the time my father had hit me and I'd fallen down the stairs, which was insane. I'd busted up a couple of ribs and couldn't go to school for a week without it looking like I was favoring my right side. *That* was real pain, but this was gnawing. I could feel the bike's vibrations in my soul.

Yeah, my *soul*.

My organs were becoming ingredients in a smoothie and my ass, my fucking *ass,* it wasn't going to survive. That was going to go first. I knew it.

And the cold? It was biting. It had jagged teeth with rabid drool, and where the pain from sitting like this for hours on end didn't reach, the cold did.

Talk about a one-two punch to the face.

The worst thing was I couldn't whine at him, not only because we were on a bike and the wind whistling past us was louder than a rock concert, but also because he was doing me a favor.

A massive favor.

Marriage might not mean a lot to some people, but there was a reason most men avoided it like it was the plague. Yet here he was, throwing himself into the fire for me. Making a sacrifice that I wasn't worthy of.

I wondered if that was a part of his nature though.

He'd thought nothing of going after that mugger earlier. Had thought nothing of dragging him back and handing the guy over to the cops while returning the purse to a woman he clearly respected from school.

When I'd called his name as I saw it go down, I didn't even know what I expected. It wasn't on him to chase after the guy. It wasn't on him to hobble back, dragging him alongside as if the guy were a dead saber-toothed tiger and he was a caveman bringing home the goods to his cavewoman.

This time, when I squirmed on the seat, it had nothing to do with how badly my ass was aching.

A soft tap on my knee was his indicator that I needed to stop wiggling—I'd learned that as we rode.

I wished like hell I hadn't left my cell phone back at the clubhouse because I could have listened to music, but instead, I was inside my head and would be for the foreseeable future.

I didn't know the exact number of hours we'd be on the road, but logic dictated it had to be upward of thirty-five.

This time, I shuffled about because my ass was back to hurting.

Deciding that I had to do something about this state of affairs, I leaned into him. Before, I'd placed my hands on his waist and used my legs to grip him, but this time, I slipped my arms around him and slumped into him so that I could redistribute some of the pressure. I didn't care that it was forward. I just needed to help my ass out.

With a sigh, I turned my head to the side, wishing the clunky helmet wasn't getting in the way as I pressed it against his back.

I could smell the road—gas and dust and engines—but I could also smell the detergent from the hoodie he wore over his leather jacket.

When I'd watched him drag on the layers, I hadn't understood why he'd put them on backward until he'd explained about needing to cover the club's insignia on the back of his leather jacket once we left the MC's territory.

He still wore his cut, a name I'd learned from the one or two (hundred) MC books I'd read since I'd first seen him, but it was beneath the outerwear.

The way he'd refused to take it off made me think it was like a second skin to him.

Without thinking, I rubbed my cheek against his back as my eyes drifted shut, trying to imagine our route, each mile moving me closer to safety, taking me farther away from Bill Murphy.

I squeezed his waist in silent thanks and shuffled ever nearer to him so that there wasn't a sliver of space between us.

His hand settled on my thigh for a second, and the heat from it sank into my bones before he returned it to the handlebars.

He was a stranger, so I shouldn't have found that reassuring, but I did.

I really, truly did.

9

DIGGER

DIGGER

SHE LASTED a lot longer than I thought she would.

Not once did she complain as I pushed us hard down I-80, taking us through Pennsylvania and Ohio.

We stopped for gas, and she didn't say a word. I felt her tense up around Pennsylvania, so I made sure to keep taking short breaks. Even so, she was as stiff as a board by Indiana but had turned into a bag of limp spaghetti in Illinois.

Still, I carried on, pushing ahead.

Not because I was a mean bastard but because my phone was buzzing away like a motherfucker, which meant nothing good was happening at home.

I doubted it was because I was AWOL. I wasn't important enough for my absence to cause that much of a fallout.

No, it was probably that some shit had hit the fan. Both the shit and the fan likely took the shape of a small-boned Irish-American woman who wasn't about to accept the future her father was gifting her.

By Iowa, I knew I had to take a break, which meant she'd get some respite, but that also meant her bones would settle and she'd feel it even worse when we started the journey again.

For a first-time rider, this was testing her body's limits, but it couldn't be helped.

We stopped off at a diner, and the second I cut the engine and the vibrations ceased rumbling, I heard her soft whimper.

Jesus, that tiny noise got to me.

I heard her discomfort, heard her pain, and expected her to whine.

Only, she didn't.

"Come on, MaryCat," I urged, gentler with her because she was being so strong. "Let's get some coffee in you."

Not rushing her, I stayed in place, letting her hands squeeze my waist for support as she made minute movements to clamber off the bike.

I liked her hands there more than I should and even missed them when they were gone.

Another soft sound whispered from her lips, but it was exactly that.

A whisper.

She was trying to stay quiet, to keep her discomfort from me, and while I was proud of her for being a trooper, it twisted me up inside too.

I shifted so I could see her. "You don't have to hide your pain from me."

Her throat moved, but she didn't say a word as, in increments, she managed to climb off the back of the bike.

When she pressed her hands to the seat and took a breather, I let her stand there.

"First time always sucks," I tried to comfort, but I knew there wasn't much comfort to be had.

Her face was white and pale, her features wooden.

When she was standing on her own, I got off too before I dipped down to grab the saddlebags.

Hooking them over my shoulder, I stopped beside her and held out my arm.

For a second, she looked at it blankly, but then her hand settled on top of it.

I let her set the pace, peering around the grimy shithole. For all that it looked ugly as fuck, it was a 24-hour mom-and-pop joint, and the smells coming from it were strong enough to diminish the stench of gas from the roads, and they were fucking awesome.

Stomach rumbling, I didn't say anything as we took at least five minutes for a fifteen-second trip, which let me scope the area.

Rolling my eyes at the Christmas trees in the window and the flashing Santas stuck to the glass, I grunted when, as we entered the establishment, holiday songs bombarded us.

Over the noise, I asked, "Need the bathroom?"

Wearily, she sighed. "I do."

I glanced around the place, found the women's restroom, then shuffled her over to it.

"You gonna be all right in there?"

Her lips quirked into a smile that gutted me. "You gonna help me there too?"

Pleased she had enough energy to joke around, I grinned at her. "I mean, I could try."

She sniggered. "Thanks, but I think I can manage. Come and investigate if I'm not back in two hours."

"Two hours? Christ. You've got twenty minutes before I send in a search and rescue squad."

"My hero," she retorted, batting her eyelashes.

The snort that escaped me had her grin widening, and because I liked seeing that over her rickshaw of pain, I teased, "You know it. Is it a bird? Is it a plane? Nope, it's Digger. On his custom hog."

Though she laughed, she asked, "Custom?"

"Yeah. Down to the tires."

"That's dedication."

"Only what she deserves."

MaryCat grumbled, "Why do guys always think their bikes and cars are girls?"

"Because they don't wanna ride other dudes," I joked. "Unless they're that way inclined, of course."

She stared at me, and her cheeks turned a delicious pink. It was so obvious against her creamy skin, even more so because of her pallor. "And you're not that way inclined?"

I had to smile.

If I'd wanted proof that she was inexperienced with guys, then I just got it.

I hadn't been a creep, but checking her out was a little too easy… If she hadn't noticed, then she was definitely not used to the signs that a guy was into her.

"I'm not. Straighter than an arrow."

"An arrow's trajectory can curve."

I hummed. "Well, my trajectory is straight ahead." Just like she was in my line of sight. Her lips twitched, so I reminded her, "Twenty minutes and I'll be in to check that everything is okay."

"Are you always this…" She paused. Something surged into being in her eyes, those fucking eyes a bastard like me had no business drowning in. "…protective?"

I shrugged. "Isn't that how a man should behave with a woman at his side?"

"Not in my experience," was her sad response. She patted my hand. "See you in twenty."

I watched her go, her wooden steps making me cringe, and then I headed into the guys' restroom to take care of my own needs.

Upon my return to the counter, I ordered two coffees and requested the menu.

The waitress batted her lashes at me, and having seen MaryCat just do that, even mockingly, I'd admit that this woman, who was my type, did jackshit for my dick. Unlike MaryCat, who would be my wife soon enough and had my cock reacting like I'd downed a few Viagra.

An interesting and totally unexpected development.

As the server set out some mugs on the counter, I didn't bother talking to her even though I was under no obligation not to flirt. I just smiled politely while I kept my focus on the bathroom door.

A couple minutes later, a hand touched my shoulder.

Twisting around, I saw the server was smiling at me. "My shift ends in thirty minutes. I know a great bar—"

"I'm just traveling through." I gave her another polite smile. "With my fiancée."

She blinked. "Oh. That's a real shame. I could have shown you a great time—"

The restroom door opened, and I shifted ass over to it when I saw MaryCat.

Her color was better, and the tiny baby hairs around her face were damp so I knew she'd washed up.

"You okay?"

"Yeah. Who knew it took so many muscles to squat?"

Surprised she was so candid, I laughed. "Better thigh workout than a cross-ski machine."

"Don't sound so proud," she groused. "God, I need coffee. Like a quart of it."

"You'll have to squat again," I pointed out.

"Don't ruin coffee for me."

Snorting, I took her over to a booth and returned to the counter to grab our drinks.

Tucking the menu under my arm, I saw the server glowering at MaryCat when a thought occurred to me.

"Spit in her food, or mine for that matter, and you'll wish you hadn't been born."

She gulped but bobbed her head double quick.

Grunting, I returned to the booth, placed her coffee in front of her, then took a seat. My ass ached too, so it was good to just sit.

I passed her the menu but didn't bother looking at it.

"I'm not hungry," she muttered.

"You need the energy. We've been on the road a long while."

"Trust me, I know."

I hid a smile but warned, "The night ain't over either, MaryCat. You should eat."

She yawned. "Maybe just a sandwich or something?"

"Go for it."

Because I always had the same order, I cast the server a glance and she stepped over to us.

Warily.

Good.

"Are you ready to order?"

MaryCat cleared her throat. "I'll have the egg salad sandwich, please."

"Meatloaf with potatoes. And cherry pie for after. Thanks."

When the woman shuffled away, MaryCat asked, "Is she going to spit in my food because you're with me?"

Amused that we'd had the same thought, I simply said, "No."

She jerked her chin up. "Okay. Not sure I can handle bodily fluids today."

I grinned. "Just today?"

Her cheeks burned hotly.

"She won't spit in your food," I assured her, the curve of my lips deepened though.

"You should probably do something about that."

Blinking, I asked, "What?"

MaryCat wafted her hand at me. "Your face. I'm going to get a lot of crap from waitresses otherwise."

My face?

I smirked.

Well, I guessed I just got confirmation that I wasn't the only one who liked how the other looked...

"I'll make sure to eat my meatloaf and smear it all over my mouth. Think that'll turn her off?"

"I think it'll help. Maybe eat like a pig too?"

"Your wish is my command," I drawled as I took a noisy mock slurp of coffee that had her nose crinkling.

"Okay. Maybe not."

Chuckling, I started rummaging through the saddlebags for the Tylenol.

Shoving the bottle at her, I directed, "Take a couple. It should kick in before we set off."

She did as I said, then both of us focused on our food which arrived a few minutes later.

It was good. Simple but tasty, and I finished all mine, not altogether unsurprised that she didn't. Not letting it go to waste, I ate hers too.

Politely, she waited until I was done, then she stood on her own two, trembling feet and headed to the bathroom without my help.

I settled the bill, also made use of the facilities, and found her waiting by the door to go outside.

It took her a few minutes to get back on the bike after I got myself situated, and though she released a couple sharp exhalations, she did it without complaint.

God, I loved a woman who didn't fucking whine.

We set off, and I took us as far as I figured the Tylenol would last her. Something she silently confirmed when her hands started clutching at my abs instead of just holding my sides.

I knew it wasn't intentional, just a way for her to process her discomfort, but I took it as a sign that we needed to stop for the night.

I pulled over at a motel that wasn't good enough for her, but I knew things were bad when, after we stopped, she made no move to get off the back of the bike.

Squeezing her thigh, I told her, "Come on, MaryCat, let's get some Zs."

Her arms tightened around my waist, smushing her tits into my back, and I had to admit that felt so good, my dick started aching from the fairly innocent contact.

That was a miracle in itself seeing as I was starting to feel tired too.

When she made no other move, I encouraged her, "There's a nice bed up there waiting for you."

"Just keep on riding," she rasped, exhaustion etching each word.

"I need some rest too, honey." It wasn't a lie, but neither was it the truth. I had a couple more hours in me, but I'd already ridden more than was wise even with all the pit stops I'd taken for MaryCat.

"Oh." Her voice was small. "I'm sorry."

"You don't have to be," I chided then twisted around to support her when she made the rookie move of getting off the bike too fast. I held her up as she sagged against me.

"Ouch."

"Yeah. It hurts." I winced.

"Hurts is an understatement. Just not sure why it hurts more this time," she grumbled under her breath while her hands came to my shoulders. "It's okay. You can let go now."

I knew I couldn't.

"Just a couple more minutes for your legs to get used to this position."

I'd be hella surprised if she didn't get pins and needles soon.

As soon as the thought struck, they hit.

"Fuck," she hissed under her breath, and I had to admit, the dirty word on her lips sounded sexy as shit coming from her.

"Wasn't sure you knew what that word meant," I taunted her, hoping to take her mind off things.

She grunted. "I'm not an angel."

No, she just looked like one.

And felt like one.

My fingers savored the contact, even as I was gradually easing my support. After a good five minutes, though, I'd admit I was disappointed to relinquish my hold on her.

"Can you walk?" I asked after she was standing on her own and I was at her side.

I sure as fuck wasn't about to leave her in the parking lot by herself at this time of the night. So she'd be coming into the motel office with me on foot or in my arms—it was down to her to decide which.

"I can manage," she whispered, exhaustion leaking into the words, never mind her expression.

Fuck, she'd look like that after she came. I knew she would. Except her eyes would be happy, not sad.

I wanted to see them happy. I really goddamn did.

Because she didn't sound all that confident, I hooked my arm around her waist after I'd retrieved my saddlebags and squeezed. "You can help keep me upright. My knees are aching."

They were, but not enough to need help. Still, it made her straighten up some and it had the added benefit of her putting her hand on my stomach to 'steer' me.

With my lips curving all the while, we walked into the motel office. I started to book us a pair of rooms, my only stipulation that they weren't on the ground floor, but she murmured, "One room will be fine. There are two beds, right?"

The clerk nodded, gave us a set of keys, and I squared up.

"You didn't have to do that," I chided, even though I was grateful.

She'd be easier to protect if we were in the same room, but I didn't want her to think I was anything like her soon-to-be fiancé.

Well, soon-to-be if our plan didn't work.

And my plans *always* worked.

So Bill fucking Murphy could get his virgin bride from somewhere else.

"This is already costing you more than it should," she grouched. "In time, effort, and energy."

"Sin will pay me back if I need the money."

"This isn't his problem either."

I wanted to say that she'd made it his problem when she'd come to the Sinners for help, but I had no desire to hurt her. She wasn't delicate, per se. Just kind and gentle. Not exactly the type of woman a guy like me should be sniffing around. Nothing about my life was kind or gentle.

Saying that, neither was her father's.

How the hell had a fucker like that reared a woman like this?

Talk about a changeling.

Especially as I'd had the misfortune of meeting Sin's succubus of an egg donor once as well.

I squeezed her side as we walked up the stairs, her leaning on me more than I was leaning on her, then when we got to the room, which was grim as fuck, I cast her a look to see if she was going to complain about the less than five-star accommodations.

She didn't appear to care, though, because the second we were inside, she let go of me, heaved over to the bed nearest the door, and face-planted onto it. The too-large leather jacket and hoodie I'd loaned her before we left the clubhouse, thick woolen scarf, gloves, and her sheepskin boots and all.

I smiled at the sight. "You'll feel better if you shower."

MaryCat wafted a hand then mumbled into musty-looking sheets, "You go first."

No way in hell if I went first would she be awake when I got out, which meant she'd end up not showering, but she was clearly exhausted...

Damning myself for a sucker, I left her alone to rest, pulled out my phone charger from the saddlebags, and got it charging before I headed into the bathroom.

Staring at myself in the mirror, I splashed water on my face and used the soap from the dispenser to clear off some of the grime from the long journey.

Even after a quick wash, I looked every single one of my years, whereas MaryCat was more like a baby in this shithole of a world we both inhabited.

She thought I was doing her a favor, and maybe I was. From her viewpoint. But she was the one who was about to forever be associated with a felon.

I rubbed my chin at the thought, wondering if I should warn her. Would it change her stance on things? Was she that desperate it wouldn't matter, or not desperate enough that it would?

Felon.

That was a label you just couldn't get away from. It fucked with everything. Your present, your future, even a fake fiancée you didn't particularly goddamn want.

I rolled my eyes at the thought then started stripping out of my clothes.

Ducking into the shower, I was grateful that she didn't want one yet because the pressure was low and it was mostly tepid, not boiling like I usually preferred. Still, it did the job, and after I was clean, I dried off, kept the towel around my waist as I grabbed my clothes from the floor, then headed back into the bedroom.

She hadn't moved, but her breathing was deep and low, indicative of someone fast asleep.

Did she feel safe around me? Or was she in possession of so few street smarts that she didn't see her position as a walking 'go' light to any predator?

Shaking my head at the sight and beyond fucking grateful I'd been the one at the gates when she showed up and not Jackson, I headed over to the other bed and dragged down the sheets before I clambered in, quickly shucking off the towel so the linen wouldn't get wet.

With her soft and low breaths as my soundtrack, the few lights from the road darting across the ceiling and gracing me with a short show before I slept, I decided to stop thinking about shit that was of no consequence and to get as much sleep as I could.

Tomorrow, after all, was going to be even harder than today.

10

MARYCAT

MARYCAT

IMPOSSIBLY, the pain I'd been in before I went to sleep was nothing to after.

Stiff as a board, I flopped onto my side, but as I did, I caught sight of Digger's back. It was muscled and inked. Nothing major, but he had a large portrait of a smiling woman on his throat that angled down to his shoulder. It was beautiful. *She* was beautiful.

His mom? Or a woman he'd loved?

For a moment, contemplating that snatched away thoughts of the excruciating toil on my bones that the journey had taken out on me thus far, and when the pain returned, I huffed.

As quickly as my aching body would allow, I hobbled off the bed and headed into the bathroom. It was damp inside so I knew he'd showered at some point, and I wiped my hand over the mirror that was still foggy with condensation to take in the state of me.

"Wow, you look worse than you feel," I muttered under my breath before I yawned and started stripping.

The bath didn't look that clean, but I really needed to soak, so I grabbed a small washcloth, poured the generic soap the motel provided onto it, and quickly wiped over the tub and rinsed it. Not ideal, not as clean as I'd like, but that was a testament to my pain level—I didn't have it in me to give more of a damn.

Once that was complete, I let the water run, and though it wasn't hot enough, it felt like heaven to just float, to feel weightless.

I nodded off in there, only for a little while, but the water had turned cold. I let some out, ran some in, then started to clean up, rubbing my fingers into my thighs where they were aching, wishing I could do the same to my ass as well.

I raised my leg high against my chest to stretch out the joint, then I used the new position to massage the back of my thigh. As I moved to switch legs, my knuckles brushed my pussy and I clenched down, surprised by the surge of sensation that hit me when I was so tired.

It was the Catholic in me that was turned on, I thought.

Knowing Digger was out there. Knowing he was asleep. The star of my fantasies from when I was younger...

I kept my leg high because it was tight in the small tub, and, intentionally this time, I rubbed my knuckles along the crease of my slit. A shaky breath escaped me as I caught my clit with my middle finger, and I rocked my hips back, parted my thighs more—

"You okay in there? You didn't drown in the bath, did you?"

My leg automatically kicked forward into the water with a splash. "I-I'm fine," I sputtered, mortified.

He grunted. "Good. Just checking."

My waking up had woken *him* up?

"Get yourself ready. If we're both awake, then we should head out."

The whine froze on my lips, much as I'd be freezing later on that damn bike of his.

"He's doing this for you," I whispered under my breath, even though the prospect of riding for several hours was akin to torture.

As torturous as being raped by Bill Murphy?

Inside, everything turned to ice.

Because of course, nothing was as bad as that.

I finished washing up without another peep and didn't utter a word of complaint when I settled on the back of the bike a half hour or so later…

11

DIGGER

DIGGER

SHE WAS A GOOD GIRL, I had to give her that.

I felt her discomfort like it was my own over the coming hours. She was cold, but she didn't complain as she huddled against me.

She was sore, but she didn't tug on my hand whenever there was a rest stop for a break.

Her silence worked in her favor because whenever a sign for a diner popped up and we'd been on the road for at least two hours, I stopped.

Whether it was for coffee or food, we took a break, and each time she sank into a booth or seat, I'd watch her face.

That expression, I was starting to be certain, would be what she looked like when she came.

Relief and need and want—in this instance, for coffee, but I'd take it.

She was hot and pretty to fucking look at—sue me.

When we'd driven through Iowa, Nebraska, and Colorado, I started looking for a motel around the Utah border.

After we found one, I also saw a drugstore, and because I knew her pain would only get worse, not better, I stopped there first.

"Come on," I told her, gently squeezing her knee. "I need to get some stuff."

Like the trooper she was—it was ridiculous to be proud of her, right?—she got off.

As we walked into the store, she leaned on me. Damn if that didn't make me feel ten feet tall to have a woman like this leaning on a man like me.

"How's your knee?" she croaked.

She'd been so silent that her words startled me.

"My knee?"

"You were limping after chasing the mugger."

"It's fine," I muttered. "I'm used to it."

She frowned. "Maybe you should see a doctor."

The suggestion was so *wifely* that I had to hide a grin. Instead of embarrassing her, I grunted and then directed, "Get whatever you need for the night."

She grabbed some soap and deodorant first, then faded away when she saw there were clothes. I thought it was cute how she blushed when she placed a package of panties on the counter.

I purchased some soap and deodorant too, but I also picked up Deep Heat.

With our stuff bought, little fuss coming from her when I paid on this occasion, though her smile was more befitting the gift of a diamond necklace than a package of panties and some toiletries, we returned to the bike.

A few minutes later, we were heading into another motel office. A room was rented for the night, and this time, we'd be staying the full night, not like we'd done yesterday. Something that was confirmed when she flopped on the bed again.

The only one in here…

Damn, I must have been more tired than I thought because I hadn't specified two beds.

Still, the way she starfished on the bedspread had me smiling at the sight, but unlike last night, I ordered, "Go and shower."

She mumbled under her breath, low enough that I couldn't hear.

"Shower first, MaryCat." I gently tapped her foot with my good knee.

"You go," she countered sleepily, making a shooing motion at me with her hand, but the second she spoke, I leaned down, hauled her into my arms, ignoring her as she yelped, and carried her to the bathroom which was much cleaner than the other place.

"If you don't want your clothes to get wet, then you need to tell me now because I *will* toss you under the spray fully dressed."

She gasped and, for the first time, glowered at me. "You wouldn't dare!"

Enjoying the return of her fire, I smirked. "Watch me."

Her glower darkened, then, out of nowhere, it faded and her bottom lip wobbled. "I can't."

"You can't?" I asked her quietly as I lowered her to the ground. "Why not, baby?"

It trembled some more. "I-I can't... I'm too tired."

I pressed a kiss to her forehead. I shouldn't have, but it felt right.

She didn't argue either. If anything, she sank into me. I let my lips remain there, content to suck in her scent before I accepted I couldn't stand like this all night.

With a sigh, I told her, "I know you are. But you'll feel better. Come on, just have a shower, and then I got some liniment for your legs." I sucked in a breath. "No funny business, but I'll rub them for you if you shower."

She peeped up at me, so fucking trusting that I wasn't sure if she honored me or enraged me.

I knew she was exhausted. I knew I'd done nothing to make her distrust me. So I had to accept that those two things combined made her let her guard down around me, but was that wise? No.

I could be lulling her into a false sense of security so I could drive off and kill her in the fucking woods.

Didn't she know how she was putting herself in danger by not—

"Would you help me undress?" Her cheeks practically glowed as the words rushed out.

Zero street smarts—*got it.*

"I'm so sorry to ask, Digger, but I really don't think I can do it on my own." She pushed her face into my throat. "I'm so sorry. I'm such a baby."

"A baby would have whined over the last nineteen hundred miles." I rubbed my chin over her hair, thanking Christ for the thousandth time that it had been me manning the gates and not another brother. "You're not a baby. You're just tired."

She was also lucky that I was a gentleman who'd been raised right. Despite my paternal parentage, Mom had done a bang-up job if I did say so myself.

Carefully, I propped her up for longer than I should've when she needed to soak. Still, I enjoyed how she leaned against me.

She was definitely a lightweight, but hell, my butt and shoulders were aching like fuckers too, and I was used to this.

I'd pushed us hard, though. I needed to be in Jersey yesterday, and we had to get this marriage signed and sealed so the Sinners would have both our backs.

"Your phone's ringing," she muttered sleepily as it started buzzing beside her ear.

I figured she knew I'd been ignoring it because the device sat in a pocket that she had to feel when she had her arms around my waist as we rode.

"It'll wait."

"Will it though?" When her weight sagged into me more, I rubbed her back and tried not to feel weird.

Weird as in... *I didn't know.* Warm inside?

It made me want to touch her more.

No funny shit, just... *touch.*

I cleared my throat. "Are you going to be okay in the shower? You're not going to fall over or anything? I can run a bath."

"A bath sounds like heaven," she mumbled drowsily.

"You can drown in a bath too," I pointed out, amused.

"Yeah, but what a way to go."

Pretty certain she was about to start snoring against me, I sighed. "Come on, let's get you in the water." I rested her against the vanity.

"Keep the spaghetti limbs to a minimum," I teased as I backed away and started filling the tub.

When it was a good temperature, I pushed in the plug and then left her there to return to the bedroom where she'd dropped the small bag with the stuff we'd purchased earlier.

Bringing it in with me, I grabbed the flowery body wash and deodorant she'd bought, squirted some soap into the water, tossed the deodorant onto the counter, and left the panties for her to deal with, knowing it would embarrass her if I handled them.

God, she was fucking cute.

As bubbles started popping into being, I turned to her and braced myself.

She was tired, fatigue etched into the lines of her face. Though she didn't mean to look that way, the heavy lids gave her a 'come hither' air that reminded me of the sultry black and white movies Mom had devoured when I was growing up.

MaryCat was like that though—*old-world glamor.*

All that goddamn red hair and curves for a lifetime.

It was difficult, when I pressed my hands to the clothes she wore, not to feel as if I were a piece of shit for even touching her. Unworthy of breathing the same air as a goddess like her.

I shrugged off the thought because it was pointless and right now, I was the only thing keeping her away from having to marry that rapist fuck, Murphy.

I might not be old-world glamor, but at least I was helping her when few others would, especially in such a permanent way.

Tugging at the borrowed outerwear, I tossed it through the door, uncaring if it landed on the floor. After dragging off her longer tufted jacket, which had a fancy name but did fuck all to keep her warm, I pulled on her scarf next, then her gloves, and then her sweater.

She moaned when I raised her arms overhead, and I knew everywhere was aching. Guilt kind of hit me, but I wasn't doing this for fun, and we needed this finalized as soon as possible.

Next came the layers of clothes she was wearing underneath, and I kept the last thin camisole for her to remove after I left.

Dropping to my knees, I unzipped her boots and helped her out of them.

When my fingers went to her fly, I half expected her to shove my hands away, but as I did, I noticed how her tits were quivering, and I knew if I looked, I wouldn't be seeing horror or disgust at my attention.

Her breathing had turned up a notch, and I knew she was reacting to me, my presence, my touch.

The princess wasn't offended by the peasant's hands on her —*got it.*

Mental note made, I flicked at the button and then dragged down the zipper. I had the makings of a boner, but I kept it under control because she was exhausted, and to be frank, I wasn't exactly wide awake.

A woman like this...

Well, she deserved more than me for her first time.

And she deserved more than this fucking motel, *and* for me to focus on what was happening between us rather than worrying over getting us to our destination.

As I pulled the jeans down, I found she was wearing thin long johns underneath, and I laughed to myself at the sight because that was unexpectedly practical.

Glamorpusses could be pragmatic—*got it.*

I wasn't about to take anything else off her, so when I moved to a standing position, I told her, "Okay, you're good to go."

Her hand reached for mine, and her breath hitched. "You know my family is Catholic."

I blinked. "I do."

She squeezed my fingers. "An annulment won't protect me and they *will* check."

I fell into her gaze as I zeroed in on what she was saying.

Christ, she'd had no privacy in her life if she knew her asswipe father would get a doctor in to check the state of her virginity.

"You're ready for what that means?" was all I said, aware that my voice had deepened, turning husky.

She stunned me by smiling. "I remember you, you know?"

"From when?"

"Westchester." Her lips quirked into a brighter smile that seemed to erase some of her fatigue. Did she have any fucking idea how beautiful she was? "I saw you there and everything about you…" She shivered. "It was so hot. You didn't look as if you'd brushed your damn hair for a month, but your face…" She tapped her forehead. "I couldn't forget that look we shared. You dismissed me when you saw my school uniform, but I didn't dismiss you."

"What do you mean?" I questioned softly, stepping closer to her so that my heat was her heat.

"I mean that you were my first crush." Her grin turned sheepish. "There's a twisted irony to life, isn't there? You've probably got dozens of bikers in that clubhouse, but you were the one on guard duty." She narrowed her eyes at me. "You're the reason I started getting into trouble."

My brows rose. "Why?"

"Because until then, I'd been all about the grades. All about toeing the line. Everything about you awakened me to boys." When I tensed up, she spelled it out, "I got tired of using my hand, Digger. Got tired of thinking about you, about what you'd look like beneath the cut, about how you'd touch me and how it would feel for that look we shared to become something else, something more.

"I knew you'd forget about me, knew that look meant nothing to you, but I didn't, *couldn't* forget about you."

I could have said a million things, could have let this turn into a premarriage celebration, but I'd always been too fucking honest for my own good.

"Do you want to know why I looked like a piece of shit that day?"

There was no denying that I remembered her. In that prissy little uniform that had made me feel like a pervert for checking her out. But I'd seen her face first, then the uniform.

I was many things but a pervert wasn't one of them, so I'd stopped looking and had focused on catching up with my messages.

I'd known she was there, though.

How could I not?

Her eyes rounded, and I knew she was surprised at what I was admitting to by asking her that. "Sure."

"Because I'd gotten out of prison about two hours earlier, Mary Catherine. Sin was my 'welcome home' party, and because we were in New York, he asked if we could stop at your mother's place.

"No one has to know we didn't fuck. Maybe there's another kid from school that you'd prefer to be with—" Just saying that made my voice lower into a growl. "We can file for a divorce if that's what makes you safer. But before you let these dirty hands touch you, think about what you're getting yourself into."

MARYCAT

I LET him storm off for two reasons.

One, because hobbling after him *wouldn't* be a power move.

Two, because I sensed him being a felon was a bigger deal to him than it was to me.

I wasn't sure if he wanted me to be outraged or disgusted by his admission like he clearly was. There was a lot to unpack there, and none of it had anything to do with what he'd actually confessed to.

Father was a felon. That was partly why Mother had cheated so often and why he wasn't high in the ranks: because he kept getting caught.

My uncle and a few of my cousins were just as bad at staying under the cops' radar.

Jail was the family's home away from home—*a real vacation spot.*

He had to know that.

I was a Five Pointer's brat, for God's sake. So the melodramatic confession confused me.

A lot.

"Paul! Oh, my god! NO!"

I jerked at the scream that came from next door. It was so loud thanks to the paper-thin walls, which made it seem as if the woman were here in the bathroom with me.

Adrenaline gave me wings and had me hauling my bag of bones out of the bathroom and into the bedroom, where I saw that Digger, the guy who was apparently a big, bad felon and whose hands were too filthy to touch me, no longer occupied the room.

Our door was wide open, and I heard him slamming on our neighbor's, yelling, "Get the fuck off her!"

Was I surprised to find him using his shoulder to break down the door when I made it outside?

Nope.

When he busted in, I rushed after him, about to help the poor woman while Digger dealt with whomever the hell this Paul was, but when I charged toward the room, my frozen feet colliding with the concrete floor, and I jerked to a halt in the doorway at the sight of *who* Paul was.

A teenage boy.

Choking on something while his mother tried and failed to pull off the Heimlich maneuver.

I reared back at the sight and then watched as Digger, that oh, so big and oh, so bad felon, took control of the situation.

A second later, a Flamin' Hot Cheeto soared out of his mouth and landed, grossly enough, beside my bare foot.

I flexed my toes at the sight, and seeing that I wasn't needed, that Digger had everything under control, I slipped away and back to our room.

If I'd been cold before, that was nothing to now. My feet literally felt like they were going to drop off, and when I rushed to the bathroom, which was steamy and warm from the running water, I undressed fully while I still had the energy to do so.

Sinking into the bath was close to painful. My skin stung and my toes burned but damn, my muscles responded to the heat.

Grateful that this motel believed in having decent water heaters, I felt myself grow drowsy as I soaked, but as inactive as my body was, my brain was whirling at a high speed.

Digger—exactly who was this man I'd be calling husband tomorrow?

Over the twenty-five or so hours of riding, I'd had nothing else to do but think and consider how fucking crazy this entire situation was.

Yet, in the little time I'd known him, he'd agreed to spare me from a forced arranged marriage, had helped a granny during a mugging, had taken down her attacker, then had gone to save some poor woman next door before sparing her son from choking.

Either I'd fallen for a Boy Scout who wore a cut or he was just a genuinely good guy.

But good guys didn't go to jail—what crime, I wondered, had he committed?

He said he'd buried bodies in his time, but there was no way he'd be out of prison this young if he'd been inside on a murder one charge…

As I let the heat sink into my aching bones, I stared at the faded, ancient tiles lining the walls and registered that, good guy or not, criminal or not, I was putting my life into his hands, and I'd take that any day of the week over my father and Bill goddamn Murphy.

13

DIGGER
BEHIND BLUE EYES - LIMP BIZKIT

DIGGER

WHEN THE DOOR unlocked to the bathroom, I was sitting on the bed, legs crossed at the ankles, hands on my abs as I watched TV.

The last ninety minutes hadn't exactly rolled out as I expected.

My shoulder ached like a fucker after busting that door down. I didn't regret that, or the two-hundred-dollar bill I'd paid for repairs, because our neighbor looked as if she didn't have money for her next meal, never mind an unexpected charge that high.

No, aching shoulder and lighter wallet aside, I couldn't regret it when the kid had been turning blue in the face by the time I'd raced in.

I had some ice from the machine outside on my shoulder, but I knew from experience it wouldn't do jack. I'd had enough injuries throughout my lifetime to know that time healed these particular wounds.

Still, the sight of her wet and warm and sleepy as she stepped out of the bathroom packed more of a punch than four Tylenol.

Her drowsy smile was like ambrosia to a wounded soldier too.

When she clambered onto the bed, did it make me a jackass that I took note of the fact she'd put on her bra under the cami I'd left her in?

She wore the long johns too, and I could see the line of her panties cut into an asscheek I wanted to bite—shoulder be damned.

Even though she was as far from polished as could be, there was something about her that felt a hell of a lot more tactile. Like she was more accessible now in her regular gear than in the CKs and the D&Gs and the CHs that she wore. Hell, even her gloves were branded.

I figured she was too exhausted to argue about there only being one bed as she lifted the sheet and curled beneath it.

"That was a nice thing you did over there," she whispered once she was settled beneath the comforter.

I'd seen her come in and head out, and I didn't blame her, not with as few clothes as she was wearing.

The woman needed a keeper—*got it.*

"Thought she was being attacked," I said gruffly.

"I did too." She curled onto her side, making the scent of her flowery soap perfume the air. Even that was innocent. "Do you want me to rub some of that Deep Heat onto your shoulder? It must be hurting."

"I was supposed to do that to you."

"You're the wounded soldier," she teased with a drowsy smile, unerringly matching my earlier thought.

"Hardly. Get some sleep," I told her, smiling back at her when I saw she didn't even wait that long to close her eyes and drift off.

With the soft hum of the TV and her gentle breaths, I'd admit, something inside me felt rested.

There was a crazy world outside these walls. The TV proved that when I switched over to the news and saw a volcano had erupted in Europe, there was an earthquake in Haiti, as well as a blizzard in Boston. Yet here, all was quiet.

I knew I should go shower off the road, but the deeper she slept, the closer she moved until she was nestled up against my side. That felt good. Like a luxury all on its own.

When I knew I was starting to fall asleep, though, I dragged the pillow out from behind my head and began edging away. She grumbled under her breath but let me go.

I collected an extra blanket from the closet and, with a grimace, settled on the floor, tucking the pillow beneath my head and covering myself with the scratchy fabric.

My bones immediately ached, never mind my goddamn shoulder, but I was so fucking tired that I drifted off pretty quickly.

God knew how long later, I woke up when a soft whoosh of air brushed my neck.

I might have been out of jail for years, but my instincts still ran high when I was in a vulnerable position.

I immediately woke up.

That was when I realized what was happening—she'd gotten out of bed and was curled into me on the fucking floor.

For a moment, I just stared at her, dead certain that my eyes had failed me.

But, no.

Her scent perfumed the air around me again—gently overpowering the mustiness of the carpet. Her silky skin slid against mine as she cuddled into me. And her hand, her fucking hand, was pressed so low on my abs that she was an inch away from touching my boner.

I didn't know if I was pissed about having zero personal space here, worried about her inability to be self-aware and to protect herself, or just fucking touched that she wanted to be so close to me, even in her sleep.

With my bones having settled, I groaned as I straightened into a standing position. Not once did she wake up.

"Fuck's sake, Mary Catherine," I muttered as I rolled her into my arms and lifted her high.

When she settled against my chest like she belonged there, it was hard to accept that she didn't.

And because I had no business thinking that shit, I quickly placed her on the mattress.

The only problem?

MaryCat, of course.

As I moved away, she grabbed my hand, mumbling, "Digger?"

I heaved a sigh. "It's me."

"Where are you going?" She blinked sleepily. "Come to bed."

My free hand balled into a fist. "No, I'll sleep on the floor."

She tutted and shifted over to the other side of the mattress, not only making space for me but dragging me with her as much as a little thing like her could with someone my size.

"Are you sure?" I asked, meaning it too.

She yawned. "Of course."

When I gingerly settled on the bed then lay out flat, it wasn't too dissimilar from how she'd fallen asleep earlier.

Except, this time, she didn't lie next to me.

No, she tucked her leg over mine, settled her face against my side, and hugged her arm over my stomach.

As I stared at the ceiling, I wondered how the fuck this had happened.

But before I had an answer, I was asleep myself—the warmest and most comfortable I'd ever been in my whole godforsaken life.

14

MARYCAT
TEMPTATION - HEAVEN 17

MARYCAT

I WOKE up with one of my legs over Digger's lap, my knee nudging his morning wood.

Was I embarrassed?

A little.

Did I react like my knee was touching hot, molten lava?

Yes.

I was more embarrassed about behaving like a frightened virgin than the morning wood or the precarious position, though. Because, naturally, a man with his background and his temperament reacted to my *over*reaction—he jolted and sat upright.

"What is it? What's going on?"

"Nothing," I told him, my voice low and husky from sleep.

He slowly sank back down. "Nothing? Then why did you jump?" he questioned, his voice still thick and raspy.

I shook my head and tried to back away from my embarrassing response to our proximity with a yawn. "I just woke up with a fright."

Bullshit if I ever heard it, but he seemed to buy it because his eyes drifted closed again and he seemed to snooze, which gave me some space to climb off the bed and to stand, ironically, where he'd been sleeping when I woke up last night to use the bathroom.

They said chivalry was dead, but Digger proved otherwise.

He'd looked so miserably uncomfortable as well as *cold* that I'd had to join him, hoping to help him get warm. The next thing I knew, he was tucking me into bed while expecting to sleep on the floor again.

I wasn't about to allow that.

Of course, that had led to my predicament—the whole knee nudging his erection thing.

Biting my lip and shoving the thought of his erection aside, I headed into the bathroom to shower.

It was impossible to believe that I'd be getting married in clothes that I'd worn three days on the run, but beggars couldn't be choosers.

I'd take my dirty clothes over a wedding dress that cost five thousand any day of the damn week if my groom was Digger.

I pulled a face at the thought and scrubbed myself harder to make up for the grimy outfit.

Once I was dressed, I headed into the room and found Digger working his arm on the bed.

Slowly, he moved it around and around, stretching it and trying to ease it, but from his grimace, I didn't think he achieved all that much.

"Let me put some Deep Heat on it."

He cast me a look. "After I shower if you don't mind?"

"Why would I mind?"

Digger grunted then got to his feet and stomped into the bathroom. As he did, it was like all the air in the room came back with a wallop, and I flopped onto the bed, trying not to fangirl about what was happening next.

For the first time in a few days, I felt like I'd slept. Really, truly slept.

After Father's announcement, I'd had bad dreams and had spent most of the nights tossing and turning. Then, yesterday, I'd woken up after a couple hours and had been aching so badly that I might as well not have rested at all.

But I felt a lot better today.

My butt was sore, sure, and I wasn't looking forward to the rest of the journey. Today would be long and grueling because I knew he wanted to hit Vegas tonight... Achieving the end goal would be worth it though.

I was going to be his wife.

I heard the shower turn on and tried not to think about a naked Digger.

Last night, he'd been the consummate gentleman, and I knew I'd put myself in a dumb position by asking him to help me undress, yet he hadn't taken advantage of me. At my weakest, my body trusted him. I knew I was safe with him, felon or not, and he kept on proving that with his actions.

When the shower continued running for a long time, I thought he was doing one of two things—letting the water soak into his bones to ease his aches, or he was jerking off.

God, I hoped it was the latter.

I'd felt his erection against my knee. The first I'd ever experienced because Kris had been shy and he'd backed away like I'd zapped him with a Taser when he got a boner.

Digger's had felt big.

Heavy.

Thick.

I swallowed.

I could almost imagine him picking up his shaft as the shower water pelted him, could see him in my mind's eye holding it in that large, tattooed hand of his...

It'd fit in his grip, but I bet it wouldn't in mine.

I spread my fingers wide and studied the size of my palm—no, it definitely wouldn't fit in mine.

Biting my lip at the thought, I tried not to get turned on, but after waking up how I had, you bet your damn ass I was thinking about sex.

With him.

Lots of sex. With *him.*

Men got morning wood every day, so I knew it didn't mean anything really. But as he jerked off, was it too much to ask that he'd be thinking about me seeing as I was the closest woman in the vicinity?

Plus, he'd slept with me. And I smelled good even if my clothes were starting to be a little worse for wear. Did that matter to men?

My brain whirred with nonsense, so I calmed myself down with thoughts about perfect and imperfect competition, running down the theories on both.

God, I hated economy class.

When the shower turned off, my heart started racing again, and I sat up, arranging my legs on the bed so that I didn't look as ungrateful as I had the last two nights.

"What the hell were you thinking, face-planting on the bed like that?" I grumbled under my breath as I turned my attention to the TV and tried not to look as if I were waiting for him to show up.

TVGM, the morning breakfast show, had Savannah Daniels talking to some celebrity about the lighting of the Rockefeller Center tree tonight, but I didn't give a damn if it was Christmas or Easter.

Would he come out wearing only a towel?

God, I hoped so—

The door opened.

I peeped out the corner of my eye and saw him.

Yes.

He was only wearing a towel. It was pulled taut against his hips, the knot too tight for my liking.

His abs were made up of more muscles than I could count from the corner of my eye, and he had pecs that belonged to a hero in a movie.

Water was dripping all over him, too, in a secret invitation to my tongue to dry him off.

Digger cleared his throat. "You okay to rub some of that liniment on me?"

I nodded without looking at him as I got to my feet and reached for the tube while he took a seat.

Squirting some onto my fingers, I was careful on the already bruised flesh, but I gently worked it into his muscles, going around the ball of his shoulder but moving across his back and down to his bicep.

"That feels much better. God," he growled under his breath, making me jump, but I carried on, working some more of the cream along his spine and over to the other side. He didn't ask me to, but I liked touching him.

Hell, my teenage self was creaming in her panties over getting the chance to touch him in this way.

When I was done, I saw that he wasn't as tense when he got to his feet.

"Thanks for that. Do you want me to do you?"

Do me?

Well, there was an invitation.

I blinked up at him, unsure if he was still talking about the Deep Heat or not. "No, I'm good. Thanks."

"You sure?" He arched a brow. "You were exhausted and aching last night."

"The soak helped."

"If you say so. We've got another fourteen hours on the road," he warned.

I died inside even though I'd been aware of that. We still had Utah and Arizona to get through, never mind Nevada.

"We're going to eat first, aren't we?"

Digger snorted. "Yeah, we are."

I smiled. "Dumb question, really."

"Seeing as I pack away three times as much as you, it was."

"We'll stop for coffee breaks?" I asked hopefully.

"We will."

"Then, I'm fine."

He chucked me on the chin. "You definitely are," he rumbled, and those three words whispered down my spine.

Lord.

How I didn't shiver, I'd never know.

I blinked up at him again. "Thank you?"

He smirked and returned to the bathroom while I wilted on the bed once more.

I was so stupid. I should have let him rub the cream into my aches. Was it too late to call him back?

I heard the sounds of him brushing his teeth and accepted it was.

We'd be sleeping in another motel tonight after the wedding cere-mony, wouldn't we?

He was right that we could lie about consummating the marriage, that I could sleep with someone I actually knew, but I'd be crazy to lie about that when I wanted his hands on me more than I'd ever wanted another's touch.

Tonight, I had the Deep Heat as an excuse.

There was no way in hell I wouldn't react to his hands on me, and if I could encourage him, maybe it would lead to more.

Maybe…

If he was interested.

He didn't seem interested.

Or I could have been misreading the signs.

I wasn't very good with this kind of stuff because I wasn't supposed to be.

It wasn't like I'd had the regular life lessons that all women did by my age. And the few experiences I had were marred by Kris' murder which was the result of *my whorish behavior.*

Father's words, not my own.

Regardless, I had a choice.

Tonight, I'd have a husband.

It was down to me if it was in name only or not.

15

DIGGER

DIGGER

WE MADE it to Las Vegas in excellent time.

The second stop at a diner, with MaryCat wilting into me, I'd let her chill out over some waffles with eggs and bacon and two coffees, then I'd ridden us hard and hadn't taken a break until we got here because I knew if we stopped again, she'd fall asleep.

I'd never had to think about another person this much, and with the long journey, my mind didn't have much else to do but wonder about her.

Ordinarily, on a run, we'd be watching out for cops, trying to stay under the radar, but I wasn't doing anything wrong for once, so my mind just had to focus on the automatic stuff like watching the road and trying not to get a boner when her hands slipped down my waist as she wiggled around for a more comfortable position.

When, with the sun sputtering its final few rays behind us, we rode past the sign for Las Vegas, I had to laugh when she hollered, "Wooohoooooo!"

I felt her relief warring with her exhaustion, and though I knew we could head directly for a wedding chapel, I didn't.

Instead, I stopped off at a jewelry store in a strip mall I'd looked up at that last diner.

It wasn't anywhere fancy, not like where Bill Murphy would go to buy a ring for her, definitely no Van Cleef & Arpels, but it was better than what they'd sell in the chapels.

When we pulled up outside the mall, parking next to a fifteen-foot Christmas tree with flashing lights that could trigger a seizure, and the engine quieted, she asked, "Why are we stopping?"

"Need to get you a ring. But we have to hurry. The store closes soon."

She tugged on my cut. "You don't need to buy me anything."

I twisted around to scowl at her. "I do. You need a ring. Your father won't believe we're married otherwise."

"I'll show him the damn wedding certificate," she groused, then her cheeks pinkened. "I don't want you to spend unnecessary money on this."

My gaze drifted over her flushed features, and I couldn't stop myself from muttering, "Damn, you're pretty."

Her eyes flared wide as she let them get snagged by mine. "Thank you?"

She'd said that earlier. It was breathy and hopeful and made me think shit I shouldn't be thinking.

For all that, I just said, "You're welcome."

She licked her lips before tugging that bottom one between her teeth.

I wanted to gnaw on that myself.

Staring at her, I watched her creamy skin turn pink. "D-Digger?"

"Yeah?"

"You're looking at me—"

"You're a pleasure to look at."

The pink shifted into red, and I decided to ease her embarrassment by explaining, "I'm not poor, Mary Catherine. I might not be a millionaire, but I can more than easily pay for a ring."

"For a fake wife?" She shook her head. "You shouldn't be out of pocket for this. You're doing me a favor..."

I *was* doing her a favor of sorts. But she was doing me one too.

She just didn't know it yet.

"I'll tell you a secret if you get off the bike."

Interest piqued, she did as I said. Unsurprisingly. She might be a good girl, but she was like every woman on God's green earth—curious as fuck.

With a groan of my own, I climbed off my hog, and when I saw her shivering at my side, I tugged her into a hug.

Surprised when she flowed with the movement, not uncomfortable by such forwardness from me, I rewarded her by rubbing my hands up and down her spine to warm her further.

"What secret?" she prompted breathily, silently telling me my touch affected her.

Fuck, I was a lucky bastard.

Especially when I thought about her admission last night—that she'd fantasized about me as a teenager.

When my dick started aching, I shifted my train of thought. She was comfortable with me—I didn't want to wreck that by scaring her with a boner.

"Remember I told you I didn't have a father?"

She narrowed her eyes at me. "Are you going to dive-bomb me with information again?"

I had to smile. "Maybe."

"Just so you know, I don't think I have many guys in my extended family who haven't been to jail." She huffed. "That came out sounding far prouder than it should have."

"It did sound kinda proud, actually," I agreed, which had her huffing again.

"Yeah, well, when you throw stuff at me as if it's a gauntlet, then I guess we can confirm I'm not afraid to pick it up and toss it back at you."

I arched a brow at her. "You have been very docile."

"Trust me, the red hair isn't false advertising. I've just been—"

"You've been a good girl. I like knowing that you might be naughty too."

Her cheeks flushed as she stared at me. "I've never been naughty in my life. Until you."

I traced my finger over her jawline. "Sometimes, it just takes the right person to free a part of your nature—"

"I want to consummate the marriage." Then, like I might have misunderstood, she stated, "With you."

Triumph might have roared through me, but I tamped it down.

I wasn't a fucking animal, and she was exhausted.

Horny or not.

I tipped my head to the side. "Not tonight. Maybe not tomorrow."

Her frown made an appearance. "What?!"

When she started pouting, that was when I knew I had to kiss her.

I pressed my mouth to hers but darted back to nip her bottom lip with a hard enough bite she was squirming against me.

Cupping her throat, I used my hold on her to angle her head back and she fucking let me. It had me growling under my breath. In response, she whimpered and gave me my in.

I'd never been someone's first time, had never wanted to be, and as I kissed her now, I got the feeling I'd be more than just her first time having sex because even where kissing was concerned, she was inexperienced.

Her hesitancy shone through, as did her uncertainty.

She was willing to follow my lead, eager and hungry but definitely not learned about these things.

I knew she'd had a boyfriend, but if he'd gotten past first base, I'd be surprised.

Oddly pleased by her inexperience, I coached her while I teased her. I thrust my tongue against hers, encouraging her to do the same in return. I tasted and savored and moaned when she mirrored my actions.

For the first time, I understood the advantage of being with someone who was a blank slate—I could teach her to be my every fucking wild dream. And she was already halfway there thanks to that goddamn hair and a body that'd make Marilyn Monroe envious.

When her hands came up to drag over my scalp, her nails scratching the sensitive flesh, I growled again, loving the mewl that whispered from her throat, proof that she was helpless and lost to the need that stirred between us.

When I pulled back with a final nip to her lip, I rumbled, "That's why it won't be tonight or tomorrow and maybe not the night after that either. Because good things come to those who wait."

And maybe, just maybe, she was exactly the 'good' I'd been waiting for. A good I didn't deserve but who seemed to want me anyway.

Even if this was just about her rebelling, about her fulfilling her teenage fantasies, I'd take it.

Hell, I'd take it all the way to the fucking bank.

Her hands reached for mine, and her nails dug into my palms. Not to steer, but to plead. "I'm scared."

Well, that helped with my boner.

"Of what?" I demanded.

"What if my father figured out what we're doing? What if he and Bill are here—"

"If they are, so what? You want to be my wife, Mary Catherine? The bullshit aside, I know it's crazy. I know you'd never in a million years want to be with a guy like me—"

"You're the first guy I got off to, Digger. You're the guy I wanted to date when I was in high school—I went for the bad boy and learned he was an emo, then I got him killed for his pains." Misery slithered into her gaze. "I don't know why, but that one glance in Westchester and I knew what desire was. I don't love you—I don't *know* you. But I'd like to. I'd like to have the chance."

"Then that's all that counts," I rasped, appreciating her answer more than she could know. One thing I couldn't tolerate was bullshit. "I'll keep you safe, MaryCat.

"They won't get to you. Whether or not they know you're here, it doesn't matter. You have no need to be scared when you're with me."

"You really mean that, don't you?"

I shrugged. "Wouldn't say it if I didn't. And you don't need to rush into sex if you're not ready just because you're scared of them."

Her eyes were massive in her face, but the heat in them told me she didn't just want me because of the situation—*got it.*

"What about you?" MaryCat asked a second later. "God, you can't want any of this."

"Maybe I shouldn't, but you've grown on me."

"Like mold. Great."

My lips twitched. "No. Not like mold. I had motivations of my own for starting this, MaryCat."

"What were they?"

"That secret I was talking about... I told you that I didn't have a dad, but I didn't tell you that I knew who raped my mother."

"You know—"

My smile was cold. "His name was Bill Murphy."

A gasp escaped her. "You're..." She surged onto her tiptoes to get into my face. "Are you being serious?"

"I'm being deadly serious." My mouth tightened. "I found out when I was twenty-four after she died. Found some letters that confirmed it." What a shitty fucking Christmas that had been.

I eyed the tree at my side with a grimace.

"Is that how you know all about his wives? I thought that was weird."

"Yes. Because I went looking."

Her eyes widened and then she proved she was clever, and I suddenly understood how she'd earned her scholarship. "He's why you went to jail, isn't he?"

"He is. My biggest regret is that I didn't kill the bastard. That I only went down for aggravated assault."

She gulped. "Wow."

"Yes."

"So, this is revenge?"

I hitched a shoulder. Sucked that it was my sore one. Fuck, that hurt. "Started that way."

I half-expected her to be hurt, but she wasn't. Instead, she graced me with a smile.

"*That* I can handle. This makes sense to me. I don't like things that don't make sense. It hurts my brain." She tugged on my hand and started trying to drag me toward the strip mall. Unfortunately for her, she was tiny and I was not. "Okay, you can buy me a ring now."

Stunned, I laughed. "It's that simple?"

"There's nothing worse than a woman scorned. You just triggered that inside me." She tugged on my hand again. "Come on. I want this done. We don't have to consummate things tonight, or tomorrow or whatever, but *you* will take my virginity, Digger. This is fate."

"Is this the equivalent of dancing on someone's grave?" I asked, amused by the fire in her eyes.

"Nope, it's the equivalent of *fucking* on someone's grave."

Weird as it was, I could get behind that too. Especially when that grave belonged to that fucker of a sperm donor of mine.

16

MARYCAT

IT WAS nothing like I imagined my wedding would be.

Nothing.

I didn't wear a white dress; I had no attendants.

It was pitch black outside, and I could hear the cheers from a drunken party just beyond the chapel in a busy bar that was rammed to the hilt.

There was no Father Doyle preaching about marriage being the cornerstone of society with the same speech he used at every service— at least, every service I'd ever attended, and that had to be in the hundreds by now.

No bridesmaids were crying about their shitty dresses; I didn't have a corsage or a bouquet in my hands.

Instead, I was serenaded by the infamous nightly fireworks display from the Gallinaro as the Grinch married us—complete with a green face, big pointy ears, and a Santa suit that really was the cherry on the sundae.

As we said, 'I do,' the relief that hit me was real.

When this guy was the only one available at that moment, Digger had offered to drive us elsewhere, but I just wanted this over.

I also wanted a room for the night to sleep in, no funny business.

Maybe that was why my laughter was a little more hysterical than it should have been as Digger carefully pushed the ring onto my finger. Then, he did the damnedest thing.

Something that made my heart twang in my chest.

That made my ovaries sing.

That made every dream of a fairy-tale wedding pale in comparison.

He raised my hand and kissed the ring. His lips touched either side of the simple platinum band that I'd argued was far too expensive, and I felt that simple caress down to my core.

When he looked at me, his mouth still on my hand, I rasped, "If you don't want me to fall in love with you, James Dane—" I'd just learned his real name. "—then you need to stop doing things like that."

A twinkle appeared in his eyes. "Who says I don't want you to fall in love with me?"

Piqued enough for my fatigue to lessen, I twisted my hand in his then plastered myself against his chest in a move I'd learned in dance class—who said the waltz had no place in modern society?

With our bodies brushing, my face tilted up as I stared at him, I breathed, "Love is dangerously contagious."

And the forced proximity we'd had and would have over the upcoming week wouldn't help matters.

"Is that a warning or a promise?"

"It could be both."

That twinkle morphed into something I could only describe as glee.

Did that mean he wanted me to catch feelings for him?

Or was it just the craziness of the moment?

We'd had a wild ride here, and it wasn't over yet. I knew we were both buzzing with adrenaline—it was the only thing keeping me upright and it *had* to be affecting him too.

My adrenaline rush, combined with the magic of his touch, had my heart pumping and sending hope zinging through my bloodstream.

The Grinch broke into our moment with, "I have another wedding scheduled in ten minutes."

Even though it was nuts, I couldn't help but think that this would be a pretty epic story to tell our grandkids…

Digger nodded. "We're heading out."

We didn't—we stayed in place.

Our gazes tangled. Our bodies remained closely tucked together. Our hearts thumped so heavily that I could feel his against my chest and I knew he'd feel mine too.

The Grinch cleared his throat.

Still, we stared at each other, and it was like that first day in Westchester.

When he'd seen me. Not my school uniform. Me. Before anything else had gotten in the way.

Wouldn't it be hilarious if something came from this?

If something impossible morphed into being out of a desperate situation and chance?

His thumb rubbed along my chin. I had a little divot there, and it seemed to settle in the nook as he tipped my head back farther and pressed the softest of breath-stealing kisses to my lips.

"My heart hasn't grown three sizes, you know? Can we hurry things along?" was the Grinch's grumble which was followed by a coughing fit that told me louder than words that the man had a nicotine addiction.

Not the most romantic soundtrack, but damn, I'd take it.

"We should go," I whispered, staring into his eyes like they held the answers to all the known problems in the universe.

"We should, Mrs. Dane," he confirmed, gently squeezing my fingers as he spoke.

God, I was married.

Married.

To a man I didn't know, but I'd always expected that. I just hadn't expected to have a choice on who that stranger would be, or for him to be my first-ever crush…

17

DIGGER

DIGGER

I PICKED one of the hotels on the strip that didn't have stupid posters plastered to it but that I knew would have luxury suites—the Gallinaro.

Fake marriage or not, a woman like Mary Catherine deserved somewhere swanky for her wedding night. Not that five stars were out of the ordinary for her.

She didn't coo at the room like other women might have.

A clubwhore would have run squealing around the place as if she were on speed, trying every seat, cleaning the mini fridge out.

Mary Catherine just sighed like she'd finally come home.

"The bathroom is over here and there's the—"

I tuned out our butler and told MaryCat, "Go and take a bath."

Her smile was sheepish, but she nodded and then moved over to the room the butler had pointed to.

Because I had about as much interest in being waited on as I did in catching VD, I gave the guy a tip to get rid of him and told him we'd buzz if we wanted anything.

I'd let MaryCat handle this bozo. What might be standard for her, sure as shit wasn't for me.

I cracked my neck the second he was gone and worked my

shoulder too as I wandered around the suite, doing what MaryCat hadn't done—oohed and aahed.

The ability to afford a place like this wasn't why I didn't stay in them. Brothers rested their weary bones in sister chapters on runs. Not five-star hotels. That didn't mean I didn't appreciate the luxury, especially after I'd pushed us both to make it here.

I grabbed a beer from the fridge even though it cost twenty-five bucks, and I sank back into a double-wide armchair that overlooked the strip.

As I stared at the mountains in the distance, I rested my ankle on my knee and chilled out some.

It wasn't every fucking day a man got married. I deserved some zen time before I dealt with the calls and the messages on my phone.

I waited until my beer was finished to grab the charger for my cell from the saddlebags I'd hauled up with us, then once it was charging, I swiped through the notifications when the device powered on.

Deciding to deal with the Prez first, I called Rex.

"Where the fuck are you?"

I didn't bother grimacing at his idea of a greeting and didn't bother wasting his time by prevaricating.

"Remember that piece of shit—Bill Murphy?"

I knew I'd surprised him because he fell silent. Then, he sighed. "Tell me you didn't beat his ass again? Rachel will not be fucking happy if you did."

It had taken our lawyer, Rachel Laker, a lot of work to get my sentence down to three years rather than the standard eight.

When I didn't say anything, he groaned. "You killed the fucker? Tell me where the body is and I'll get Cruz to come and boil his bones."

My nose crinkled. "I didn't kill the fucker. Even if he deserved it."

"Won't argue."

"Good," I grunted. The club knew I had daddy issues.

"If you didn't kill the bastard, then what about him?"

"Stole his fiancée."

Rex sucked in a breath. "Explain."

So I did.

I told him everything.

From beginning to end.

I even included saving Mrs. K's purse from a mugger, just because I knew Rex had always had a soft spot for the teachers and staff at our old 'alma mater.' Dude had set records in the classes there.

If he hadn't been born and bred to be the Prez of the Satan's Sinners' MC, then I was pretty fucking sure he was born to be the president of something.

Maybe even the good ol' United States of America.

"Jesus Christ, Digger. Why am I blessed with you dipshits for brothers?" he grated out when I finished. "And don't think that mess with Mrs. K gets you off anything. Why the fuck didn't you come to me before you took off for Vegas?"

I grinned to myself. "Because it's easier to say sorry after the fact?"

He growled. "Motherfucker."

"You heard what I said, didn't you?" I argued. "Bastard was going to rape her—"

"You don't know that."

"Don't I? Ain't I living proof that the fucker doesn't care about raping poor girls?"

Rex huffed. "Don't get me in my feels."

"Why not? I'm in mine. What's with all the calls anyway? Were you guys concerned about me?"

My mocking tone had him grunting. "Fucker disappears from the clubhouse, can't be found anywhere on the compound, and was acting sneaky as hell after he switched guard duty with another brother?

"Throw in our text conversation and you bet your ass I was worried. You're beyond reliable. *Usually.* I was thinking someone had fucking hijacked you or some shit."

"It's nice to know you care."

I received another grunt for my pains.

It wasn't a lie, though.

It *was* nice to know he cared. Especially when I took in the hundreds of missed calls I'd had from brothers the club over. None of which, it seemed, were related to MaryCat.

Before we grew ovaries, I checked, "The Five Points been sniffing around?"

"No. Doubt they realize the girl knows about her half-brother. Not sure it's something Sin's skank mother would advertise."

I'd admit, my relief was real. I didn't want to bring war to the Sinners, but serving my sperm donor a sweet 'fuck you' and saving the girl from his miserable hide was worth it any day of the week.

"You're really married?"

I heard his astonishment. "Want to see a picture of the marriage certificate?"

He snickered. "No. I believe you. Just can't believe you're fucking married. Weren't you the guy who used to get hammered on vodka and Red Bull, declaring that marriage was for pussies?"

"Vengeance tastes nicer than vodka and Red Bull."

"It fucking better." I could almost imagine him shaking his head. "Why did you have to go all the way to Vegas, dipshit? There are plenty of one-day states where you could have gotten married without heading off to the other side of the country."

My mouth rounded. "What?"

"Lemme see… Colorado, Utah, Nebraska, Indiana, Illinois, and Ohio. Yeah, they're all one-day states. I mean, fuck, why didn't you stay in Coshocton? We have a sister chapter there, you complete dumb-ass." He snorted. "Some digger of truth you fucking are. Use Google next time. Google is your friend."

He couldn't see me, so I flipped him the bird. "Jesus." I thought about MaryCat's exhaustion and pulled a face. "Crap."

Marriage hadn't exactly been a priority of mine, so I hadn't thought to look.

"Sums it up." Rex cackled.

"How do you know that?" I jibed. "Been looking at getting married?"

He sniffed but didn't answer me. "Bill Murphy's like a bad

goddamn smell you can't get rid of. I almost wish your mom had kept

your sperm donor's identity a secret."

"I don't."

"You wouldn't," Rex groused. "Instead, I've got one of my best men going half-fucking-cocked on vigilante missions against a Five Pointer. It's a wonder we haven't gone to war yet."

When I'd beaten the crap out of Daddy Dearest, I hadn't worn my cut. Ties to the Sinners were there if the Five Points looked, but apparently, Bill wasn't worth even a glance.

Either that or he'd gone out of his way to keep the court case quiet because Rachel had worked her wiles on the jury about my reasons for assaulting the bastard.

Although, I wasn't sure why he'd bother now that I knew about MaryCat's situation. Wasn't like the Five Points' grunts didn't use rape as a bargaining tool anyway.

If we *did* go to war with them, I'd ride to the O'Donnellys' compound in Queens and shove the truth in their faces about how their women were being treated on their watch.

Never let it be said that I wasn't a fucking feminist.

I said none of that, though, just queried, "Since when am I one of your best men?"

"Don't get too big-headed," Rex grumbled. "You're still the dipshit who married Sin's sister. *In fucking Vegas!*" He hooted. "I don't need to beat some sense into you. He'll do that for me!"

I knew he wasn't wrong, but I still weaseled, "Sin will see that what we did was the right move."

"If you say so. You going to make a go of this, or is it in name only?"

"Why do you ask? That's a pretty fucking personal question. Are we gonna have a sleepover too?"

"Yeah, yeah, smartass. Just remember that I ain't the one with the rep of beating people to death when I'm mad." I grimaced as he continued, "Sin might take to the idea easier if you're head over heels for the girl.

"Last thing I need is for you to stir his temper. I like your skull attached to your neck, and after this, he'll probably try to break it off. You know how he is when he loses his shit."

Fuck if I didn't.

I rubbed my throat, reminding myself that I liked my skull attached to my body, too, and muttered, "I don't know what the game plan is."

"Well, I'd figure it out before Sin gets back if I were you." Rex laughed. "Tell you what. You just got married? Never let it be said I'm not generous. You guys need a honeymoon. I want you back in Jersey in seven days. You hear me?"

My brows lowered. "You're giving me time off?"

"Yeah, I am. Maybe you can figure out how to stop Sin from making an ashtray out of your corpse in that time.

"I'll be in touch if the Five Points come calling. Be ready to head back if that's the case," he warned. "They're going to need to see proof that she went of her own volition and that the marriage is signed and sealed."

I blinked. "I understand."

"Good. She has our protection. Either way."

My relief from before was nothing to now.

Knowing she'd be safe no matter what happened, I closed my eyes and dug my fingers into them.

That was when a thought occurred to me.

"I need to tell you something."

"What now? You rob a bank too?"

I smirked. "MaryCat found the clubhouse's address on some blog."

Rex snapped, "Fuck off."

"I'm being serious, Prez." This time, my tone brooked no argument.

There was a silent pause, but I knew he was listening which meant the buck stopped with him and not me. "Send me the URL. I'll get Maverick on it. See you in a week."

As he cut the call, I glanced around the suite and smirked.

This was home for the next three days.

18

MARYCAT

MARYCAT

I WOKE UP IN A BED.

I'd fallen asleep in the bathtub.

My cheeks burned like they'd been set alight as I realized *who* had transferred me from the tub to the mattress.

He'd seen me naked.

"I tried to wake you," he murmured, making me jump.

I peered at him and squinted at the only light in the room aside from the windows—the screen on his phone. Which, I noticed, had the Kindle app open.

Rather than focus on the mortifying aspect of him dealing with my pruney nudity, I focused on the interesting. "What are you reading?"

"Why?"

"Because I'm curious," I whispered.

Plus, I needed to change the subject.

I already knew I was naked between the sheets, and call me a damn prude, but this was the first time in my life I'd ever slept like this.

Did it feel good? Or just weird? I was the kind of woman who lived in her bra, who didn't like her tatas on the loose. To feel them liberated was unnerving, especially with Digger at my side.

Was he wearing clothes?

My hot cheeks turned molten.

"*Lord of the Flies*."

It took a few seconds for my brain to process what he was saying. *Lord of the Flies?* "Really? Why?"

"I like it."

"Why?"

"Because I do?" he joked. "Been obsessed since we read it in school."

Ugh, I hated that book. "You're rereading it?"

"Yeah. I read it at least twice a year. Reminds me what bastards we can be when we don't even try."

"Do you need confirmation of that in your line of work?"

"You'd be surprised."

"What do you mean?"

"I mean, sometimes, you have to do stuff that doesn't sit well with your conscience. And then, you read a book like this. About innocent kids who turn into fucking monsters. It's a nice reminder that we're all capable of evil shit."

"That's a nice reminder?" I whistled under my breath. "We need to get you reading romcoms."

When he laughed, I smiled into the darkness.

In the distance, with the curtains open, the strip was clear. A million lights blared, but it was a comforting glow in the pitch-black room. It had to be near dawn, but it was still as bright as ever out there.

"I can't believe I fell asleep." To be honest, I was more surprised that I'd woken up when I didn't need to.

"I can. You were exhausted. I pushed you hard."

"For my own good."

"Yes."

"How's your shoulder?"

"Better. My knees are fine too before you ask." He tipped his head to the side. "How about you? You feeling okay now?"

"My head's clearer. My butt still aches.

"To be honest, I'm more worried about things outside of my control. I know my father." I tensed. "He won't like being foiled."

"You're my wife now, MaryCat."

In name only…

Huskily, I whispered, "Am I?"

"If you want to be. But in the eyes of the MC, you are either way, and they'll kill to keep you safe."

I bit my lip at the thought. I really shouldn't find that reassuring, but I did.

"What if I wanted to try being your Old Lady?" I whispered, having learned the phrase from *Sons of Anarchy*.

He grew still. "I'd say you were crazy."

"What if I *were* crazy?"

"Then I'd tell you that I don't live in a place like this and that I can afford plenty of shit but not five-star pads."

"More to life than luxury."

"You're used to this."

"Didn't see me complaining about the motels on the road over here, did you?"

"No," he said slowly.

"They were gross. I can deal with gross. Sometimes, end goals matter more than the journey."

"That's because you were desperate."

"I was," I agreed. "And exhausted. But…"

"But?"

I placed my hand on his abdomen. My fingers spread over the lean muscles, and the sixteen-year-old me squealed inside at touching him. Touching the guy who'd starred in my wet dreams for over eight months before I'd done something about it and had decided to get a boyfriend who'd kissed like a fish and had *not* been the Adonis I'd truly craved.

The one I was now married to.

"MaryCat," he chided, a warning in his voice.

"What? I want to touch you." My fingers slipped down, trailing along his torso until I felt goosebumps stir into being at my caress. "I've wanted to touch you for years."

"I'm not a teddy bear."

My hand stilled, and I snorted out a laugh. "What made you think I thought you were?"

He grunted. "I don't need stroking."

"No? What a shame. You can stroke me if you want."

"MaryCat!"

"What?" I countered, surprised by his grumbling.

"I'm trying to be a gentleman."

"I wanted you to be one last night, but not tonight."

"You're sore from the trip."

"Not that sore." I huffed, but my feelings were definitely hurt. "Jesus, if you don't want me then just tell me."

His hand slapped out to grab mine, and he shoved it between his legs.

The move was predictable, but give me predictable any day of the week because, holy shit, he had a boner.

A big one.

A frickin' delicious one that made his morning wood look small.

There was no misunderstanding what that meant.

My hand trembled as I held his dick in my palm, a pair of boxer briefs the only thing between him and me, while he ground out, "You're not ready for what I want to do to you."

Why did that sound more like a promise than a threat?

"Is that for you to decide or me?"

"Me, seeing as you've no idea what you'd be getting yourself into."

"A lot of dick, by the sound of it."

He released a choked laugh. Then I squeezed his length. He growled. And all of a sudden, his hand was on me, around my throat. The tips of his fingers pressed into the soft flesh, and though my heart began racing, I held him as firmly as he held me.

A dual threat.

God, this was hotter than I imagined.

I spread my legs as an ache surged between them.

"Touch me," I breathed. "Please?"

"You'll regret this in the morning," he grated out, but he shuffled onto me, resting that delicious thickness of his right where I needed it.

"Why? Do you think I'll want an annulment?" I nipped the pad of his chin with my teeth. "I have no idea what I'm doing, and I don't think you do either, but that doesn't mean I'm unhappy about just going along for the ride. Don't you feel the same?"

He was silent for so long that I kept expecting him to throw himself off me, to fall onto the other side of the mattress, and to tell me to go to sleep.

Then, he rasped, "I do."

I could tell he didn't want to admit that. I knew it and understood, but maybe I'd read too many Russian classics in literature because there was a fatalism about us being here.

So many moving parts had led to this moment, and it just felt right.

Carefully, so as not to deter him, well aware that he wasn't all in yet, I spread my legs wider and cupped his hips with them.

My butt rocked up and back as I moved them, and I mewled as his length settled deeper into my softness.

A short breath escaped him before he repeated, "You'll regret this in the morning."

"I won't."

"You will." His fingers flexed as his mouth lowered to mine. I felt his breath brush my lips. "You'll hate me."

"I won't." *I didn't think I could.* "I've been waiting for this for a long time."

"Sex? I guess there aren't many twenty-one-year-old virgins in Manhattan."

"Not outside of the Irish Mob," I drawled my agreement, but I didn't mean that. Not really.

I'd been waiting for him since I was sixteen.

Arching my hips again to get that delicious contact between us, the frisson of sensation sizzled down my spine, drawing a bunch of nerve endings to life that had yet to see the light of day, and I closed my eyes, loving having him looming over me more than I could say.

This could have been so different.

If he hadn't helped me… God, this could have been Bill Murphy. Everything in me would have died *and* dried up at the same time. Whereas here, now, I wanted this more than Digger did.

Enjoying the pressure of his fingers against my throat, I snatched a kiss from him.

"Are you always so honorable?"

"No," he intoned. "But you bring out a strange side of me."

I'd asked the question, then I realized I shouldn't have had to ask.

I already knew.

In less than seventy-two hours, the man had proven himself to me. Here he was again, proving himself to me.

"I'm glad, and you *are* honorable. I shouldn't have asked that. You've shown me you are."

"I have?"

"Do you always save old ladies from muggers and bash down doors to get to choking teenagers?"

"Random shit happens to everyone."

Lips curving, I denied, "Never happened to me. Not until I was around you."

"Maybe your guards stopped you from seeing those things."

"Maybe." I doubted it though.

He rested his weight on his knees and leaned into me. I heard a few rustles of fabric, then I yelped as his weight pushed me into the mattress, and his thick erection branded me with its heat.

There was nothing between us now.

Nothing.

I moaned.

He let loose a hissed breath, rasping, "You sure there's no pretty boy in your college who you'd prefer to pop your cherry?"

Narrowing my eyes at him, and though it made no sense because it wasn't like he'd been crushing on me for as long as I had on him, I whispered, "Why would you want someone else to pop it?"

I felt his growl rumbling in his chest like some wild animal that I needed to avoid.

I felt that growl in my core.

I felt it in my ovaries.

"You trying to piss me off?"

"No, but you're the one who asked," I retorted, deliriously happy that that question could have angered him. "You're the one who prodded first. Remember, I'll bite back."

"You will, will you?" His hand finally moved, tracing my throat, up my jaw, over to my cheekbone. He stroked along the crest with his thumb. "I'll taint you. I'm a Sinner—"

"I'm a Fecker. A daughter of the Irish Mob. I'm not exactly innocent."

"I'm a felon," he disregarded.

"Already talked about this." Irritation hit me and I slammed my hands against his shoulders. "I'm not about to convince you to fuck me—"

It happened in a flash.

One second, I was the aggressor; the next, his hand was around my wrists and he was hauling them overhead. His strength was... frightening. But also intoxicating.

In less than five seconds, he incapacitated me.

His face loomed over mine. "Don't bitch at me for trying to protect you. That's what I do." His grip flexed around my wrists. "Now, are you going to be a good girl? Or do I need to keep restraining you?"

Everything about those two questions made me melt.

I *wanted* to be a good girl.

His good girl.

But I also wanted to keep being restrained.

I blinked up at him in the darkness, knowing he couldn't see my expression yet also knowing that he sensed my answer because he laughed.

Low, slow, deep.

"Ah... that's the Catholic in you."

Was it?

His nose dropped down to run along mine, but though his touch was affectionate, his words weren't as he told me, "I won't be your bad boy."

"Who says I want you to be, *Mr.* Dane?"

He laughed again. "True, Mrs. Dane."

"Digger?" I whispered. "If you can't feel how much I want you, then you're the crazy one."

In answer, he rocked his hips, sliding his dick along my *wet* folds, which had me whimpering.

"Fuck. You're the sweetest temptation I've ever come across, Mary Catherine," he mumbled, his lips pecking at mine. "Sweet and soft and so fucking out of my league…" Before I could argue, he growled again. "Fuck it."

And that was when he let go.

Not of my wrists, but of whatever it was that was holding him back.

He snarled as he plundered my mouth, rougher than he'd been before, and I loved it. I loved how he devoured me and explored me and tasted me. I loved feeling like I was a bowl of ice cream he needed to eat before it melted. I loved being the cherry pie he always ordered, wanting him to feast on me.

He didn't savor and caress—he consumed me.

Whole.

His cock continued tunneling along my sex, making me feel all kinds of things that had me whimpering into his mouth as he stole my breath and replaced it with his own.

With the pressure of his cock against my clit, I was seconds away from… *something.*

I thought it was an orgasm, but it was so different from the ones I experienced on my own that I didn't think it could be.

Normally, they weren't like this.

They didn't feel so good.

So strong.

So powerful.

When it exploded or imploded inside me—I had no idea which—I cried out, tearing my mouth from his, head falling back as I let the pleasure roar through me, screaming with the glory of it, the sheer joy of knowing what *this* felt like at long last.

His mouth sank toward my throat, and that was his next feast. The contrast of his stubble, the hard graze of it with his lips, the soft caresses, had me moaning even more as it made every nerve ending along my spine stand at attention.

"I'm clean," he whispered against the tender flesh of my neck.

I could smell his body wash—

Oh.

Oh.

Stupid, stupid.

"Me too," I whimpered like he didn't already know that. Like my virginity wasn't a massive clue.

With another growl, he reached between us, taking his dick away and replacing it with his hand.

As he sucked and nibbled, marking me with a hickey that, tomorrow, I'd wear with pride, his fingers toyed with my clit before they sank down to my slit.

When he pushed one inside, I gasped, mouth agape as I sucked in air like it was in short supply while he carried on moving down, lips working on my breasts, the nipples being teased and taunted by his teeth and tongue.

One finger stretched me, then another circled the hole before he thrust the tip into me.

He bit my nipple, enough that it hurt, and as I yelped, he pushed the second finger into me entirely. The burn was real, but so was the sting from my breast.

"Ouch," I squealed, wriggling around on the bed.

His hand squeezed my wrists. "Be still."

I pouted. "That hurt."

"My dick's a lot bigger than my fingers, sweet girl," he rumbled, but he was laughing—it vibrated against my breast.

That felt good.

Almost as good as the orgasm he'd just gifted me without even doing all that much work.

Ten minutes with my fingers and watching porn on Twitter, and I was huffing on the mattress, trying and failing to climax.

Five minutes of contact with his dick, and I was going off like a Fourth of July fireworks display.

Go figure.

"Sweet girl?" I whispered, liking the nickname more than I could say.

He hummed, and then he killed me.

Stone. Dead.

"*My* sweet girl." His tongue curled about my nipple, making me squeak as he spread his fingers. "There," he crooned, "you can take it."

I twisted a little, spreading my legs wider, finding that made it easier as I rested them on the bed. I stopped clutching at his digits as I muttered, "I'm trying."

"Such a good girl," he agreed with a purr, and his voice keyed into every fantasy I'd never known I had.

A third finger made an appearance, but as I squeaked again, he groaned. "So beautiful taking my fingers. Imagine how beautiful you'll be taking my dick."

I whimpered at the thought, thinking about how thick he'd feel, how hot. He'd hurt but it would be so good.

He bit down on my nipple again, harder this time, and as the pain soared through me, his third finger was no longer seeking entrance but was there—deep inside.

I was breathing hard by this point, confused by the pain, aware that my clit was throbbing with the need for more.

"D-Digger?"

"James for you, sweet girl, when I'm between your thighs."

Eyes flaring wide, I licked my lips. "*James*, please, stop teasing me."

His laughter made my heart happy again, and he flexed his fingers —both around my wrist and inside me—before he liberated me. "As my girl wishes."

I gulped as he angled my legs about his hips. When they were riding high there, I felt his cock, and it was *a lot* bigger than those three digits, but I forced myself to be calm.

Forced myself to relax because I knew it would be easier in the long run.

Reaching up, not wanting us to be apart, I slipped my arms around his shoulders and drew him into me so that his breath was on my mouth again.

As the tip of his dick brushed my slit, I moaned. "I wanted this the first time I ever saw you."

"Second I saw your uniform, it was like a punch to the gut. Knew you were way too young."

So, he *had* felt it. I hadn't been on my own.

"Do I feel too young now?" I demanded as he started to thrust into me.

"You feel like fucking heaven." Then, he took me.

Claimed me.

Branded me.

And he was careful. *So careful.*

He was patient, never rushing me. When his cock brushed my hymen, he grabbed my hand and settled a kiss on my palm before he twisted it around to press his lips to my wedding ring.

"Together," he stated.

And somehow, that meant more than the vows we'd uttered in a cheap wedding chapel in Vegas with the Grinch grumbling as we wed.

"Together," I whispered back.

Just as he thrust home.

I mewled as the pain hit me, but it disintegrated a short while later as he let me get used to him. In the meantime, his mouth ran along my throat again, and he sucked on my beating pulse.

For a second, I could only stare blindly at the ceiling, processing the odd sensations that were rippling through me.

It hurt.

It felt good.

He was too heavy.

But he blanketed me just right.

His lips were a sweet form of torture.

I was hungry for something.

And as I stared, as my mind whirred, not a single thought was about the expediency of this.

There wasn't a murmur in my head that revolved around Bill fucking Murphy. Or the last time someone touched my sex—the doctor who'd checked my hymen.

Nor was my head focused on annulments and divorces and how this protected me as nothing else could.

It was about how, at long damn last, I knew what *this* felt like.

What *he* felt like.

I understood now how the fullness and the stretch could be so good even as it hurt.

I recognized now the glory there was in my body heat entwining with another's, for our skin to be cleaved to each other.

I knew now what it was to experience the pressure of his weight against me, to be blanketed by his strength, to be held in his arms, and to be cherished and caressed and pleasured.

My mind was exactly where it needed to be.

Then, he shattered my thoughts as easily as tossing a pebble into a window by brushing his lips against mine and whispering, "You ready, sweet girl?"

"I was born ready."

He chuckled like I'd wanted him to, and this time, as he did so, I felt it inside me.

That was even better.

I wanted his laughter, I realized.

I wanted it all.

His forearms settled on either side of my ears, and his forehead rubbed against mine.

He was slow, at first. Not exactly careful, but he didn't pressure me.

It burned then it ached. I wriggled my hips back and squirmed, and it was like, 'Open Sesame.' I moaned and dug my heels into his ass, then I rocked up higher so that I was meeting him slow thrust for slow thrust.

My mouth snagged his, and this time, my tongue started the war and he fought alongside me as his pace quickened, faster and faster. I didn't feel that impending explosion, not like before, but damn, it was good. Too good.

When tension hit him, I knew what that meant, but he didn't rut away on top of me. He pulled back. His hands clasped my hips and he rearranged me before one moved between my legs to my clit.

I groaned, head flip-flopping to the side as he strummed that nub, making that sensation whirl to life in my belly again.

It was so deliriously wonderful that it hurt, and this time, with his pace increasing, I understood why I'd never reached this height with my fingers alone.

When I came, my choked cry echoed through the room, tangling with his as he did too.

It was everything I expected and nothing I imagined.

All at the same time.

It felt even better than before, yet that had already been more than I could have anticipated.

The pleasure sank into my very being, making me feel like my *soul* had lit up with the electrical sensations that scorched a path through my center.

But what made it so much better was that it was him. *Him.* Digger. James. Whichever—I wanted both. *Needed* both.

There was something about him, something in the brooding looks, in his massive form that made me feel tiny, in the way he protected me and shielded me.

God, I'd never experienced anything like it, and I wanted more. So much more.

The pleasure was drugging and awe-inducing, which was so damn good that I now understood all the shit I was taught in Sunday school.

Because there was a reason lust was a sin. It didn't have a damn thing to do with boyfriends being killed by insane fathers and everything to do with *this*.

This was worth pining over.

This was worth going to war for.

This made the world go round and it made it churn to a halt, and at long last, I was invited to the party.

And there was no going back.

19

DIGGER

I WOKE up in the crispy forebears of the wet spot.

Immediately, I grimaced.

"Shit," I rumbled under my breath.

My curse word stirred her, but she stirred even more as, with some gymnastics, I got us both standing before I picked her up and carried her into the bathroom.

"Wasrong?" she slurred, her forehead tipping onto my shoulder.

"Ever heard of honeymoonitis?"

"Huh?"

I rolled my eyes. "Don't Catholics teach their girls anything?"

"Not a girl." Her voice turned smug. "Not anymore."

I almost grinned, but I was mad. More at myself than her. Not only had I fucked her raw, I'd left her like that all goddamn night.

"You're going to need to clean yourself up."

She rubbed her forehead against my throat. "Don't want to."

"I know you're sleepy," I chided. "But do you want a UTI?"

MaryCat tensed. "No. Why would I get one?"

Jesus.

I was going to have to teach her everything.

For a second, I felt the burden of that, but then I thought about last night. How she'd followed my lead like the fucking trooper I knew she was, and how, with every kiss and caress, I could mold her into what I needed…

The control freak in me liked that way too much.

I'd never wanted a virgin. Never thought I'd get one with how I lived my life, so it hadn't been a problem. Yet here I was, an ex-virgin as a wife.

Shaking my head at the thought, I muttered, "You're supposed to pee after sex."

"Why?"

I huffed. "Because."

"Because?"

"Didn't you do any research?"

"No." She sounded more awake, at least. "Why would I?"

"Because it's the 21st century?"

"And I couldn't have sex without my boyfriend being killed," she drawled, shoving at my shoulder. "I figured it was best to steer clear of temptation."

"You didn't watch porn?"

"Yes, but I mostly used my imagination," was her prim retort, which swiftly turned mocking. "I'm a good Catholic girl, don't you know?"

"Well, that must have been boring."

She sniffed, but the effect was spoiled as she kissed my shoulder and, with a tenderness that got to me, gently massaged it. Much as she'd done yesterday.

Fuck, her fingers were like magic.

"It *was* boring," she concurred. "After a while. That was when I turned to Twitter. It made it worse and gave me repetitive strain injury."

I grinned. "I'll bet."

"Don't tease."

I shrugged as I stepped into the shower booth. "It's funny. I'm gonna have to teach you everything and it's not like I'm the fucking encyclopedia on this shit. I guess you could talk to the clubwhores—"

"The club *what*?" MaryCat squeaked. Then, she sobered. "Oh. They're actually real? Women do that? For rent? I thought it was a fictitious device."

I blinked at that. "A fictitious device?"

She wafted a hand. "Never mind. Women genuinely sleep with guys in the MC to pay rent?"

"They do."

She pulled a face. "That's kind of sad."

I'd expected a bitchy retort. "Why is it? If it's what they want to do?"

My mom had been one, so whether she knew it or not, she was walking on thin ice.

Her brow furrowed. "In *Sons of Anarchy*—" Of course, she'd watched that. "—they always try to be with bikers though. As if that's the gateway to them." Her shoulders wriggled. "To each their own. I just..."

"You just what?"

"I don't think I'd want that for my daughter if I had one."

Well, she had me there.

For a second, the only thing I could see was a mini MaryCat, all red hair and big green eyes, growing up and pulling moves clubwhores did...

I couldn't argue with her.

"Would you want your daughter to be forced into the same situation as you? Clubwhore or daughter of a Five Pointer, doesn't it all boil down to what's between your legs?"

Her eyes rounded, and while I expected her temper, I didn't get it. She nodded. "You're right. It's very, very wrong."

"Agreed."

"Was your mom a..." MaryCat winced. "I don't want to call her that."

"She was. She was desperate after she had me."

"That's even sadder," she said miserably. "Especially with her... you know, that she was raped? It must have been difficult for her to be... intimate."

I swallowed.

Why had I never put that particular two and two together?

My poor mom. Fuck, she'd had it rough.

Closing my eyes a second, I forced myself to stop thinking about this because if I didn't, Bill Murphy would be wearing a body bag next.

Mom wouldn't want me to spend another thirty years in prison because of that asshole.

God, the temptation, though.

Especially now.

Shit, maybe Nyx and I were more alike than I realized.

"I guess." Because I could see her misery was real and because I felt it too and was glad for her empathy, I pressed a kiss to her temple. "Turn on the faucet." I was kind as I maneuvered us so that my back would be blasted with the cold water. She reached around me and did as I asked. I tensed when the water hit but changed the subject: "It might be too late for the UTI. But we can go to a clinic if that's the case."

"This isn't a very romantic conversation," she complained with a pout that I wanted to kiss.

So I did.

Because I could.

"Sometimes, sex isn't."

"That sucks," she said breathily, flushed now and not because of the hot water.

"I'll teach you how to do that later."

Her eyes widened. "You will?"

Well, damn. I'd been teasing, but I saw her curiosity was clear.

"If you want."

"I want," she admitted huskily. *Eagerly.*

Laughing, I shook my head.

It made sense, I guessed.

Deny a woman pleasure for all these years and she'd have a lot of pent-up needs. I was more than willing to be the sacrificial lamb as she burned them out of her system.

"You going to clean yourself up, or do you want me to do it for you?"

She slumped against me. "I want to do it."

Talk about a mixed message.

Smirking at the wall when I realized what was going on, I murmured, "You're a brat."

"I was your sweet girl last night," she muttered indignantly, straightening up.

My tone turned serious. "You liked that, huh?"

Our eyes collided and she gulped. "I really did."

She'd responded to 'good girl' more.

I hummed as I stroked my hand over her spine. "Come on. We need to get you Plan B too. I should have used a rubber."

"You really didn't anticipate last night, did you?"

"I never anticipate anything. Makes life more interesting."

"I think I like the fact you didn't plan that."

Chuckling, I told her, "You're weird."

"You're weird too," was her prompt reply. "But I like you."

She had me there as well.

"I like you too."

20

MARYCAT

MARYCAT

ENDURING Digger's initial amusement in the elevator as I preened in the mirror at my hickeys was worth it when he pressed me to the wall and kissed each one, stating, "Gotta make sure people know who you belong to."

My legs were still shaking when we finally made it into the lobby, where it registered exactly how tired I'd been upon our arrival because I hadn't noticed the decorations.

How the hell I'd missed twenty or so Christmas trees in a circle around the Gallinaro's entrance, I'd never know. Not when each one was dressed in gold and silver and was sparkling with a thousand lights.

The circle had a life-sized Santa's sleigh in the middle, with gift boxes tumbling off the back and false reindeer made out of more lights.

As if the place couldn't be gaudier…

Still, it made me feel festive and added a bounce to my step.

I was probably going to get a UTI, but I was also about to receive a lesson in oral sex, *and* Digger had told me as we ate breakfast for lunch —waffles and maple-glazed bacon in bed—that we had at least three days here before we had to start back.

Three days.

A UTI and Plan B would put a crimp in my plans to try everything sexual under the sun, but the fact that Digger wanted those three days too made me happy.

This was all unexpected, and so much better for it.

As we headed outside, he clicked his fingers. "That reminds me. You never did tell me the name of the blog with the clubhouse's address on it. I need to send Rex the URL. Do you remember it?"

I shrugged. "Not off the top of my head, but when I have my phone, I can send you the link. It was a pretty interesting article."

He grunted.

When we approached the bike, I groaned internally but didn't say anything as he straddled it.

My ass, hips, and legs ached from the ride and also from last night, but I clambered on too, eyes crossing with discomfort until the engine started.

The vibrations weren't soothing, but they did do something to my inner thighs…

Was it possible to get off on the vibrations?

I hadn't felt that yesterday on the bike or earlier on in the ride, but like I'd told him, I tended to avoid as many lustful thoughts as I could because not only did they get me nowhere, but Father Doyle was harsh on those kinds of things in confession.

I had no desire to spend an hour on my knees going through dozens of Hail Marys all because I'd jilled off during the sex scenes on *Game of Thrones*.

I'd learned shortly after I'd seen Digger in Westchester that Father Doyle punished lustful thoughts and masturbation with the same severity as if I'd gone on a murder spree.

Heck, with our faction, he probably went harder on the masturbators than the murderers.

Before we set off, he said, "Remind me to rub Deep Heat onto you when we get back from the pharmacy. That should help when you sit down."

I melted into him, breathing, "My hero."

He snorted then set off, but he squeezed my hand before he did so I knew he liked hearing that.

As we rode away from the hotel, it was difficult not to feel like those hounds—hounds shaped like Father and Bill Murphy—that had been baying at my heels, chasing me and forcing me down a certain path, had been diverted.

It was impossible not to feel safe when I was with this man and his ring was on my finger.

In less than a week, he'd already protected me more than any other had, and while it might not last forever, I was happy to take each day as it came.

If that made me snuggle into him, then so be it.

For the moment, he was mine.

If I could convince him, maybe he could be mine forever...

The thought hit me like a two-by-four to the temple, but I let it form fully in my mind.

Forever.

It tasted good on my tongue as I whispered it. The wind snatched it away, but I said it again. And I squeezed his waist.

His hand dropped to my fingers, and he squeezed them back.

Hope burned inside me, a fragile flame that I'd have to cultivate to keep steady.

His life was so different than mine—I'd learned that already. But mine wasn't exactly nice. There were definitely similarities between them.

Crime and felony charges were run of the mill, and women were nothing but pussy to be bargained for. He wore a cut and Five Pointers wore Brioni... Could a clash of two cultures work?

Was it impossible?

When we made it to the drugstore, I was in a world of my own.

He tapped my leg, murmuring, "Come on, sweet girl. Let's get you sorted."

I smiled at the term of endearment as it made that hope in my chest blossom some more.

Sweet girl.

I wanted that. More of it. Wanted to be *his* sweet girl for longer than a semi-permanent marriage.

Clambering off the bike, I winced as I straightened up.

His glance was apologetic. "If you want, I'll ride back on my own and you can catch a flight."

"No."

His lips twitched. "No? Just like that?"

"No."

There was no way...

Didn't he sense that?

Or would he prefer for me—

His own smile appeared, but it was sheepish and so boyish that it made my heart melt. "I should make you get a flight because you'll be sore as hell but..." He jerked a shoulder and tugged at my hand. "I'm kinda glad you don't want to."

We grinned at each other like a couple of lunatics, hope making me dizzy throughout that prolonged stare, then his phone rang.

His grin faded—I immediately missed that smile.

"I gotta take this. You go and get what you need, sweet girl," he said absentmindedly, handing me a hundred bucks.

Accepting it, I nodded and took a step back, but as I walked toward the store, I heard him mutter, "Jesus. Already? You said I could have a week, Rex."

I'd never met this Rex before, but I already didn't like him and wasn't looking forward to meeting him either.

Turning around, I watched his expression darken, and then he caught me watching him.

His grimace said it all.

The honeymoon was over.

21

MARYCAT

AN HOUR LATER, after we returned from the drugstore, it was clear that the situation was more worrisome than Rex had first thought.

Barely a foot over the doorstep, Digger's cell was ringing again.

Then, for Digger, at any rate, the unimaginable happened—Rex asked him to put his bike in the cargo hold of a plane.

It was the first time I'd seen my husband be anything other than cool and calm.

For a moment, he gaped at nothing.

Then he spluttered.

Then he went through the phases of grief.

Over. His. Bike.

If the situation hadn't worried me, I'd have found it hilarious.

Then, because I figured it was a wifely thing to do to offset his grief, I cleared my throat to remind him that I was in the room and offered, "I really can fly by myself, Digger. You can ride it up. It's me my father wants to see."

His scowl was immediate. "MaryCat, now isn't the moment for being brave."

"What is it the moment for?" I asked, trying to keep my amusement from my words.

His inhalation was noisy. "Me. Sucking it up." I thought Rex heard that and commented on it because Digger's scowl clouded over, dropping a few shades to the depths of Vantablack. "As if you'd want to put your bike on a plane, Prez. It's a fucking tragedy is what it is." He paused then glowered at the wall. "No, it doesn't help, Rex. It doesn't help at all."

When he hung up, meekly, I inquired, "What did he say?"

He grunted. "That if the plane went down, the hog and I would both die at the same time." I had to snort. He squinted at me. "I didn't hear amusement coming out of you just now, did I?"

I rolled my lips inward. "Nope!"

"I think I did."

Something had his eyes lighting up. Something...

God, I couldn't put a word to it.

It was both teasing and dark.

One second, I was hovering in front of the dinner table in our suite, and the next, I was shrieking as he surged to his feet and started chasing me.

For a moment, the scantest second, fear filtered through me.

It grabbed me in a chokehold.

The teasing in his expression was forgotten, and only that darkness lingered in my memory banks.

A lifetime of being a toy in the games my mother and father played together, an adulthood of being the victim of my father's torment...

Then, my brain caught up.

The time we spent traveling shifted to the forefront of my mind.

Digger *saved* people.

He didn't break them.

No matter how dirty he considered those hands of his as being.

He chased down muggers and spoke kindly with an ex-administrative assistant at his school.

He broke into motel rooms when he thought a woman was being attacked then, after he saved her son from death by Cheeto, he paid for the goddamn repairs to the busted door. Something I'd learned the following morning, when the motel owner, grumbling all the while, had been begrudgingly repairing what Digger had broken.

And, more importantly than that, he traveled across the country to save a girl who'd showed up at his 'doorstep' one random day, who was the sister of a buddy of his, and had married her.

All of that swirled around my head, swooping in like a storm front to whisk away my dumb fears with the speed of a hurricane.

So I let loose a second shriek that faded into a hoot and ran across the room, aware that I barely evaded the brush of his fingers as they swept over the hem of my shirt.

I yelped as I stepped onto the sofa, feet sinking into the plush, white leather cushions before I leaped over the back.

By the time my feet collided with the floor, I was darting to the dinner table where this chase had commenced.

"You can't catch me," I crowed, ducking from side to side, a wide grin splitting my jaw.

Then he chuckled.

It was deep, rumbly, and had me stilling in place.

Umm, why was I running?

Before I could answer that very valid question, he rushed toward the left so I twisted right. Then, he chuckled again, sounding more lighthearted than I'd heard him even when he was teasing me, and there was only one destination that I had in mind.

Running toward the bedroom, I slipped behind the door, and once he followed me, I jumped on his back.

The chuckle morphed into outright laughter as he grabbed a hold of my legs while I curved my arms around his neck, careful not to hurt his bruised shoulder, and clung to him like a spider monkey.

"*I* caught *you*," was my smug retort. "Bet you didn't expect that, did you?"

He snickered. "I didn't. You're full of surprises, huh?"

Mary Catherine wasn't.

Mary Catherine was, to be honest, boring as fuck. Studious and obedient. The 'goodest' of good girls.

Ugh,

MaryCat, on the other hand, was out from under her father's thumb.

So, I didn't bother answering verbally. I just nuzzled my face into the side of his throat and gently pressed a kiss there. He had a bunch of ink on his neck, shapes that I couldn't make out from this angle but ones I vowed to explore when I had time.

Father wouldn't take this away from me, wouldn't rob me of the man who was my first crush and my now husband.

I wouldn't let him.

I wouldn't.

The surge of rebelliousness whipped through my body like quicksilver and, perversely, it turned me on. I wasn't an adrenaline junkie by any stretch of the imagination, but everything with Digger was different.

Turbo-charged.

His shaky breath as I nipped that sensitive patch between neck and shoulder only turned me on even more, making me grateful I'd convinced him to hold off on me taking Plan B until we were traveling.

I licked the area, smoothing my tongue over it before nibbling where I'd laved.

His fingers tightened around my calves. "Do you know what you're starting, baby girl?"

The heat at my core shot up. "I do." Then, I took the bull by the balls. "I'm wet, James."

"You're sore."

"I'm not."

"Don't you ache?"

I rolled my eyes—the Lord save me from white knights. "Yeah, but it's the kind of ache only you can get rid of."

His chuckle made a reappearance. "More surprises."

Then *he* startled me.

He flopped onto the bed, twisting us around in some ninja magic so that, suddenly, I was on the bottom and he was very much on top of me.

God, he was *so* heavy. Such a solid presence, a grounding one. Fuck, I hadn't known that would feel so good.

He loomed over me, his massive shoulders taking up my whole line of sight as he studied my expression. "You know what's coming, don't you?"

"Better than you do, probably. Uncle Aidan will get involved."

His hand cupped my cheek, those inked fingers so gentle as they stroked along the curve of my jaw. "Are you scared?"

I was only capable of focusing on the tenderness of his caress.

Did he know what that did to someone chronically starved of affection like me?

"No," I croaked out the truth.

It was illogical that I had been before, but now that the shit *had* hit the fan, I wasn't.

I had no idea why but the butterflies inside me had nothing to do with anxiety and everything to do with him. His touch. His proximity.

"Why not?"

Knowing he wouldn't give up until I answered, I stumbled around for something that would satisfy him. "Because I'm your wife." When he just blinked, I clarified, "I'll tell Uncle Aidan that I consented to marry you. That we can't get the marriage annulled. That'll stop him."

He shook his head. "Don't be naive, Mary Catherine."

Annoyance whipped through me. "MaryCat," I corrected. "You said the Sinners would defend me if I was yours."

"And they will. I'm not saying they won't. I'm saying that when we get back, there could be a war." His gentle brown eyes darted over my face. "Men die in wars."

Now, fear flushed through me. "I won't let that happen."

"You won't be involved. Hell, you should probably stay here. I can go alone—"

"No!"

"I'll take you to Sin's house, then. You can lie low there."

That begged the question of why he hadn't suggested *that* in the first place.

But, I didn't let that trip from my lips, not when I knew he had his reasons for enjoying robbing Bill Murphy of the chance to wed me.

Instead, I murmured, "They'll want to see me. Hiding me away in Vegas or in my brother's house won't be good enough for them. If anything, *that* will be what triggers the war."

"I'm not putting you in their line of fire."

I swallowed. "If you don't, then you'll get hurt. I won't let that happen either. Don't act as if you're expendable, Digger."

"I'm a felon, MaryCat. My brothers would mourn me but no one else gives a—"

Wrath burned my fear into ashes. "My father took my choices away, Digger. Do *not* be like him." His eyes widened in surprise, but I wasn't done. "*I* would care. I would mourn you.

"You think I'd be okay with letting you get hurt when you're only involved in this because I burst into your life? You think I'm that self-centered that I wouldn't be a part of this?" I sucked in a breath. "You might think I'm a pampered princess, and sure, that's fair. When I wasn't being imprisoned in my room, I was spoiled.

"But if you try to leave me at Sin's home, I'll find my way to Queens and I'll make Uncle Aidan listen to—"

His lips were on mine before I could finish that sentence.

And to be honest, I was both mad about that and glad.

Glad because I wanted his kiss. Mad because he was doing it to shut me up.

But I'd show him.

Digger was going to get over this self-sacrificing shit because now that I had him, I wasn't going to let him go.

He didn't know it yet, mostly because I hadn't known until I'd slept eight hours through, but I'd meant every one of those vows I'd pledged to him with the Grinch and a couple of staff members from the chapel as our witnesses.

Death wouldn't be parting us for a *long* time.

To some, it'd seem too quick for me to know that I wanted him forever, but not to me.

Not.

To.

Me.

"You're living up to your name, MaryCat." He pulled back to nip my bottom lip. "I can feel your claws. Hissing and spitting. Bristling at me.

"Do you know how fucking beautiful you are right now?"

I didn't answer because the time for words was gone. I arched up and urged our mouths to reconnect.

Only, I showed Digger what I wanted.

Him.

My tongue slid against his, tangling and teasing until the battleground wasn't my mouth but his.

He grunted into the kiss, bobbing lower so that I had more of his weight on me.

My arms slid around his shoulders, and I stroked one set of fingers through his hair, simultaneously scraping my nails over his skull as I dug my knees around his hips and, with a surge of strength that surprised him, urged him to roll over.

I knew he permitted the move—he was too big for me to shift him on my own—but when I was straddling him, power rushed through me.

Maybe I was David playing with Goliath—and I didn't mean with Digger—but I just wasn't going to allow other people to dictate my life anymore.

Mary Catherine was gone.

Long live MaryCat.

With that surge of power came the ripples of need that I'd experienced ever since he'd rode into my life.

I retreated only so that I could drag my shirt overhead, uncaring that a couple buttons popped away in the process. Next, I unclipped my bra, and all the while, my eyes were locked on him.

Then, I caught his hand in mine and pressed a kiss onto my palm before I drew it to my breast.

"Touch me, James. Touch me like I've wanted you to for years."

A grunt escaped him at that, but his fingers, callused and rough around the edges, scraped over my breast.

When he tweaked the nipple, my head fell back at how damn good that felt. My groan was guttural as I rocked against him, grateful that my center was experiencing his hardness full throttle.

"Does that feel good, baby girl?"

Head rolling on my neck, I whimpered.

Then, he tutted. "Good girls answer questions when they're asked."

I froze.

Good girl?

Oh, fuck.

Fuck.

He'd said it before but had used sweet girl more.

Now, in that tone, *good girl* did things to me. Things that I shouldn't feel. Things that should be illegal.

But Digger, in that way of his that unnerved me, that took the wind from my sails, that put me on my ass, had given it a different connotation.

A connotation I didn't just like... one that made me melt.

Then, he broke into the stasis he'd set me in by chuckling. Gracing me with more of that deep, rumbly goodness, except this time, my knees were next to his sides and I *felt* it.

"You like that, huh?" His hand scraped over my abdomen, bringing the skin to life in a wave of goosebumps. Then, his fingers dipped below the waistband of my jeans. I groaned at the heat there. "Talk to me, Mary Catherine."

"MaryCat," I snapped, more insistently than before.

"Only good girls get called by their nicknames," he vowed.

I shuddered then stunned myself by lying, "I don't want to be a good girl."

His brow arched as he started to unfasten the fly of my jeans. Wordlessly, he worked, lowering the zipper so that he could thrust between the tines. When he scraped over the front of my panties, I cried out, "Oh, James. Oh, my god."

"I think all this slick tells me how you feel about being *my* good girl, MaryCat."

I swallowed as he traced over my sex, not aggressively but… *thoroughly*.

That was the only way I could think to describe it.

Over the cotton fabric, he explored every inch of me, leaving me unable to deceive him about how his dirty talk affected me.

When he rubbed my clit then retreated, I whimpered.

"Tell me if you want to be my good girl, MaryCat."

I licked my lips. "In bed, yes."

He laughed. "Good save."

My hand fell to his abs as a thought drifted into being—an important one. One that I had to clarify.

"I needed to be rescued. I don't want to be saved."

That had him stilling, his eyes narrowing on me, but I held his gaze without blinking. His hand retreated from my jeans, and though I wanted to cry about that, I didn't.

He might have incapacitated me, might have turned my body into a traitor, but that didn't mean I was going to concede defeat on this.

"I won't let you get hurt," he rumbled eventually.

"Then protect me. Defend me. But this isn't a battle that needs fighting with fists. Words should do."

His brow furrowed. "How can you say that? Why are we even here if that was enough?"

"Because your ring on my finger protects me. I'm a married woman. You took my virginity. In their eyes, I'm spoiled goods."

"What kind of piece of shit thinks that?"

"I told you, we all play a role in this life." I swallowed, wishing we could get back to the good stuff, but this was too important. Digger, if I didn't stop him, would martyr himself unnecessarily. "But that's the point. You saved me from that and you've given me a voice, one I didn't have before."

"Why didn't you?"

"Because I'd never have been able to speak with Uncle Aidan. Now, he'll demand to talk to me."

"Why not? If you're family?"

I chuckled. "Don't be naive. What would the head of the Irish Mob speak to a college student about? A college student who happens to be the daughter of a Pointer who isn't as high up in the ranks as he should be."

"Why isn't he?"

"He gets demoted a lot. His temper makes him rash and he makes mistakes, so he ends up in jail."

His jaw worked. "The idea of him hurting you, MaryCat, pisses me off."

I leaned forward, cupped his chin, then pressed a kiss to it in silent thanks.

"You think if you talk to O'Donnelly, you can stop things from escalating?"

"I do." I sucked in a breath. "Uncle Aidan is unusual."

"He's fucking insane is what he is. *Unusual*," he muttered disparagingly.

"Do you know that you can lose fingers if he catches you in a lie?"

"What!?"

"I'm telling you—he's Old Testament, Digger. I-I just can't believe that if he knew what was happening, he'd be okay with it. His sons are too good for that anyway."

"What do you mean?"

"Exactly what I said—they're good men."

"They're mobsters," he dismissed.

"You're a biker, yet you're the only guy who has ever held me with kindness, who's cherished me, who's made me feel like more than just a commodity," I said simply. "Some things don't have to make sense to be true."

His eyes narrowed on me, and though I saw his confusion at my statement, a confusion that was formed in him accepting that I was telling the truth, he decided to focus on the unimportant stuff.

Men.

"You're close to his sons?" he demanded.

I hitched a shoulder. "No. Or I'd have gone to them. Whenever I see them at events, they're always kind to me. And the women talk—"

"Don't I know it," he groused.

My lips twitched. "I need to revisit this conversation because you're stubborn. I'd much prefer to have your dick inside me again."

He smirked at me. "Okay."

"Okay?"

The smirk faded and was replaced with a somber look. "We'll do this on your terms."

The relief that flooded me was stark. Hell, it was *sharp*. It should have pricked at my heart, but it couldn't because that organ was too full of the feelings he inspired in me.

"We will?" I croaked.

He half sat up, tossed his tee overhead, then with one of his hands settling between my shoulder blades, he drew me into him. "We will. Now, *are* you going to be my good girl, MaryCat?"

I sagged. "Yes."

His mouth tipped up at the corners. That was the last thing I saw of it before it was on a direct collision course with mine.

I shuddered into the kiss, shivered and shook, especially as bare skin was finally brushing against bare skin.

"I want you, James," I whispered.

Humming, he tongued my Cupid's bow. "You've got me."

The question was… for how long?

22

DIGGER

THING CALLED LOVE - ABOVE & BEYOND, RICHARD BEDFORD

DIGGER

THE PRISSY PRINCESS wasn't averse to a dirty biker defending her but she had a voice of her own—*got it.*

For all that MaryCat's spitfire nature worked its wiles on me, her soft laughs and gentle smiles, her kind eyes and kinder words brought me to my knees.

Tenderness had never been something I'd sought out, mostly because I'd never been on the receiving end of it. My mom had loved me, but aside from a kiss on the cheek and a random hug, that was about it.

MaryCat was a toucher, and I was realizing that I liked being touched.

If anyone else had leaped on my back the way she had, I'd have dragged them off me, pinned them to the ground, and strangled the ever-living fuck out of them.

Prison had shaped me. You didn't show someone your back, not without expecting to be stabbed in it.

Which meant the unthinkable was happening—I'd started letting my guard down around her.

It was too much, too soon, but hell if I could pull the brakes on her.

When she shivered against me as our torsos brushed, I lowered my mouth, dropping kisses to her chin, to the line of her jaw. I savored her soft scent a moment before I tugged on her earlobe and then suckled it.

The husky cry she let loose made me smile. Her innocent responses fired me up more than the crassest of clubwhore dirty talk ever could.

I ran my tongue over the curve of her ear then retreated to her throat where I sucked on the sensitive flesh, palpating it against my teeth, making sure there were more love bites there for her father and O'Donnelly to see.

It was a dangerous stunt to pull, but... I had faith.

In her.

There was no reason for her to know that I trusted no one apart from my brothers. And sometimes, I didn't trust them either.

I licked along the sinews in her throat, moving to her collarbone.

While she trembled in my hold, I buried my face between her tits, careful because I knew my stubble would scratch her skin.

I brushed my mouth over her curves, enjoying the way she arched her back as if encouraging me to dive even deeper.

Finding her nipple, I sucked on the tip then bit on it, raking it until it was puckered and taut. Only then did I leave it and find the other.

When she whimpered, "James," I obeyed the silent plea for more, mostly because I loved the sound of my birth name on her lips.

James was something I hadn't been called for decades. Even Mom ended up using Digger more than James before I was fifteen.

It was fitting, I thought, that it belonged to her. That it was for her sole use.

My hand moved to her open fly, but this time, I slipped beneath her panties too. When my finger found her clit, her folds wet with arousal, she sobbed my name again.

God, I didn't think I'd ever tire of hearing it fall from her lips.

As I brushed her clit, I decided to be kind.

Her past and her upbringing had shaped her. Meaning that, like a teenage boy could blow his wad in less than two pumps of his dick, MaryCat was quick to react to stimuli.

I was *not* going to complain about that. Especially as I thought it was tied to me. *My* touch.

Crying out as I gave her what she needed, her fingers tightened in my hair, pulling at it as she wailed through her orgasm.

Her hips rolled and rocked with an eagerness that spoke of greed, and because I wanted her to be greedy for pleasure, pleasure I'd willingly give her, I let my hand slide down, the butt of my wrist settling against the tender area as I circled her slit.

She froze, a shaken breath drifting from her lips as I thrust the digit deeper.

"Sore?" I asked then, before she could answer, warned, "Good girls don't lie."

She whimpered and her cunt turned into a vise around my digit. "Yes and no. B-Be careful and I'll be fine."

"You tell me and we can fool around in other ways."

Her pussy fluttered. "Y-You mean it?"

My brow furrowed. "Of course I do."

A wail escaped her at that, then she rolled off me. Just as I was cursing myself about touching her when she was tender, she was writhing on the mattress, jerking her jeans down her legs.

My lips twitched at the sight. "It'd have been faster if you stood up, baby girl."

"No. Too far," she panted. "You'll change your mind."

I didn't have much time to wonder what I might change my mind about, and I found I didn't care because when she was naked, she straddled me again, but she wasn't done.

Her hands scrabbled at my fly this time and her fingers delved inside to find my cock.

I hissed as she rubbed her thumb over the tip, but then, she was straightening up and settling the glans against her slit.

That was when I clicked my tongue to stall her.

She'd already convinced me that she'd take Plan B once we were traveling home, but I wasn't going to risk it. I'd stocked up at the drugstore, so I grabbed a condom from my pocket and covered myself with it.

She watched with eager eyes, taking in the motions with the hunger of someone who craved information as badly as a beggar gorged himself at a feast.

Still, sensing she wanted some control over this, I let her ride me once I protected us so that she was coating my dick with her juices.

Every time she bumped her clit, she shuddered like she'd been zapped by a spark of electricity.

"Fuck," she said thickly. "You feel so good."

Wanting to watch the show, I leaned on my hands and rumbled, "How good?"

"Perfect. So perfect. You're so big, but I know you'll be…" She mewled. "I know that you fit me just right. Only you. Only you," she whispered feverishly.

It was too soon to be thinking the kind of shit I was thinking.

Shit like, 'You'll never know anything but my cock.'

Like, 'Get used to my dick, baby girl. It's yours.'

Before I could spiral into territory that questioned whether I was good enough for her again, whether I was insane for even letting my mind go there when we came from different sides of the same track, she settled the tip at her slit and started to sink onto me.

She was slow. Torturously slow. But I kept my eyes locked on her face, watching for the faintest hint of pain in her expression so that I could bring this to a halt sooner rather than later.

But there wasn't any.

She was careful, adjusting to my girth with every inch she accepted inside her before attempting to take more.

It was probably the most patient I'd ever been in my goddamn life, but it was worth it for her to take all of me.

My head rocked back slightly as I savored the feeling of her tightness clinging to me, then she mumbled, "J-James?"

I grunted.

She rocked her hips.

It was… awkward.

I blinked then, understanding hit, and I reached for her waist. "This way," I instructed, guiding her, encouraging her, and helping her when she needed it.

She wasn't a natural, but it didn't matter. She still felt like fucking heaven. *Like fucking mine.*

"You're doing so well, baby," I praised. "Your pussy is so goddamn tight. You've taken me fucking beautifully."

She shuddered, the rocking of her hips faltered, and I guided her again then started to take over when her cunt began fluttering around me—that was the first warning sign.

With one hand on her hip, a chunk of her ass in my grip to keep her moving, I focused on her clit with the other.

The second my thumb rubbed over it, she released a cry, her entire being tipping forward as her fingers found my shoulders, her nails digging in, clawing at me in a way that'd leave marks.

"You feel so big."

"You're perfect," I replied, surging up so that I could press my mouth to hers. "Such a good girl." Her cunt strangled my cock. "So fucking good. My good girl. *Mine*, MaryCat. Mine."

A few more strokes to her clit and she exploded around me, her pussy gripping me in a chokehold that I didn't care if I survived.

As she orgasmed, I encouraged her to continue her pace because I was so fucking clos—

I growled as I came, the noise brushing her lips as she sobbed through the comedown from her climax.

We froze like that, a still-life tableau of need and want and pleasure.

For myself, I was thinking about shit I had no business feeling this early on.

Didn't mean I *wasn't* feeling it, just meant I wasn't going to admit it out loud.

But sweet fuck, what she did to me.

It was the difference between jerking off and sliding home for the first time in the only pussy you were okay to ever experience again.

It was enough for the lights to fade, for sounds to disappear, for the earth to quake beneath the fucking bed.

That this small Irish-American spitfire was capable of bringing me to my knees shouldn't be such a surprise after last night, but it was.

It fucking was.

Then, time kickstarted. The world continued turning. Her mouth fell on mine and my arms slid around her as I tumbled her onto the sheets.

As I kissed her, she pulled back a little to mutter, "I want to stay like this again."

Shaking my head at her, I smirked. "We ain't borrowing trouble. You can sleep after we shower."

Though she was fascinated as she watched me deal with the condom and strip off my jeans, after, she griped and groaned through clean-up duty, a task she let me take on completely which was cute as hell, especially when I sprayed her right in the pussy with cold water and she leaped a foot in the air.

She glowered at me but, cuter still, didn't vow revenge, just let me apply the liniment to her thighs then trudged to the bed and waited for me to climb in.

Once I was there, she slid in beside me, hooked her leg over mine, and settled her head on my chest as if we'd been doing this for a hundred years.

Maybe in a parallel universe, we had.

Crazy though it might be, that would make sense of why this felt so fucking right, why shit was so easy between us.

As I covered us with the comforter, I ordered, "Sleep. We have errands to run if we're going to get my hog on a plane tomorrow."

She hadn't needed my permission.

Before I finished the sentence, she was asleep, her soft breath brushing my throat.

The trust she showed in me was insane. How she settled into me like this was *her* spot blew my mind. The sense of home I had with her at my side was even more bewildering.

As I stared at the ceiling, I had to wonder if a sinner like me had earned this paradise…

The problem was that I knew the answer was no.

So, the only real question worth asking was one that I didn't know she'd asked herself too—how long would I get to keep *this* for?

23

MARYCAT

MARYCAT

I WOKE up to his head between my thighs.

For a second, the world was a hazy mess of dim lights and darkness beyond the windows that were half-shielded by the drapes. The TV was on, and the light illuminated the space, which was the moment I realized *why* I'd woken up.

Digger was tasting me.

There.

I shuddered as the tip of his tongue slid through my folds; a word I'd always hated in the romance books made sense now. Each little piece of skin was sensitive. And when he gently bit on it, testing its resilience with his teeth?

Mary, Mother of God.

My eyes rolled back in my head as I spread my thighs wider.

That rumbly chuckle of his told me that he knew I was awake, but I didn't give a damn if he knew. I just never wanted him to stop what he was doing.

The flat of his tongue thrummed over my clit before he suckled on one of my labia. My brow furrowed as I realized that actually felt kind of nice.

He nipped and sucked my clit then he did this thing that made a slurping sound.

Before I could do more than jump, he was moving down, his tongue penetrating me, and I was—

"James," I sobbed.

"Let go, baby girl," he mumbled.

God, I was *so* wet.

I was noisy.

Like, noises were coming from down there.

Was that normal?

Was I *ab*normal?

Sarah had never mentioned anything about being wet if Anthony touched her. As troubling as her situation was, it made sense that she loathed his touch.

For a second, my mind drifted as embarrassment took hold at the sounds he made as he ate me out because of my response to him.

It was a ridiculous defense mechanism, but it let me process my feelings of mortification.

After meeting Digger, and after experiencing him, *experiencing this*, the urge to save Sarah from her horrible marriage was strong, but first, I needed to be selfish—there was no saving anyone if I couldn't save myself.

And right now, my problems were on the East Coast, I was on the West, and I had *Digger's* mouth on my pussy.

On my clit, to be precise.

"Good girl. That's it. Come back to me."

How did he know I'd lost focus?

"You taste so goddamn fine, baby."

His tongue started doing this flittering thing that robbed me of all thought and had my mouth gaping as I stared at the ceiling.

"J-James," I warbled, the alien sensations from this type of caress doing crazy things to my system.

"What, my sweet girl?" he rumbled so that the vibrations hit my clit.

"I-I wish there were a mirror on the ceiling," I blurted out.

He chuckled, which made me moan. "Want to watch me eat you out like you're a five-course meal, hmm?"

I shuddered. "Y-Yes."

His smile was wicked before he dove back in for more.

Jesus.

Fuck.

Oh, God.

"D-Do the noises bother you?" I questioned in a rush, hating how naive I sounded, but the hotter he made me, the more evident they became.

He peered at me from between my thighs, those velvet brown eyes soft yet wicked. Hungry yet patient.

"Why would they bother me? You're fucking wet, baby girl. Wet for me. I turn you on and I get you hot. That's never going to be a problem for me."

A shiver whispered down my spine as I stared at him.

"Look at all this." His fingers stroked over my sex and came away coated with juices. "I could fucking drown in you."

The embarrassment began to fade away when I saw his genuine appreciation of my response to him. The next noise that came, I didn't bother worrying about it, just groaned and writhed and shuddered through his every caress as he tongued my slit in a manner that had his face gleaming with my arousal.

Then, when he used his fingers to pull apart my labia and it exposed my clit, I cried out when his mouth returned to the nub, and, as I quaked beneath him, aware that the most sensitive part of me was exposed now, he gently sucked on it before palpating the tiny nub with his tongue.

All thoughts faded.

Nervous ones, anxious ones, embarrassed ones—gone.

Like that.

As if they never existed in the first place.

Eyelashes fluttering, I urged myself into sitting up some, leaning on my elbows so I could watch.

"Such a good fucking girl."

Moaning, I took in our sizes as his words filtered into my consciousness.

I was so small in comparison to him. His shoulders took up a lot of room between my thighs, especially now that he'd settled into place for the long haul, and *what a long haul it was.*

"So fucking good. You like what I do to you, baby girl?"

"Y-Yes. So much. T-Thank you, James."

"You're fucking drenched." He slurped on my clit. "*And* you taste like heaven."

One of my hands, of its own volition, scraped over his head, digging into the slight waves of his hair. I didn't realize I was doing it, guiding him where it felt best, but he let me be bossy, mumbling soft words against my cunt that had me dying right then and there.

"I love that you know what you want. All this is for me."

A sharp cry escaped me.

"MaryCat, you're my good girl. You take what you need, baby. You take it and make it your own."

I shuddered each time he spoke, and with every statement, he took away more nerves that surged into being when I worried I was taking too long to come. He didn't care, so why should I?

Then, his tongue thrust into my slit again and he started to stroke delicate flesh.

The nerves were raw, the flesh sore from his attentions.

It felt… uncomfortable.

And he knew.

Immediately pulling away, he muttered against my clit, "You're going to come for me like a good girl, MaryCat. I ain't gonna stop until you coat my lips and jaw in your cum, you hear me?"

The imagery combined with his tongue's lashing of the tender nub had me sobbing, "I-I hear you."

God, did he know how his words drove me to distraction?

An urge hit me—I flopped onto my back and then allowed my legs to rock upward so that the front of my thighs were against my belly. Then, I slipped my hands around my feet in a yoga pose that was great for stretching out the hamstrings and lowering the heart rate—I needed that because he was going to put me into cardiac arrest.

Suddenly, I was there.

I didn't know if it was the shift in position, the fact I could kind of see the artist at work or his tongue's wicked skills. Hell, maybe it was a combination of all three. *Whatever.* I was there and I was going to die and it felt so good and it was too good and oh. My. God!

My fingers clenched around my toes as I strained toward release, a release he gave me so generously. It pummeled me, had pleasure zipping around my being. Only, he didn't stop once I'd come. No, he doubled down by flicking his tongue along my sex.

I knew what he was doing too.

He was tasting me.

My arousal.

Gross?

But…

God, that felt good.

Maybe nothing he did was gross. Nothing between us, at any rate.

The weight of holding my head up strained my neck as he kept me there—high, high, high. But he'd let me come. I didn't understand why I still felt so on edge. So ready to explode when the explosion was a thing of the past.

Yet, he wasn't stopping.

He didn't pull away.

If anything…

Oh, fuck.

He flicked his tongue quickly over my clit and alternated between that and deep sucks.

Suddenly, I knew the soft climax of before was just a warm-up.

Lights flashed behind my eyes as if we'd invited the Vegas strip into our room.

My ears buzzed, my lungs burned, and my stomach twisted as he flew me to greater heights, greater still, higher. We were entering a different stratosphere, and then one of his hands shifted to my breast.

He found my nipple. He tweaked it. He rolled it between his fingers. He thumbed it. Then, he pinched.

Hard.

And that was me done.

Gone.

RIP, MaryfuckingCatherine.

The orgasm hit me like a sucker punch.

I screamed as the pleasure washed through me, suffocating me, choking me. The cry was torn from me, loud enough that later, I'd be grateful for the soundproofing in our suite.

My sobs turned to moans entwined with soft shrieks as I rocked through it, needing to offset the sweetest agony I'd ever known, and then, out of nowhere, I was sinking down, down.

Floating on endorphins.

When I came to, it was because he was pressing a kiss to either side of my inner thighs.

My eyes kickstarted and my ears could hear and my lungs weren't burning anymore.

Fingers stroking through his hair, I stared at him with a vision that was fuzzy at the edges and slurred, "Morning."

"No sex for at least three days."

My mouth rounded as he might as well have thrown a bucketful of ice water on top of me.

"What?" I shrieked, jerking upright then regretting it—who knew oral sex was great for the core?

He arched a brow at me. "You're sore."

"I'm not."

"You are."

"I'm not! *I'd* know!"

"You're your own worst enemy," he retorted, flipping over so that he was on his back. "Anyway, you won't want sex once you take Plan B. It'll trigger a period."

Shit. He was right. It was the reason I'd convinced him that I'd take it once we started traveling.

Still, I huffed. "You can't take them away."

He snorted. "Take what away?"

"Orgasms. I like them."

That curve of his lips made another appearance. "I can tell. Thought I was gonna drown in your pussy juices. What a way to fucking go though."

Before our conversation, I'd probably have been embarrassed. But I heard his delight and mumbled instead, "Don't be a pussy tease."

"I'm not. Did I not just give you two orgasms?"

He didn't even seem smug about it. Just matter of fact as he slung his arm behind his head and propped it up in the sexiest move I'd ever seen.

"You did," I said breathily.

"Anyway, you'll be all shy once you get your period," he predicted.

"I won't."

He winked at me.

Ugh, so cocky.

Speaking of cocky…

That was when I saw his erection.

It was there.

Just there.

Against his abs.

Minding its own business.

Didn't he know it was there?

He had to, right?

Men always thought with their dicks.

I cleared my throat. "You can't leave things out to tempt me like that."

"MaryCat, don't be ridiculous."

"Ridiculous?" I huffed. "I'm *pleasure-starved*, James. I'm *deprived*. I've got carpal tunnel from masturbation. Well, before Father Doyle switched up his punishments."

"What? Punishments?" he sputtered, casually reaching up and swiping his jaw.

Which gleamed.

With me.

My cheeks were back to burning.

"Confession sucks," I grumbled, watching him, wondering if it'd be weird to kiss him now that I glossed his lips better than Vaseline. Because I was unsure, I continued, "There was no way I could buy a vibrator either. Father would find it, and—"

"Why would he look for a vibrator in your things?"

Because he wanted to find reasons to punish me.

I didn't say that though.

If I did, I knew that delicious erection would disappear, and I wasn't entirely sure of how to get it back again.

I mean, I *knew*, but Digger was Digger.

There was no arguing with his stamina, and there was no ignoring the fact that he'd just gone down on me with zero expectation of recip-rocation. That much was clear from how his fingers had found my shoulder and he was making circles there.

No, Digger was definitely a different breed of man.

Not entirely displeased by that fact, I let my hand flop onto his muscled stomach. He wasn't even tensing up and there were ripples.

I'd married a man with a six-pack.

What world had I moved into?

"It doesn't matter. I just couldn't buy a vibrator," I muttered eventually.

He cut me a look. "You can't convince me with puppy-dog eyes. No sex until you're not sore *or* bleeding, and I'll test that out for myself, seeing as you can't be trusted."

Though I huffed, inside, the cogs started working.

Deciding to shift gears, I mimicked him and made circles on his abs with the tips of my fingers. "Was I really not too wet?"

"You really weren't. No such thing, baby," he said easily, his gaze on the TV where Savannah Daniels was making a yule log with what appeared to be a group of grandmothers.

I swallowed. "Promise?"

That had his focus veering onto me. "Look at my cock and tell me you ain't relieved you get that wet?"

When he offered, it'd be rude to refuse.

I looked at it.

Every inch of it.

Thick and fat and long.

Who knew those three words, when combined, could ever be a wonderful thing?

Was it purple or just a deep, dark red?

The tip was super taut and small dots of pre-cum dripped onto his stomach.

That wasn't hot—that wasn't hot—that wasn't hot.

Fuck, that was hot.

His lips twisted a second before he controlled his grin. "Your cunt was drenched. Say it."

"My cunt was drenched," I whispered.

"Because of me."

I nodded. "Because of you."

"Now tell me that you know I fucking loved it."

I swallowed. "I know you loved it."

He tutted. "I *fucking* loved it."

I smiled a little. "You *fucking* loved it."

"And your cunt is so tight that it's a great thing you get so goddamn wet."

I released a breath. "And my cunt is so tight that it's a great thing I get so goddamn wet." Cheekily, I added, "Because you have a massive cock."

Laughter drifted from him. "This, here, it's ours." He traced his finger along my jaw. "Sacred. Weird crap happens all the time when you're fucking. Part of the fun."

Curious, I leaned over him. "Can I kiss you?"

"I'll taste of you," he said, still matter of fact.

"Do I taste bad?"

"I didn't mean that. I meant you might not like it."

"Can I try?"

"Sure."

I nestled into him, my fingers still super close to his dick. A glance showed me bigger droplets of pre-cum were starting to bubble from the tip—that had to be a good sign.

I kept up with the circles as I pressed a quick kiss to his lips.

"That ain't a kiss," he dismissed.

I scowled at him. "That's totally a kiss."

"You're more playful when you've had sleep."

That came out of left field. But he was right. Except this was the side of me that Sarah usually had to deal with. I guessed I'd let him past my walls.

Not wanting to admit that out loud, I countered, "You got a problem with playful?"

He snickered. "Nope. Now, if you're gonna tell me that you're going to kiss me, at least fucking kiss me, MaryCat."

I bit my lip, let my nose approach his jaw, and…

Huh.

It wasn't the *best* smell in the world, but it wasn't unappealing. Especially when I knew that was me and he'd done that to me.

I rubbed my thighs together at the thought.

Allowing my mouth to find his once more, I slowly fluttered my tongue around it. Then, he parted his lips and I dove deep. His hand found the back of my head and he kept me there as I explored him.

My thumb drifted over his abs.

Pre-cum coated the side of my nail.

I was getting closer to my target.

I moaned as he shifted higher, turning this from my playing field to his as he stroked his tongue against mine. It was gentle at first, then it wasn't.

It was raw and hungry and deep.

He pulled back when I started mewling, nipping my bottom lip before he plunked his head down on his arm again.

"Why did you stop?" I complained.

"Because you're not ready for anything else."

"Says who?" I groused.

As my breathing calmed, I peered at his cock.

For a long time, I studied the one-eyed beast, then I drew up the courage to state, "You said you'd teach me to blow you."

Not a question or a request—he'd probably say no. My husband was too good at denying himself. He was definitely better at it than me: the die-hard Catholic.

"I will."

"You have an erection now."

Yawning, he said, "My dick likes you."

Though his words took me aback, I preened. "It does?"

"It's attached to me, MaryCat," he chided, but he was chuckling. "If I ain't shown you enough that I like you too then we need to work on your self-esteem. You got problems with your self-esteem as well as daddy issues?"

My cheeks flushed. "Don't mock."

"Ain't mocking. Just telling the truth. Technically, I got daddy issues too." With a wink, he grabbed my hand and lowered it to his cock.

More matter-of-fact moves.

I was starting to think he'd patented them.

"Hold it tight like this," he instructed. "You won't break it. I'm rougher than you could be."

My brow puckered. "I want to see you do it too."

"I'll add it to the list," he teased, more amusement lacing his words.

Moving his fingers aside, he let me hold him and then placed his hand over the top of mine to better instruct me.

I shuddered at the feel of him. He was soft and hard—simultaneously.

Silently, he taught me how to jack him off. It wasn't clinical, more informative. I could hear from how his breathing quickened that he liked my touch, so it made it more fun for me.

"You play with my balls and I'll come faster. You grip 'em and twist them in your palm, it'll hold me off."

"Why would I want to do that?"

His lips quirked. "Not everything's a race to the finish line, Mary-

Cat. Plus, I ain't like you. You get to come over and over and over—"
Each 'over' made me feel dizzy with the prospect. "—but I've got a
few goes in me a night."

"A few?" I croaked.

A hiss escaped him when I reached down with my other hand to
caress his balls. Which was when I moved lower on the bed so that I
wasn't at eye level with him anymore.

It helped that he didn't lean on his elbows as I had so that he could
watch me. If anything, the breathing room made me more adventurous.
Especially when his fingers moved to my hair and he started playing
with a few strands.

It was remarkably liberating to be given such freedom to pleasure him.

I shuffled nearer then pressed a kiss to the tip once I let it lay flat
against his stomach, then I flicked my tongue along the little slit that
had pre-cum gathering there already.

I guessed his pre-cum wasn't particularly funky or bad. Just...

"Why do you taste like salt?"

His chuckle made another appearance. "It's what cum tastes of."

Though I crinkled my nose, he just carried on toying with my hair.

Which was the moment it came to me—the realization.

He'd answer anything I asked.

He was free with himself.

Open.

I liked open.

I hated closed.

He didn't talk in doublespeak and didn't withhold information.
Every word wasn't a battlefield, and every conversation didn't leave
me feeling interrogated.

I loved that he lay there and let me touch him. He'd gotten me off
so many times, but there was no rush here. Hell, there wasn't even any
expectation. He was calm and relaxed and it slithered into my bones.

I wanted this.

More of this.

All of this.

I wanted it every night.

Forever.

The thought made me woozy.

Because of that, to hide the depth of that craving, a craving that let me see how it could be ten years down the line, him still calm and caring, me irate over one of our kids, maybe, breaking a wrist...

It was a jarring image, but I liked it even more.

"Lick the tip then move down the length of my cock," he directed. "Get it wet. It'll make it easier if you want to suck it."

Eyes wide, I obeyed.

There were ropes of veins and a thick, long one at the back. From human biology, I knew what it was, but seeing it in a textbook and exploring it with my tongue were two very different learning experiences.

I much preferred the practical approach when Digger was my workmate.

"Never use your teeth unless you want me to fuck you, and I won't fuck you today so keep them to yourself."

My eyes flared wide. "Biting's a good thing?"

He hitched a shoulder. "To each their own."

I hummed as I worked, enjoying giving him the pleasure he so freely gifted me. And I knew I pleased him. For all that he was lying there like a lion lazing under the sun, he'd tense, his thighs shifting, his abs clenching if I did something he enjoyed.

Luckily for him, I was a quick study, and though I'd been raised as one big, fat inhibition, I was too eager to know *everything* to let them get in my way.

As he guided me on what worked or didn't work for him, I found myself with his cock in my mouth.

At long last.

Honestly, there should have been a choir singing a salutation at how happy I was to have him inside me again.

I knew it was big—my pussy *was* sore.

But I loved his size.

I enjoyed how he shuffled more on the sheets and how his hands would fist in my hair if I sucked hard.

I appreciated the taste of him, and how his pre-cum would lubricate my path as I slipped down as far as I could.

As the power dynamic between us shifted and flowed, I found myself feeling more exhilarated than when he'd popped my cherry.

I was in control here. His pleasure was mine to give.

It lit me up inside and made me realize how good it felt to be with someone so unabashed and unashamed where sex was concerned. Damn, not just sex, but everything. *Everything.* Not even the prospect of war had made him lose his temper with me.

If anything, when I'd laughed at his predicament with his bike, he'd teased me and chased me, no aggression, just... *Digger.*

Tears pricked my eyes with gratitude, but I shoved the thoughts aside, wanting to give him everything he'd gifted me.

So I sucked, and I licked, and I nuzzled his balls, slipping one into my mouth even though he hadn't said that I should. I twisted them together in my palm once they were slick with spit as I focused on his glans, then I slurped my way up and down his length like he was a popsicle before I bobbed my head and sucked on him as hard as I could.

When both hands fisted in my hair, the sweetest sense of satisfaction surged through me.

He was half-sitting now, and I didn't mind the attention because grunts were escaping him, soft groans, and finally—

"Look at you, MaryCat. So fucking beautiful with my cock in that pretty mouth," he growled, fingers tugging at my hair as he held me to him. "Such a good girl."

I whimpered.

Then his hips started to rock and I realized he was thrusting into me from beneath.

Excuse me while I fainted.

Not really, but God, it felt good knowing that I'd taken him to this point.

He didn't shove me down so that I was choking. It wasn't a close-won thing—even in this, Digger was controlled.

When he tensed, his fingers tugging on my hair, more praise spilled from his lips as his cum landed on my tongue. His abs were against my ear as he loomed above me, surrounding me with him on all sides.

For a moment, I didn't know what to do with the cum on my tongue. It was salty and bitter and there was so much of it.

Then, he rumbled, "Spit it on the sheet, baby girl."

The strangest thought occurred to me—*wouldn't a good girl swallow?*

I moved away from his dick, well aware that his seed was leaking from the corners of my lips, and I made sure he was looking at me.

I showed him my tongue, watching his nostrils flare at the sight, then I swallowed.

His eyes closed as he flopped back on the sheets, his fist landing on his forehead in a display of masculine despair.

Bobbing down, I licked up the few drops that had landed on his abs, which was when he rasped, "You're going to be the fucking death of me."

Once I'd cleaned up the mess I made, I smirked at his statement and settled into his side. "How did I do?"

"You want a grade?"

"Would you give me one?"

"Ah, Christ, you were a teacher's pet, weren't you?"

"As if you didn't realize that before."

He grunted. "A teacher's pet with a cum fetish."

"What's a cum fetish?"

"What does it sound like?"

It sounded like I was obsessed with cum. Had I been around it enough to be obsessed though?

Before I could pepper him with more questions, he drawled, "A-."

My eyes widened with delight and it immediately shifted my focus away from obsessions and semen. "So high? Where could I improve?"

He hissed out a breath. "We'll train your gag reflex so you can take more of me."

It was my turn to flop back on the bed, my hand covering my eyes in a display of feminine need.

"When can we have sex again?"

His chuckle had me huffing. "When you didn't just drain my dick *and* when your period stops."

"So, what you're saying is, I have to wait a lifetime?"

He snorted. "Yeah, MaryCat. That's exactly what I'm saying."

24

TEXT CHAT

Sarah: I want to kill HIM. Jesus Christ, I did something wicked in a past life if this is the asshole I have to be with until he dies.

Sarah: If I strangle him, I need you to be my alibi. Ya hear me?

Sarah: Remember when I took the fall for you busting your dad's side mirror on his BMW? This is payback time.

THREE HOURS LATER

Sarah: Mary Catherine?

FIVE HOURS LATER

Sarah: Mary Catherine!

ONE MISSED VOICE CALL
FOLLOWING DAY

Sarah: Babe?

Sarah: Mary Catherine, what's going on? I called your dad but he isn't answering either.

TWO MISSED VOICE CALLS
FOLLOWING DAY
THREE MISSED VOICE CALLS
FOUR MISSED VOICE CALLS
FIVE MISSED VOICE CALLS

Sarah: OMG, where the fuck are you? Anthony just said the Five Points have a red alert out on you. Yes, Mary Catherine. I actually spoke to my jerk-off of a husband to ask about you!!

Sarah: WHERE. ARE. YOU?

SIX MISSED VOICE CALLS
SEVEN MISSED VOICE CALLS

Mary Catherine: *peeps in*

Mary Catherine: *ducks for cover*

Sarah: Holy shit, you'd better run for cover!!! Are you safe?! Who do I need to kill?

Mary Catherine: No one. No deaths required. Look, I don't have time to talk right now. Things are crazy here. My phone's not with me. I'm using a computer at the airport to check in because I knew you'd be freaking out.

Sarah: Since when don't you have the time to talk to ME? WTF? And where's here?

Sarah: Wait.

Sarah: THE AIRPORT? Which airport?

Mary Catherine: Vegas.

Sarah: Vegas. What in the ever-living hell is going on?

Sarah: Mary Catherine, what are you doing in Sin City and why wasn't I invited along for the ride?

Mary Catherine: I got married, Sarah.

Sarah: Hahahaha. Great joke.

Mary Catherine: It's not a joke.

Sarah: Of course it is. There's no way in fuck that you got married without me there.

Mary Catherine: I did. And the Grinch was the officiant.

Sarah: Are you tripping?

Mary Catherine: Maybe. ROAD-tripping.

Sarah: Oh, my god. You're being serious!

Mary Catherine: I am. Beyond serious.

Sarah: Who did you marry?

Mary Catherine: Well, it wasn't Bill Murphy.

Sarah: Eww. I heard about that from Anthony today. What was your dad thinking?

Mary Catherine: I don't know, but whatever it was, he can't get to me now.

Sarah: Honey, don't you remember what happened before? To Kris?

Mary Catherine: Of course, I do. But I picked someone who's not afraid of my father, Sarah. Someone who would make HIM scared.

Sarah: Who? I can't imagine anyone from college being scary enough for that...

Mary Catherine: You're right. He isn't from college. He's a biker.

Sarah: Like a cyclist?

Mary Catherine: No. A BIKER. Jesus.

Sarah: A biker? You? My God, you ARE tripping.

Mary Catherine: I'm not! GRR. Anyway, I have to go.

Sarah: No! Wait!

Sarah: I'm sorry. I wasn't mocking, I swear. I'm just concerned. You genuinely married a biker?

Mary Catherine: I did. He's my half-brother's friend.

Mary Catherine: You know, Padraig?

Sarah: I remember you telling me about him, of course. Wow.

Sarah: Fuck.

Mary Catherine: You remember when Padraig came to the house?

Sarah: Of course lol. You hoped he'd killed Mommy Dearest. That's not a conversation you forget.

Mary Catherine: Well, the other biker...

Sarah: Your Charlie Hunnam-lookalike crush?

Mary Catherine: Your memory is disturbing.

Sarah: Be grateful I can keep up with your massive brain.

Mary Catherine: Har. Har. Har.

Mary Catherine: Anyway, it's him. The Charlie Hunnam-lookalike.

Sarah: Who is?

Mary Catherine: My husband. He's the one who rescued me from Bill Murphy.

Sarah: Him? Wow. Mary Catherine, you're really married to him? You don't know him.

Mary Catherine: I don't know Bill Murphy either.

Sarah: God. So true. I have no idea why I even said that. SMH.

Sarah: I'm kinda speechless. And proud. I thought you were a good girl.

Mary Catherine: I am. :P

Sarah: Hahahahaha.

Sarah: Ugh. Do you know what I hate?

Mary Catherine: What?

Sarah: That you couldn't come to me about this. :(It sucks.

Mary Catherine: It does.

Mary Catherine: Do you know how the red alert was sounded? Was Mother involved?

Sarah: I don't think so. Anthony would have said. You know he hates her since she told him he looked like Mr. Potato Head. It's the only time I've ever appreciated anything that bitch has to say.

Mary Catherine: Interesting.

Sarah: Oh.

Mary Catherine: Oh?

Sarah: I didn't think anything of it because I was too busy trying not to strangle Anthony at dinner, but I'm sure the MIL from hell was talking about your mom the other night. I tune out normally so I'm not certain, but could she be in rehab?

Sarah: Someone's in rehab lol. Whether it's your egg donor or someone else's.

Mary Catherine: Could you find out for me if it IS her?

Sarah: Of course. Give me five mins.

Mary Catherine: Thanks, babe.

Mary Catherine: What did Anthony do to make you want to strangle him, btw?

Sarah: Started talking about having a family again. I'd prefer to have Lucifer's spawn than his. *shudders*

Sarah: Okay, I texted the bitch.

Mary Catherine: <3

Mary Catherine: Father's already gotten Aidan Sr. involved so we're heading back to the East Coast now.

Sarah: If Senior's involved... you know what that means, don't you?

Mary Catherine: Yeah. War.

FIVE MINUTES LATER

Sarah: Mary Catherine, you still there?

Mary Catherine: Yeah. GTG in a minute. Our flight's boarding soon. Everything okay?

Sarah: Your mom IS in rehab.

Sarah: Is that important?

Mary Catherine: It means that Father found out where I was without her input.

Sarah: Eww. He's got a trace on your phone?

Mary Catherine: I think so.

Sarah: Jerk off. That's so creepy. Especially with all the cameras.

Mary Catherine: I know. God, I hope I never have to see him again.

Mary Catherine: Is that too much to ask?

Sarah: Considering who I'm married to hasn't dropped dead of a heart attack yet... yes. :/

Mary Catherine: I know I don't say it often, Sarah, but I love you. You know that?

Sarah: Jesus, do you think you're going to die or something?

Mary Catherine: I'm not a virgin anymore. If Digger can't help me... if Father...

Sarah: Yeah.

Sarah: Jesus.

Sarah: Still, this biker. You trust him?

Mary Catherine: I do.

Sarah: Then I do too.

Sarah: You're more persuasive than you think, girl.

Mary Catherine: Meaning?

Sarah: Meaning that not all wars have to be fought with fists OR bullets.

Mary Catherine: I have to log off. Our flight's boarding. I'll let you know everything as and when it happens. xo

Sarah: You'd fucking better.

Sarah: And, hey, I love you too.

Sarah: Now, don't suck at being my BFF and make sure you come back to me.

Sarah: Ya hear me?

Mary Catherine: I hear you. :P

25

MARYCAT

MARYCAT

"YOU STROKE ME LIKE THAT."

Digger's brows lifted. "I do not."

"You do," I teased, but my tone wasn't malicious. Mostly, it was amused.

Watching him inspect his ride for any little scratch in the paint was pretty sweet.

His bike had been tucked up safe and sound in the cargo hold of the airplane we'd flown on.

Which, in my mind, was far safer than the highway.

"Then, you know I touch you with reverence," he informed me, his tone as teasing as mine was, but there was a semblance of truth to the words that made my heart twinge and prompted me to leave him alone as he checked his ride over.

The red-eye to Jersey hadn't been painful. Digger had to blow too much money on getting his bike, sorry, *hog*, prepared for being flown freight, but on the plane, it had been nice to just sit there and talk. Side by side. Instead of shouting over his shoulder and ingesting too many calories from bugs I accidentally swallowed.

Then, of course, I'd thought about my conversation with Sarah.

Unfortunately, he'd been right about me getting embarrassed when the Plan B triggered a period, or I might have even asked him to join the mile-high club to take my mind off things at home.

"Why are you pouting?"

Though I jerked in surprise, my pout twisted into a sheepish smile. "I was just thinking."

"What about? No, I won't fuck you on my hog. Before you ask, I mean."

I gaped at him. "That's possible?"

He groaned under his breath. "I should have kept my fucking mouth shut."

"You should've," I agreed, especially when I'd been thinking of sex on another mode of transportation. "But, how do you do that with-out... dying?"

"You're not that much of an adrenaline junkie, MC."

Somewhere over Chicago, he'd started abbreviating my already abbreviated nickname to MC.

I liked it.

It was far superior to Mary Catherine.

"Maybe I am," I grumbled. "You don't know I'm not." Then, I squinted at him. "Have you done it before?"

Lips twitching as he stopped polishing the body, the part that had a fire ombré on it, he mused, "Jealousy looks good on you, baby girl."

I huffed. "I'm not jealous. I'm curious."

"Just you watch that curiosity doesn't kill the MaryCat, hmm?" he chided, but he strode over to me and cupped my chin. "You shouldn't ask questions you don't want the answers to. I'm not a choir boy, MC."

"I don't want you to be a choir boy."

His gaze pierced me with his intensity. For whatever reason, my words or tone supplied me with an answer. "I haven't done it on my hog. But I know someone who has and he only did it because he has a death wish."

I blinked. "A brother?"

He grunted. "Name's Nyx."

"Nyx? Like the makeup?"

Digger's mouth twitched. "It's a makeup brand?"

"I mean, yeah? They do the best lipstick."

He scraped a hand over his jaw. "I'll have to tell him that when he's back." With amusement still lighting up those gorgeous brown eyes of his, he returned to his hog and then, in short order, declared, "Okay, we can go."

"Any injuries?"

Though he knew I was mocking him, he just arched a brow at me. "Nah. It was packaged well. How's your ass?"

I shot him a wry grin. "Grateful we didn't have to ride across the country on that thing."

"Figured as much." He winked. "Think you can manage a twenty-minute trip to West Orange?"

Deciding that was the moment to suck it up, I stated, "I think we should go to Aidan Sr.'s compound."

His head tilted to the side. "The one in Queens?"

Surprised, I asked, "You know where it is?"

He hummed. "I know *of* it."

"Why?"

"I just do. You can't have a secret with me around."

I smiled at that. "You can't know everything."

"I can try," he said with a wink.

A soft thrill whispered through my veins as he curved an arm around my shoulder.

I could never have imagined that a biker would be affectionate, but I was either thinking stereotypically or he was breaking the mold.

"Where's your mind at, MC?" he asked, his tone more serious. "They won't let me through the gates of the compound. Not unless it's in a body bag."

"Auntie Lena, Senior's wife, she's there."

"So?"

"I might be able to get her on our side."

She could be the key to the Sinners, i.e., Digger, walking away from this unscathed and me never having to see Father ever again.

His brow puckered. "With the intent to do what?"

Nervously, when it was ridiculous to be nervous around him, I blurted out, "I genuinely don't think the O'Donnellys know what goes on in the lesser ranks."

"That'd make sense. Rex doesn't know what the Prospects get up to at all hours of the day. He relies on his council to keep their ears to the ground. Surely, they're the same?"

"Maybe. They have their crews, but if those crews are a part of the problem…"

"I see what you mean." He pursed his lips. "You want to talk to Magdalena O'Donnelly first."

"I do. I want to offset the tension in the situation. I want…" I hesitated, sucking in a breath. "…to allay the chance of the Five Points declaring war with the Satan's Sinners."

"You think you can do that? You think you can be that persuasive?"

For a second, I bit my lip, then I mumbled, "We're married, aren't we?"

He snorted as he chucked me under the chin. "Some women wouldn't think I was that much of a catch."

"Some women are fools."

He didn't acknowledge my comment. "*I* brought up the idea of marriage."

"Something in my story made you listen and offer that to me. My desperation isn't unfeigned. I have to believe that Auntie Lena will respond to that and react accordingly."

Everyone knew what the Aryans had done to Magdalena O'Donnelly.

All these years later, NYC was still reeling from the aftermath of Uncle Aidan's wrath as he punished those who'd dared hurt his wife.

How could a man do *that* then allow women in his faction to be similarly abused?

No, something wasn't adding up.

And every Five Pointer knew that the only person who could ever get through to Uncle Aidan was his Achilles' heel—Auntie Lena.

"Digger?"

"What?"

"I know I'm your wife."

His eyes darkened—he liked hearing me call myself that. "You are."

"I want to stay that way."

"You can't—"

I shoved his arm. "I *can* know that. I *do* know that. I even…" This was where things got embarrassing. "I know in the books, bikers—"

"Wait. What books?"

"MC romance books."

His lips twisted. "That's a thing?"

"Well, of course."

"Ain't you just a treasure trove of information." Digger hooted. "I mean, I know there are chicks who dig bikers. Hell, half of the rich bitches in West Orange sniff around the clubhouse for a rough lay, but romance *novels*? You being serious?"

I scowled at him. "Are you trying to shove in my face how many women want you?"

"No." His arm tightened around my shoulder. "You back to being jealous, MC?"

My scowl darkened.

His grin widened. "Not a wise question to ask, hmm? Okay, let's shift to the topic at hand. Why did you bring up MC romance books?" He paused. "Wait, they know we run drugs and guns and shit, right?"

"Who's they?"

"Readers."

I shrugged. "I knew."

"Well, fuck. Women be crazy." He scratched his stubbled chin. "Right, so, you were saying."

"In the books, they say that when a biker claims a woman, he brands her."

He stilled. "You're talking ink, not hot pokers, yeah?"

"It depends on the books."

Scratching his jaw, he muttered, "There are some hardcore chicks out there."

"You have your arm around one of them," I retorted.

He whistled under his breath.

"I want a brand."

"You do, huh?" He smirked at me before he pressed a kiss to my nose. "In the MC, that ring on your finger don't mean much."

I knew it.

"I figured," I admitted.

"A brand is usually what it takes to get protection from the club."

"Why didn't you take me to a tattoo studio, then?"

"Because it wasn't necessary. Not with you being Sin's sister too, something Rex confirmed the first time I spoke with him. The ring was more for your father. Plus..." His hand shifted to my throat, and his thumb traced over the sinews there. "If I brand you, MaryCat, then there's no getting away from me. That's a big step. A massive step, in fact. Let's not run before we can walk, hmm?"

My mouth twisted as hurt surged inside me.

Why would he want me anyway when he had all these 'rich bitches' in town wanting to get hot and heavy with a biker for the night?

God, I'd been stupid to bring that up!

I was lucky he wasn't laughing at me. But I'd thought... How he'd looked at me...

Mortified, I cleared my throat. "Fine." When I pulled back, he frowned at me, but I erased all remnants of sadness from my expression, rasping, "What do you think about my idea?"

"I think it might be a good one, but they won't let me through the gates to the compound."

"Then don't go through the gates," I said stiffly, staring down at his hog.

"I'm not leaving you in there by yourself!" he argued.

"I won't be by myself," I told him, my words calm. God, all those years of living with Father had helped improve my acting skills. "Auntie Lena will be there. She'll help me. I know she will."

"You don't know that for sure."

"I do. She was gang-raped by the Aryans, Digger. You have to know that. She won't let..." This whole idea of mine revolved around that being the truth.

God, don't let me down, Auntie Lena. Please help me talk to Uncle Aidan.

He grimaced. "Christ, I forgot about the Aryans."

It was what had been playing on my mind the whole flight home. That, and the fact Father had traced my phone.

If Digger hadn't told me to leave my stuff at the compound, Father *would* have followed us to Vegas.

The thought sent a shiver down my spine.

For what felt like an endless moment, he studied me. How I didn't squirm was beyond me, but I kept myself contained, barely, by focusing on his bike.

"You really think this will work? Why didn't you try this before?"

"I had no way of getting to the compound, not with so many guards on me. Going to Queens might be easy for most people, but I might as well have been aiming for Timbuktu.

"You know I spoke to my friend?"

"Sarah."

I nodded. "She told me that my mother's in rehab. He dumps her in there sometimes. I didn't know for sure until then, though, that he must have a trace on my phone.

"Then, there's the fact that this…" I bit off the words 'might mean nothing to you' as I showed him my wedding ring. "…exists now. As you said, this changes everything on my end. This makes them look at me differently. It gives me a leg to stand on."

"It could make them look down on you," he warned. "They think they're better than us. They might judge you for tying yourself to me."

"Maybe they will, but it gives me a shield of defense from Bill Murphy." I straightened my shoulders. "I have no desire for anyone in your club to get hurt on my behalf." For the first time since I'd brought up brands—*stupid, stupid, stupid, Mary Catherine*—I looked at him. Stared him straight in the eye. "And there's no way I'm going to let the Five Points hurt you when you've been so good to me." I tipped up my chin. "I have to try."

26

DIGGER

MY FAVOURITE FADED FANTASY - DAMIEN RICE

DIGGER

IT DIDN'T SIT RIGHT with me, leaving her on the O'Donnelly compound defenseless, but there was no way in fuck the Five Points would let me in, not when there'd be red alerts out for any Sinners' patches on their turf.

But, these were her people.

She knew them better than I ever could, ever fucking wanted to. So, maybe she could negotiate our way out of this problem…

What neither of us had said when she'd declared that her wedding ring 'changed everything' was that all it took was for me to have a bullet to my head for things to get real messy, real fast.

But I'd seen the hope in her eyes when she'd talked about brands, so I knew she was already thinking ten steps ahead.

Too many steps ahead.

Being with a Sinner for a handful of days was one thing.

Being with a Sinner *permanently* was another.

But one thing I knew about my wife was she was overeager—I wasn't about to tie her into something that had more ramifications than a wedding vow when she didn't know what she was getting herself into.

Even if that meant dealing with puppy-dog eyes that made me want to kiss all her woes away and sad smiles that made me want to punch someone.

The ride to Queens was awkward at first.

Her hurt at the perceived rejection made her want distance between us and that didn't work on the back of a hog.

Sometimes, MC heard what she wanted to hear—*got it.*

She soon shifted into the position we'd grown accustomed to, however—her hand on my stomach, her thighs cupping mine, her torso curved around me.

One thing my brothers had never warned me about was that you could measure how pissed off your woman was by the distance she shoved between you on the back of your bike.

Maybe they hadn't told me because it was obvious.

Or maybe they'd known I didn't give a fuck if the woman didn't matter, and they never had until her.

Around ten minutes away from the compound, she tugged on my waist.

I knew what that meant and rejected it with every fucking bone in my body, but I pulled over.

"I should walk the rest of the way."

"There are serial killers out here," I argued even though it was morning and the roads were busy with humdrum traffic.

Her gaze turned analytical. "There are technically serial killers everywhere. I'm actually going into the house of a serial killer, and am probably married to one, and am definitely the daughter of one... I think I'm safe from the saturation of serial killers in my life. Statistically speaking, I mean."

"Is that supposed to reassure me?" I groused, not mentioning that she was right about me too.

"Well, yes, but also to remind you of who and what I am," she declared as she climbed off the back of the bike.

A move I only allowed because that prissy little answer had me growling at her, jerking to my feet, grabbing her by the arm, and dragging her deeper into me.

I pinched her chin between my thumb and pointer finger then snapped, "What you are is *mine*."

Her nostrils flared. "Make up your mind, Digger. Am I or aren't I? Stop sending mixed messages."

Dammit, she was right. In a way. But I was trying to protect her. Didn't she get that?

"What's mixed about this?" I snarled, urging our mouths to collide.

As she sagged into me with a whimper, triumph roared inside my Neanderthal brain, which was ridiculous, but said Neanderthal didn't give a damn.

I thrust my tongue between her lips, uncaring that we were standing on the side of the road. I fucked her there like I couldn't fuck her how I wanted to, uncaring that my bike was propped up by me and me alone.

Crazy as it might be, I knew I was all in. She was too fucking innocent and too deep in the shit with her family, however, to be able to make that decision for herself right now.

The only thing that mattered was my prissy princess knowing that she fucking belonged to me, which, in the long run, meant I'd save her from herself if I had to.

A moan escaped her, one that I swallowed, as I took the kiss too far. She was sweet and kind and gentle and all things soft and tender, but this kiss wasn't.

I claimed her with my body like I couldn't with my brand.

I owned her at that moment, and her sweet supplication was proof of that ownership.

My hands held her waist fast, fingers digging into her curves while hers moved over my shoulders, unable to settle, needing to touch me wherever and however she craved.

When I pulled back, her mewl of distress set itself on repeat in my brain. I knew I'd never forget that soft sound, knew that it would haunt me for years because the moment she walked through those gates, I had a feeling I'd never see her again.

It made it harder to let go of her.

Made it impossible to do anything other than press kisses along her jawline, savoring the scent of her, enjoying how she melted into me.

"Will they frisk you?"

My words didn't match my actions, but she was goop in my arms and she mumbled, "Doubt it."

"Good. I'm going to give you a piece and another cell phone. I'm going to wait out here until I hear from you, okay?"

She stiffened in my arms. "Then what?"

"I'll wait for your call. Whether that's to invite me in or to tell me what's going on," I said calmly. "If you want to do it this way, MC, then you gotta accept the fact that they're more than likely going to put a bullet between my eyes for stealing you away."

She blinked at me slowly, *dazedly*. "No! I didn't... No, that's not what I want..." Her fingers clutched at me. "I just don't want your people to get hurt."

"Neither do I. That's why I'm going to let you go in there when every goddamn bone in my body is saying that if I do, this is the last time I'll ever see you."

Her eyelashes batted again, not in a coy way, just in a bewildered one. "You don't really think that, do you?"

"I don't think they'll kill you. I just don't think they'll let us be together." My mouth tightened as I cupped her jaw. "But, here's the thing, MaryCat. The only orders I obey are from my Prez. Not a bunch of fucking mobsters.

"You were talking about brands earlier. My life ain't easy. My life is dirty. You think your father's is, but it ain't by comparison. Your people wear slick suits and four-hundred-dollars-an-ounce aftershave. They dress their women in designer labels and go to church on Sundays. They *appear* outwardly respectable.

"The Sinners don't do that. We don't wear suits and sure, some of us wear aftershave, but hell, I don't even fucking shave every day. I don't give a damn about seeing you in designer labels, not when I'd prefer you to wear nothing at all, and I definitely don't go to fucking church unless the Sinners' council has hauled my ass to a meeting. Nothing about us is respectable—"

"Maybe I'm not either," she retorted indignantly.

Unable to stop myself, I grinned at her. "Baby girl, you're the most respectable thing I've seen in decades. I just bet you wear a hat and gloves to church, don't you?" When her cheeks turned bright pink, I had my answer. My grin twisted. Sagged. "You're too good for the likes of me."

"No," she ground out. "That's not true!"

"It is." I trailed my thumb along her cheekbone, enjoying how she shivered at the simple caress. "But my point is, MC, I ain't perfect." Her brow furrowed in confusion so I continued, "I'll let you go onto that compound even though every fucking instinct I possess is telling me not to.

"I'll let you deal with this in your own way even though I want to take over and make shit better for you. I'll even let you handle the situation and retreat from my life *if that's what you need.*"

"I don't understand," she breathed.

"Sure you do," I rasped. "You've had every single choice taken from you, MaryCat. Every. Single. Choice. From who to date to what to wear. From how to be to what to do with your life."

"I'm a Sinner. We're all about freedom.

"So, what you're going to do is, you're going to go in there, and you're going to convince the matriarch of the Five Points that what's happening in the ranks is wrong, and you'll use your wedding ring as a defense against Bill fucking Murphy.

"You'll make shit right, and then, you'll live your life however you want because that's what a sweetheart like you deserves."

She gulped. "You're scaring me, Digger."

My smile was sad. "No, I ain't. We both know you're braver than you realize, MC." I brushed her bottom lip. "You're going to make waves and then, and only then, will you make a decision about your future. Including…" I sucked in a breath and put myself on the line. "…whether you want me in it or not."

Her eyes rounded and she straightened up, spine erect, chin angled belligerently, hands balling into fists at her side, practically vibrating in her shoes.

"It's all your decision, baby girl," I informed her huskily. "It's on you."

Though she still looked as if she were ready for war, she declared, "No, it isn't. What about you? Do you want me in your future?"

I tilted my head to the side and reached for the hand that wore my ring. I kissed it. "Might be crazy, but yeah."

I retreated at that, not letting the joy in her eyes filter into me. I wasn't about to get my hopes up. The moment she realized what she'd be relinquishing by being with me was the moment she'd forget about me.

She'd agreed with my plan of action only because she was desperate.

A man with my past wasn't about to brand a woman like her, no matter how much I wanted to, not when she was in 'fight-or-flight' mode.

So, I pulled away, kicked my leg over my hog, and knelt on the gravel as I unfastened one of my saddlebags. I grabbed one of the extra burner cells I always carried with me. "This has my number in the contacts." I collected the Glock, then I turned to her. "You know how to use this?"

She bit her lip. "For the most part."

With an eye roll, I walked her over to a small alleyway, showed her where the safety was, and ran through the basics.

"If you feel threatened, you knock off the safety, point, and shoot."

"What if I miss?"

"Don't." I studied her. "I doubt you'll need it today."

"You think they'll take me back to my father's."

"I do." I angled my head to the side. "But I wouldn't be dropping you off here if I didn't think your powers of persuasion couldn't work a miracle too."

Her smile was incandescent.

It hit me then that a woman like her had never been shown that a man could have faith in her...

"But if you do get taken back to your father's, then you shoot first and ask questions later, do you hear me?" Her smile started to fade.

"The club has a brilliant lawyer and she'll get you off the charges." I didn't care who we had to bribe to make that happen. "You don't anger him so he hits you in front of people. You don't do a damn thing to him until you're alone.

"The second you feel threatened is the second you shoot. If you let him get the drop on you and he hits you, I will be pissed at you. Remember, you shoot first and I'll worry about sorting out the repercussions later.

"But bear in mind, the moment you shoot is a moment you can't take back."

"I don't care if I kill him," she whispered, then she closed her eyes, shame filtering into her expression. "God, that makes me a horrible person."

I shook my head. "I didn't mean it that way, baby. I meant if you shoot and don't hit him, you've got a raging bull on your hands. We haven't gone through this together for me to lose you to your goddamn father.

"So, you let him get close, and you make the shot then, do you understand? You can't miss. You *have* to take him down. Doesn't matter if he dies or if you just incapacitate him, you hit him. You give yourself some breathing room and you run the hell away from him, get yourself in public, and then you call me. Understood?"

She swallowed. "I understand."

"I'll come for you. I won't be far away, so it won't take long—"

"You're really not going back to West Orange?" she interrupted, those big green eyes of hers extra wide.

"Hell, no!"

"What about Rex?"

"Fuck Rex. We sort you out first. MC, you call me no matter the time or the day, you got me?"

"I got you."

I sucked down a breath. "There's a diner a few blocks away. I'll stay there for the rest of the day if need be. When you're in, if you can text me so I know you're safe, I'd appreciate it." Her eyes softened.

"And if, when you have an update on what's going to happen next, you text me so I can prepare, even better."

She threw herself at me, arms clinging tightly, face burrowing into the soft Henley I wore beneath my cut.

That was when I admitted to myself that it was going to suck ass letting go of her and hugged her back.

Then, tucking her head beneath my chin, I murmured, "Men become monsters when they're pinned down. Your father may come for you and he might be kindness itself in front of his bosses, but the second he gets you in a car is the second he could change." She tensed. "That'd be a good moment to shoot. Just saying. Maybe the O'Donnellys will drive you home—I don't know. Either way, I won't leave the diner until you tell me to, okay?"

"Okay," she breathed.

"Are you sure you want to go through with this?" I repeated. "You don't have to. We can meet with O'Donnelly Sr. on Sinners' turf."

She was silent for so long that I knew she was second-guessing herself, and it probably hadn't helped that I'd frightened her. But that was what I'd intended. Reality *was* frightening. I knew, point blank, that when Sin realized I'd let her return to the lion's den, he'd probably smack the fuck out of me.

But...

Choices.

They were important.

We had autonomy over our actions for a reason, and a man who'd been jailed knew exactly how vital autonomy was.

My mom had her choice robbed from her by a Five Pointer, and she'd raised me with love despite where I'd come from.

I'd had the choice to say no when MC had come to the Sinners' compound. I could have made her wait for Sin, could have tossed her out on her ass.

The only real choice MC had had was to marry a man she'd never met to evade the octopus-like reach of another piece of donkey scrotum.

"I want to go through with this."

Disappointment unfurled inside me.

"Okay."

It wasn't okay.

"I know I can make Auntie Lena help me." She peeped up at me. "I know she will, Digger."

I sighed. "You know when my mom was raped?"

Her eyes rounded even more than before, and I took that for an answer.

"She heard women walking past as it happened. She cried out and no one helped her. No one." With a final trace of her cheekbone with my thumb, I rumbled, "Women aren't always 'sisters.'"

Hell, if I hadn't seen that for myself when it came time for the Old Ladies to get into catfights with clubwhores.

"I-I promise I won't forget what you told me. Shoot close range. Text when I get in and when, *if,* they send me home with Father."

"Pack the burner and the gun somewhere you don't think they'll check."

MC eyed the gun. "Where the heck do you think I can put *that*?"

I had to laugh. "That's between you and God." I turned around and scanned the streets to make sure no one was watching. "Now, go on. Hide 'em."

She huffed but didn't argue. I heard grumbles and grunts, the sound of sighing, and then a yelp as the cold metal of the Glock collided with her skin.

"Right, done," she grouched.

I turned around and stared at her. She wore one of my Henleys, so it was baggy on her, but she had several layers beneath it to fight off the winter chill and that offset the overlarge fit.

Her jeans were skinny so there was no hiding it in the waistband.

While she wore boots and thick socks, they were slim-fitting so she couldn't tuck anything there. Her new gilet was padded, though, and it provided *some* cover.

I regretted not buying her more clothes when we'd hit another store in Vegas to grab her some essentials before our flight.

Motioning with my hand for her to twist around, I looked at her, really looked at her, and couldn't see where she'd hidden both.

"Good job," I praised, watching her beam a gratified smile at me. Inwardly, I smirked at her reaction, then I pressed a final kiss to her lips and sealed the deal. "Now, be a good girl and own your future, hmm?"

When she did, that was when I knew I could keep her because fuck, I wanted to.

I didn't want to lose this sweetness, didn't want to lose the way she looked at me, how she made me goddamn feel when I was with her.

Whether she knew it or not, I was all in. To the point where I was starting to think about her needs more than I thought about my own.

Her eyes widened. "A-A good girl?"

I nodded as I climbed onto the back of my hog. When I started the engine, I shouted over the noise it made, "Yeah, *my* good girl."

That was when I took off.

I didn't look back.

Because if I did, I wouldn't let her go.

"Choices," I muttered under my breath. "Why you gotta decide to be a gentleman now, Digger?"

Hell if I knew.

Getting a wife made a brother lose his fool mind—*got it.*

27

MARYCAT

MARYCAT

IT TOOK me a ridiculous amount of time to stop gaping at Digger's back.

So long, in fact, that he'd disappeared into the cacophonous traffic by the time I realized that I needed to get my butt in gear.

Sure, the man sent more mixed messages than a radio station, but that 'good girl' stuff…

Goddamn, it frazzled my brain.

In the best way.

And with my past, it really shouldn't.

Behave, Mary Catherine.

Don't disappoint me.

Be a good girl.

All things I'd heard over the years, words that had been indoctrinated into me by both my parents.

Ugh, I much preferred it when Digger said it.

With that thought locked in mind, I turned on my heel and started toward the compound.

As I walked, I processed everything he'd said, and as I processed, I tried not to freak myself out.

I'd barely spoken to Auntie Lena in the past, aside from wishing her a 'Happy Easter' in church and telling her when I was eighteen what I intended to study at college. Oh, then there was my confirmation. She'd given me a necklace but she hadn't spoken much to me.

She was, I'd found, an odd woman. Most said that the Aryans had fucked up her mind, twisted it, but surely, she wouldn't let others be treated the same way she'd been?

God, I was pinning a lot of my hopes on a woman I barely knew and who had a few screws loose.

A woman who was married to one of the most insane men on the East Coast...

I released the breath I'd sucked in. "You can do this."

Jesus, who was I kidding?

I couldn't do dick.

I was—

"No! Digger had faith in you. Even if it goes wrong, he gave you a contingency plan. He's there. He'll come if you need him."

The pep talk might have made me look like a crazy person on the side of the road—New York was used to worse—but it wormed a path inside me, lighting me up with hope.

To offset the cold, I was practically jogging on the road to the compound. That had nothing to do with the pounding of my heart though. Nothing whatsoever.

When I reached it and saw the guards at the gates, I gulped.

"You can't be a chicken now. Not when Digger gave you that big speech. He wants you to pull on your big girl panties and own this. You can do it. You beat Kitty Frasier in debate class and everyone *knows* she was Mrs. Ridley's favorite," I muttered beneath my breath. "If you can beat her, you can persuade Auntie Lena."

The guards, I realized, had noticed me before I noticed them.

They stood at attention at the sight of me, and they grew tenser and tenser with every step I took.

Biting my lip, I didn't bother announcing myself, aware that they'd know who I was.

Instead, I called out, "I'd like to speak with my aunt—Lena O'Donnelly."

The guards flicked each other looks, but they didn't have the chance to respond. The gates suddenly opened behind them and a Mini Cooper pulled off the driveway.

I stumbled out of the way, deciding that I didn't need to end the day in the ER, and that was when the window rolled down and I realized I was a dumbass because there was only one brother who drove that car...

"Mary Catherine?"

I nearly sobbed with relief.

"Conor," I breathed, rushing forward, my hands flattening on his door even though the metal was frigid against my palms.

"Where the hell have you been?" he demanded. But before I could answer, he rumbled, "Move aside." I blinked at him but obeyed, then he jumped out. "Jonesy," he called. "Ring my—"

I grabbed his hand and tugged on it, begging, "Conor, no! Please, listen to me first. Please."

His eyes flickered over me. "Mary Catherine, you've been kidnapped and you escaped." That was when I realized he was cataloging any injuries I might have. "You're in distress. You need to be with your family—"

"No," I barked. "I wasn't kidnapped, and the last place I need to be is with family. Conor, I know you don't know me well, but you have to know that I wouldn't want to marry a sixty-year-old man."

"I didn't know you were getting married." He frowned at me but he tapped his chin. "I've been busy with..." He cleared his throat. "Well, you don't need to know with what. Who's the sixty-year-old?"

Biting my lip, I mumbled, "Bill Murphy."

He snorted. "This isn't the time for joking, Mary Catherine."

"I'm not joking!" I cried, and, God forgive me for being a fool, I shoved him in the shoulder. Hard enough for him to stagger back a step. "My father's decided that he wants me to marry that old pervert! Conor, please, *please*, you have to help me. If you don't, I'm screwed. Literally.

"I managed to run away the day after Father told me who I'd be marrying, but the moment Bill and I'd have met for him to propose, you know what would have happened, Conor. We wouldn't have left that meeting until I didn't have a hymen anymore—"

He gaped at me. "Excuse me?"

I swallowed. "You heard me."

"No. I didn't. What does your hymen have to do with anything?" His brow furrowed, then he rubbed his temple. "Mary Catherine, I'm functioning on two hours of sleep in the past five days. I need you to speak slowly and clearly."

"Should you be driving if you haven't slept?" I chided.

"What are you? My ma? I just escaped her clutches," he groused.

"Yes, well, maybe you shouldn't have if you're so sleep-deprived. Didn't you know that that's the equivalent of being drunk when you're behind the wheel?" I folded my arms across my chest. "I mean, I'm glad you're here because I need your help, but you could have gotten into an accident."

He stared down at me, and a smile started dancing on his lips. "You're right, Mary Catherine. *You* can drive me home."

I gaped at him. "Me?"

"Yeah, you." He beamed at me. "We have a solution. You can drive and talk at the same time."

"No," I argued. "I need to speak with your mom."

"You really don't. She hasn't taken her meds in a few days. She's kinda cranky."

Nerves fizzled to life in my belly as my plan went down the crapper. "Oh, God, what am I going to do?"

But Conor tugged me into a hug that, I thought, surprised us both. "You're going to drive me home and tell me all about your non-kidnapping and almost-engagement, and then we're going to fix things."

Tears made my eyes sting. "You'll take their side."

"Whose side?"

"Your da's side. Father's side. Bill's side."

He snickered. "Mary Catherine, we don't know each other that well, you're right, but surely you realize how crazy that sounds.

Since when do any of my brothers and I *ever* agree with what Da says."

My soft sniffle morphed into a watery chuckle. I pulled back to look at him. "You promise you'll help me?"

He tapped my cheek. "What's family for?"

28

MARYCAT

MARYCAT

HOPE WAS A BEAUTIFUL THING. Deadly, venomous, but beautiful nonetheless.

It drowned me with the force of a tidal wave as I watched Conor warn the guards, "Any of you mention who you saw today and I'll hack into your bank accounts and make your savings fit into a piggy bank, ya hear me?"

Then, he clambered over to the passenger side and waved a hand at me to get behind the wheel.

As I adjusted the driver's seat, I turned to him to thank him, but his head was against the rest and his mouth was open as he started snoring.

"How the hell did you fall asleep that fast?" I muttered under my breath.

But, it gave me a couple of moments to text Digger once I found his number in the contacts.

> Me: Change of plan, Digger. Conor (he's the nicest brother) was at the compound and I'm driving him back to his apartment in the city. He's promised to help me. If you want to follow me, here's my live location.

LIVE LOCATION SHARED FOR EIGHT HOURS

I didn't wait for him to reply but saw the two ticks that meant he'd read the message.

Feeling much better than I had before, I saw Conor's phone was in the cup holder, being charged, and I unplugged it then hovered it in front of his face so it'd unlock.

I flipped on the 'silence' switch at the side of my device and called myself with his cell phone so I'd have his number in the future, just in case, before I plugged it back in and took off.

I tightened my hands to the point of discomfort around the steering wheel because they were sweaty with nerves and kept sliding as I drove us to the city.

My eyes constantly drifted to the rearview mirror as I sought out my husband's hog. Around ten minutes later, when I saw it sliding into the lane a few cars behind me, my anxiety faded somewhat now that he was nearby.

It wasn't normal how he could calm me down just by being close—I barely knew the man, after all—but soothe me he did.

In our short acquaintance, I'd come to associate him with protection. Safety. Fairness. *Kindness.*

Maybe it made sense for my old crush to be morphing into something else.

I'd never imagined that day back in Westchester that the scruffy biker could be so much more than just hot.

A smile danced on my lips at the thought, and during the drive, I allowed my mind to drift to the days I'd spent with Digger.

They kept me better company than Conor did who, for someone so cute, snored loudly.

Though, two hours of sleep in five days *was* kinda crazy.

By the time that we were on the island, I had no idea where to go. I'd checked his GPS for a 'home' address, but no dice, so I tapped his knee. "Conor?"

When that didn't work, I slapped his knee instead.

Nada.

I patted his cheek next.

Nope.

Tugged on his ear.

Still snoring.

Getting annoyed now, I grabbed a chunk of his hair and—

"What the fuck?"

I jerked in my seat and nearly veered into the next lane at his sudden awareness *and* his volume.

Slapping my hand to my heart, I cried, "You scared the shit out of me!"

Conor heaved a sigh and rubbed his eyes. "Just don't touch my fucking hair."

"I didn't want to touch your hair, but you weren't waking up and I have no idea where you live."

He grunted but tapped a few buttons on his console and then waved a hand at it. "There."

Then, he was back to sleeping.

Jesus Christ, did he have an on/off switch or something?

Still, I had directions at least. That was better than nothing.

Traffic was crazy as always so the short ride took longer than it should, and by the time I was pulling outside the parking garage of his building, he popped an eye open, telling me he'd been faking it, and ordered, "Drive in. The system recognizes my license plate."

I huffed. "Yes, sir."

"I don't remember you being this sassy."

"No. Quiet as a church mouse, that's me," I agreed grimly, pulling into the garage and driving down the squirrelly lane toward the underground lot.

As he directed me to his space, he yawned a few times, then, when I'd parked, he admitted, "Think you saved my ass back there, Mary Catherine."

"I did?" I queried.

"Yeah. I needed that sleep more than I realized, even if it was only an hour."

"I thought you were a genius."

"I mean, I don't like to brag."

I rolled my eyes. "What genius thinks he can function on so little sleep?"

"Done it before."

"You got a death wish or something?"

"Don't think so. Normally I can do it, but you're right. It was dumb."

"And irresponsible," I tacked on.

His lips curved. "And irresponsible."

"And dangerous."

"And dangerous."

"To yourself and other innocent drivers."

"To myself and other innocent drivers. Now, if that's everything, *Ma*, maybe we can get upstairs and we can solve your problem, hmm?"

Sheepishly, I nodded and clambered out from behind the wheel. Throwing the keys at him over the roof, I checked my cell phone as he collected some of his stuff from the vehicle.

> Digger: Will be right there.
>
> Digger: You okay?
>
> Digger: Good girl for not texting and driving.
>
> Digger: I'm outside the building.

> Me: Grab a coffee. I'll text you soon. I think Conor will let you up once I explain everything.
>
> Me: I like being your good girl.

"You want to tell me why a bike was following us?"

I blinked at that then jerked when I saw Conor standing beside me, reading my messages to Digger.

With a squeak, I held my phone to my chest. "Conor! That was rude."

He smirked at me. "You tugged on my hair. I think you deserve some minor embarrassment. You got a praise kink, huh? Interesting."

I stared at him. "Excuse me? I don't have a kink!"

What was it with him and Digger trying to make out like I had fetishes and kinks?

"Sure you do. 'Good girl?'"

At his arched brow, my cheeks blossomed with heat. "Don't be—"

"Facetious?" He yawned. "That's my job. Come on. Let's get upstairs. It's fucking cold down here."

Still gaping at him, still embarrassed as hell, I followed him as he wandered over to an elevator. He tapped in a few buttons that I realized were a keycode, then he murmured, "Well? Who was the biker? This Digger guy who's got your panties in a bunch?"

I swallowed. "He's my husband."

That gained his full attention.

But he raised a hand. "I need a gallon of coffee before we can have this conversation. I already know that it's going to give me a migraine."

"Welcome to my life," I muttered.

At his grunt, I fell silent, but my cell burned a hole in my pocket when it vibrated with Digger's replies.

Thankfully, we were delivered to the penthouse in short order. As the doors opened, Conor snagged a hold of my hand and dragged me behind him when he saw there were bags on the floor.

"Who's there?"

"Conor!"

"Aoife? What are you doing here?"

"Brought you some leftovers," the other woman chirped from someplace in the penthouse.

I knew Aoife was the money man's bride—Finn O'Grady. Hers was the wedding my family hadn't been invited to and which my father had raged over for days. Even with the bloodbath ending.

"Leftovers?" Conor crowed, surprising me by triumphantly fist-pumping the air. "What about apple pie?"

There was a soft chuckle. "How could I forget about your damn apple pie obsession?" she called out.

Smirking, he loped off, forgetting me when apple pie was in the vicinity and leaving me to linger in the foyer.

For a moment, I took in the minimalist living room, complete with a white leather couch that would seat fifteen and odd lighting that either belonged in a strip joint or a lab.

Perplexed, I decided that I'd get nowhere hovering by the elevator.

Tracing Conor's path, I followed the sounds of chatter, too, and discovered the kitchen.

I'd seen Aoife in church and had taken note of the kindness with which she spoke to Father Doyle who was a douche. I'd also noticed how the O'Donnelly brothers teased her and how she teased them back.

The rumor mill said she was pregnant, but I didn't have a clue if that was true or not, if it was just the usual bitches being bitchier than normal.

Most of the women my age were always griping about how a hottie like Finn O'Grady had ended up with a woman of Aoife's size, which epitomized why I loathed my social circle.

Father insisted I hang out with them, but the only person I genuinely liked was Sarah. And whenever Sarah, who was as curvy as Aoife, heard those bitches, she always blanched and escaped to the restroom. Though I followed, she never admitted how much that stung.

We might have left school long behind, but bullies were still everywhere and neither of us were brave enough to stand up to them.

Sarah, because she was shy around anyone who wasn't me. Me, because those bullies reminded me of my mother. While she was the queen of insults and, by comparison, they were wannabes, I'd never been very good at fighting bitchy fire with fire of my own.

Seeing Aoife bustling around Conor's kitchen as if she belonged there, I realized that this was a common occurrence—she fed him.

"God, you're the best, Aoife. Thank you." He was groaning as I walked into the room.

"Would you like help with the bags?" I offered quietly, feeling guilty that I'd never really introduced myself to her. That I'd never defended her to the bitches in our circle, either.

Either this situation with Bill Murphy had made me braver or being around Digger was rubbing off on me.

Aoife, not expecting a second person to be in the apartment, jumped at my question, and Conor, turning around with a dish of pie— an actual pie dish—in his arms, shook his head. "Nah, I'll bring them in in a second."

"It's not a problem," I dismissed, rushing into the hall to bring in the carrier bags.

I caught Aoife whispering something to Conor, but he was too busy eating pie, then she shut up when she saw me and sent me a smile.

It didn't hit her eyes.

The kindness with which she'd looked at Conor was absent, amplifying my guilt as I muttered, "Here you go."

"Thank you," she said, her tone regal.

Conor, not entirely unable to read the room, pointed his spoon between us. "What's going on with you two? Do you know each other?"

"No," I answered awkwardly.

"I've seen her at events," Aoife said.

My cheeks pinkened. "I spend most of my time in the restroom with my best friend, Sarah Mulhearne. The women pick on her because of her size."

Conor's spoon waggled in the air. "What's wrong with her size?"

Aoife sighed. "Men."

"Nothing's wrong with her size," I countered. "She's healthy. That's all that matters."

"You know women can be catty, Conor," Aoife chided.

It was clear, from her tone, that she thought *I* was catty too. Which was unfair. I *wasn't* catty. My mom was, but I wasn't.

Flushing more than ever, I muttered, "I hope I've never said anything to offend you."

"Of course not," was Aoife's bland retort. "You really hang out in the restrooms?"

I hunched my shoulders. "Those parties aren't my thing."

"Mine either. I'd prefer to be in my bakery."

"I'd prefer you to be in your bakery too," Conor agreed, which made her smile.

Clearing my throat, I admitted, "I don't like…" *Anyone?* "…most of the people in my age group." There, that was more politically correct.

Aoife studied me. "What are you doing here?"

"She got herself kidnapped," Conor mumbled, his head in the freezer before he retrieved a carton of ice cream. "And I think she liked it."

"I didn't get myself kidnapped!" My flush deepened to dangerous levels at Aoife's raised brows. Agitated, I muttered, "It wasn't… There was no kidnapping. I willingly went."

"With a biker. Who you're married to now. That's right, no? I think I remembered that much correctly."

I huffed. "You forgot the part about me being raped if I didn't take the situation into my own hands!"

Aoife gasped. "Excuse me?!"

Conor dolloped a massive chunk of ice cream on top of his pie. It was more like a meteorite than a scoop. "That's what you meant about your hymen?"

"You're a virgin?!" Aoife squeaked. She spun around to look at Conor. "Conor, this is no time for food!"

"I haven't eaten in two days," he argued, holding the pie dish to his chest like it was a teddy bear. "You can't deny me food. How am I supposed to solve this problem if I'm starving?"

Aoife plunked her hands on her hips. "You need to explain, Mary Catherine."

"You know my name?"

Her tone was cold as she informed me, "I know your mother."

Oh, shit.

Suddenly, her standoffishness made sense.

It had nothing to do with the bitches my age who called her fat because they were jealous of her wedding ring and everything to do with my cunt of a mother.

"Whatever she's said to you, I'm really, really, really sorry," I said in a rush. "Trust me when I say that I've been on the end of her vitriol too many times over the years. I know how her words sting."

Mother cut cleaner than a freshly sharpened butcher's knife.

Aoife bowed her head at me, the move graceful. "I appreciate that." Then, she granted me the ultimate sign of forgiveness in a hostess' arsenal. "Would you like some tea? Coffee? A slice of Conor's pie?"

"Not my pie!"

Despite my anguish, I hid a smile. "I couldn't eat anything. But maybe some water?"

Aoife shoved Conor away from the refrigerator and collected two bottles of water. Then, as if she owned the place, she moved over to a cupboard, gathered two glasses, and settled them on the breakfast bar where she perched herself on a stool.

As she patted the seat at her side in a gentle offering, I murmured, "I'm too nervous to sit."

Nodding her understanding, she waved a hand at my drink in silent invitation. I snatched the bottle and gulped the water down.

Having drunk almost three-quarters of it, I apologized, "Sorry. I didn't stop on the journey down."

Aoife cast Conor a glance, but the question was directed at me. "You were at the compound?"

"Yes. I wanted to speak with Auntie Lena."

"And I told her she's loopier than a rollercoaster at the moment."

Aoife grimaced. "That last lockdown didn't do her any good."

I shared the grimace. "I hate lockdowns."

When the Five Pointers went to battle, we were 'imprisoned' in a separate, secure compound for our protection.

The experience never failed to suck.

"Me too. Now, what happened?"

On a deep exhalation, I blurted it all out, keying this relative stranger into the intimate details of my life so that Conor would help me.

I watched her already pale peach complexion blanch as I explained about what Anthony had done to Sarah and how I knew that fate had awaited me if I'd met with Bill Murphy. Then, I told her about my half-brother, Sin, and how I'd put my hopes into him.

By the end of my miserable tale, Conor had finished his pie, and

Aoife was sniffling a little—maybe she *was* pregnant?—and I felt ragged and worn out.

"Digger's waiting for you downstairs?"

That was the first thing Conor had said in the good forty minutes of my soliloquy.

Biting my lip, I nodded.

"Invite him up."

"He thinks he'll be shot—"

"If he were Brennan or Declan, *maybe*," Aoife answered. "As it stands, it's Conor. He doesn't shoot. He destroys lives through his computer."

"That sterling character assassination would make another man cry."

Aoife winked at him. "But you're not *another* man, are you?"

He sniffed. "I'm not about to shoot him, Mary Catherine. Aoife's right—that isn't my style. I'll save him from my brothers too, but I don't make the same promises for your father."

I swallowed. "You mean that?"

"Of course I do."

His brow furrowed. "Sarah Mulhearne's husband might not be so lucky either. Da doesn't like rapists."

"Sweeter words I've yet to hear," Aoife grumbled.

Conor nudged her with his elbow. "Not after Ma and the Aryans."

"You mean, before he was okay with that?"

"Not entirely. I just don't think he thought about it. It's not his style, and because he's so…"

"Depraved," Aoife tacked on helpfully.

To which Conor hummed his agreement. "I don't think it occurs to him. Not among his people. It's something enemies do to attack a made man, not something that happens in-house, if you see what I mean." Aoife's scowl said she didn't like his logic. "Take the Russians, for example. It's well known that Vasov's wife was raped, butchered, and murdered under the Pakhan's roof when the Italians stormed his compound."

"It's like living in a book about pirates. Who acts like that when the world isn't at war?" she reasoned. "And it's not as if we should do that if we *are* at war."

Conor shrugged at her harrumph. "Our world is constantly at war. And anyway, there's always somewhere that's feuding. We're not a peaceful species."

Aoife huffed. "I refuse to debate this with you."

Deciding that an angry discussion was in the cards if I didn't bring things back on track, I cleared my throat. "I appreciate you listening to what I have to say."

Conor pinned me with a stare. "We're family. We might not be close because your mother's a grade-A bitch, but that doesn't mean we're not family. You should have come to us immediately."

Aoife snorted. "She really is, and Conor's right."

"I know," I admitted. "But I couldn't come to you. I didn't have the means of contacting you."

Conor frowned. "Why not?"

"I don't know," I mumbled, shoulders hunching. "I wouldn't have wanted to impose anyway. Not unless it was a crisis."

"Which this is," Aoife remarked.

"You're family," Conor reiterated. "We'll get this fixed. Call your... Christ, feels weird to think of you being married, Mary Catherine. Let him come up here."

I needed more than that. "You *promise* he won't get hurt?" I didn't care if the request was childish.

"I promise. No one, not my brothers or my da, will hurt him. Not without me stepping up for the man who helped you when we failed you. Understood?"

His words had me closing my eyes with relief.

"Understood. Thank you, Conor."

"The only question is, do you want to see their punishment for yourself?"

I swallowed then blurted out what I knew, "Bill Murphy... Conor, he's more dangerous than you know. Digger's his son. H-He raped Digger's mom. They got into a fight years ago and Digger served time for it. H-He says Bill murdered his exes."

Conor frowned. "That's not true. They were sick, weren't they? I mean, he's known as the merry widower, but it's just a joke."

"Not according to Digger."

Conor's frown darkened. "Tell your man to get his ass here. We need to have a conversation."

29

MARYCAT

MARYCAT

THOUGH I HAD Conor's promise, I was still nervous when Digger walked out of the elevator.

I noticed his tension as he peered around, his hands burrowed in his pockets, then relief lit up his expression when he saw me.

About a split second before I collided with him.

"Conor's said he'll help, Digger," I whispered shakily, my arms sliding around his waist as I hugged him tightly.

"You often get a woman to fight your battles for you?"

"Conor!" Aoife hissed, making me realize both of them had joined me in the living room. "Behave."

"That's not fair," I retorted, twisting around to glower at him.

Against me, Digger stiffened but drawled, "If I have faith in that woman, why wouldn't I bring her on board? There's more than one way to win a battle."

"That's a good answer," Conor mused, scratching his chin, his gaze turning distant for a moment. Then, he flicked a look at his sister-in-law. "You should go home, Aoife."

She hooted. "Not on your life."

"If you don't, then Finn will come looking for you."

"He can. I already told him where I am. He'll probably—"

Conor's phone rang. "Jesus Christ, Aoife."

She just smirked at him.

"What do you want?" Conor complained into his cell. "No, you can't come up. I'll send your wife down, though." He paused. "I thanked her for the pie."

"He didn't!" Aoife called out, even though I knew that was a bald-faced lie.

"I did!" Conor huffed. "Fine. Okay. Shut up about it. I'll thank her when we cut— Jes— Fuck off, Finn. I'll text you the entry code. Oh, screw—" He scowled. "He disconnected the call."

"Probably didn't appreciate you cursing at him like a sailor," Aoife preached as she wandered past me to the elevator, clearly waiting on her man to make an appearance.

Conor, grumbling all the while, retreated to the kitchen. I tugged on Digger's hand and urged him to follow.

"Are they always like this?"

"I don't know them well enough to say, but I know whenever they're together, they're always bickering," I said in a whisper.

"Even Finn O'Grady?"

"You know him?"

"Baby, my name's Digger, remember? No secrets with me around."

"Oh, you should get along well with Conor then," Aoife chirped from over by the elevator. "Never asked him a question he can't answer."

I cast her a look and smiled gratefully at her before I tugged on Digger's hand again and dragged him into the kitchen.

"Finn and Aidan Jr. are best friends," I whispered. "Finn is like a foster son to the O'Donnellys."

"I knew the former but not the latter," Digger confirmed.

"Da covered up most things about Finn when he was a teenager, and I compounded that so *digger* or not, he's a hard man to trace," Conor informed us as we made it into his kitchen. "Want a sandwich?"

That grabbed Digger's attention. "What you offering?"

"Fried bologna."

"Leave it," Aoife called. "I'll make everyone something to eat while you plan. Otherwise, your arteries will clog forever."

"Works every time," he whispered at me, moving around the counter to the table just as Finn and... oh, jeez, Aidan Jr. entered the room. Conor frowned at his older brother. "What are you doing here?"

I barely knew Finn, and while I was better acquainted with Aidan, everyone knew since the drive-by shooting at Aoife and Finn's wedding that had seen Junior's leg shattered into a million pieces, he was *always* biting someone's head off.

"What a welcome," Junior intoned.

"I don't *try* to be welcoming."

"Like I didn't know that already." Aidan looked at me. "Hello, Mary Catherine. You've had us worried."

Embarrassed, I ducked my head. "I'm sorry, Aidan. I didn't mean to—"

"Yes, you did," Conor corrected. "With good reason. Aidan, if she hadn't run off and gone to the Sinners, she'd have ended up with Bill Murphy of all asswipes."

"Bill Murphy?" Junior repeated. "Isn't he like ninety or something?"

"If only he'd be so close to death's door," Digger rumbled.

"Oh, yeah, Digger's Murphy's kid. He raped his mom."

As tension flooded my husband, I whispered, "I'm so sorry, Digger."

But Finn bit off, "Fuck's sake, Conor, there was a kinder way to word that."

"What are we? On *Dr. Phil*? I'm telling it how it is. Murphy's a piece of shit who deserves Da's wrath." Conor's face tightened. "You *know* I don't like rapists, Finn."

"Who does?" Junior countered, his gaze settling on Digger. "I don't think I know you."

Digger, his features stony, stated, "Name's Digger."

"And you're a Satan's Sinner?"

"Yes."

"You've caused a whole lot of shit for your people."

"Wasn't about to let my old man hurt Mary Catherine. The moment she said his name and his affiliation, I knew what the asswipe was capable of. He's a fucking murderer, not just a rapist."

"How do you know that?" Conor demanded.

"Because I dig."

Finn, Aidan Jr., and Conor cast each other a look.

"What—sandcastles on the beach?" Junior mocked.

"For answers. The first poor bitch married off to him died in a car accident, and the second one died when they were vacationing at the Grand fucking Canyon.

"How no one suspected he was involved in that one is beyond me. He must be flush with more cash than you guys know for the amount he must have laid out on bribes."

Weakly, Aoife asked, "I thought you said they were sick, Conor."

"Bill's been around since the dinosaurs. I never thought to look into his past," Conor muttered uncomfortably.

"But why would he kill them?" she peppered.

"No divorce," Junior stated.

"And none of them gave him any kids," Digger rasped as he motioned to himself. "I'm aware of the irony.

"His third wife disappeared around the same time as he applied for permission to get some work done in his backyard. Work that involved digging the space out and refilling it with concrete for some fancy seating area. She was filed as missing until he logged her as dead after three years. Cleared out a nice insurance policy on that one."

"How do you know all this?" Junior demanded. "It's insane how much you've uncovered."

"The Sinners have ways of finding things out. Just like the Five Points do," Digger stated.

"You got this kind of info on each of his wives?" Finn inquired.

"The ones that met a weird fucking end, sure. Which, ya know, was all six of them. The fourth's brake lines were damaged, and the fifth died of a shellfish allergy. As for the sixth, there was a mishap with her meds."

"What kind of fancy seating area?"

"That's what you focused on, Conor?" Aoife complained.

Conor just shrugged.

"One with a hot tub," Digger said flatly.

"So, he stews himself in a hot tub on top of wife number three's bones." Conor clapped his hands. "Well, I think he needs to die. Everyone with me?"

Junior snorted, but aloud, he mused, "Surprised Da didn't think something weird was going on."

"You know he doesn't wade into the men's personal lives," Finn remarked.

"But still. *Six* dead wives?"

"Why didn't he pick up on the stink when the notion of marrying Mary Catherine off to Murphy came up?" Aoife argued.

"You know how he gets when Ma's like this. When she's manic, he loses his shit. Since that last lockdown, she's been nuttier than a bag of acorns."

Still feeling guilty for sharing Digger's secrets, I clutched at his hand. "Father gave me no choice. He told me I *had* to marry him."

Junior frowned. "Da would never have forced you to marry someone decades older than you if you'd come to him. Did your asshole father say why he'd made the arrangement?"

"Does it fucking matter?" Digger snapped. "This ain't the Dark Ages. Fathers don't make decisions about their kids' spouses anymore."

"They do in the Irish Mob. My brother's due to get married to a daughter of the Bratva," Junior said calmly, but his expression was anything but.

"The age gap is nothing on this though," Finn muttered. "Twelve years or thirty-five."

Aoife, who'd been chopping onions, shuddered. "Even worse when Murphy's gross."

Finn cast her a look. "It'd be okay if he was a hunk? I need to delete your kindle library."

Aoife cackled. "You'd be the one who'd suffer if you did."

That had the twinkle in his eye gleaming.

"And no, it wouldn't be better if he was a hunk. I'm just saying it adds insult to injury."

"Mary Catherine says Murphy would have forced the issue, Aidan," Conor tacked on.

Junior frowned as he folded his arms across his chest. "How?"

Feeling even more mortified with Finn and Aidan Jr. watching me, I started stuttering, but Aoife saved me by answering, "Their first meeting, he'd have raped her to make sure she didn't have a hymen anymore.

"Because, you know, the Irish Mob values a sliver of skin and prioritizes that over a woman's safety and believes that's her only worth. How ridiculous," she finished, her tone scathing.

At her sniff, Finn grimaced.

"You don't know he'd have raped you," Junior pointed out.

"I know it's what happens," I whispered. "Anthony Mulhearne did it to my best friend."

"The Five Points are okay with allowing a rape culture to fester in their lower ranks, are they?" Digger sneered. "And you fuckers look down on bikers for being trash when you're letting that kind of shit happen on the daily."

Junior's eyes narrowed. "You're picking a fight with the wrong person."

"Am I? Seems like you're the one asking dumb questions to a member of your family who felt as if she were in physical danger."

At that, Junior blinked. "You're right. I'm an asshole."

"Only took nearly four decades for you to admit it," Conor mumbled.

Junior strode over to the dinner table and took a seat. His limp was more pronounced than ever, and when he sank onto the chair, the relief that filtered through his expression was raw and made me uncomfortable for him.

When he was settled, he released a heavy breath. "Da's already contacted your Prez, demanding Mary Catherine's return."

"I know."

"It's why we flew back from Vegas," I said softly.

Digger's tone was oddly smug. "Where we got married."

Junior's gaze flickered onto the hand I had around Digger's arm. He glanced at my ring then focused on my husband. "And you decided to come here first?"

"No, I found Mary Catherine outside the compound," Conor answered. "She wanted to speak with Ma."

"You thought she'd help?" Junior asked me kindly.

"I hoped she would," I whispered.

"If we want to call Da off, we have to switch the bait. You know he hates the Sinners," he mused, uncaring that Digger was standing here, listening in.

"Why the hell does he hate us?" my husband demanded.

Junior shrugged. "Da hates everyone. It's the Catholic in him."

Snorting, Conor sank back in his seat at the head of the table. "Well, there's an option." He scratched his chin. "Rather than going to war with us, how do you think your Prez would feel about going into business instead?"

The brothers shared a look that went over the head of everyone but them.

Digger hitched a shoulder. "I'm not that high up that I could say either way."

Conor studied him. "You know we'd win."

Digger tensed. "Excuse me?"

"Numbers alone says we would. We have more manpower than you do, and Da's got his fingers in a lot of pies on the East Coast. West Orange is being gentrified, isn't it?"

Digger's mouth pursed. "Lots of rich Manhattanites are moving in, yeah, but they don't have allegiance to you."

Conor hummed. "Wouldn't take much for Da to poison your backyard."

"Conor," I grouched. "Are you trying to annoy him?"

Conor grinned. "There's nothing more annoying than the truth, Mary Catherine. And the truth is that the Five Points could take the Sinners in their sleep." He turned to Aoife. "What are we eating for lunch, Aoife?"

"She's not your cook," Finn grumbled, shoving him on the shoulder.

My experience with them one-on-one might be meager, but even I knew how these guys bickered.

Well aware that the situation was about to devolve, I turned to Digger and asked, "War or business?"

He sighed. "I'll talk to Rex."

Junior, who'd been listening to us, not the argument in the background, grunted. "Wise choice."

30

DIGGER

DIGGER

"WHERE THE FUCK ARE YOU? You were supposed to be here hours ago. Wasn't that the point of taking the fucking red-eye late last night?"

I grimaced. "Sorry, Prez. Got waylaid."

"*Got waylaid*? What are you? A set of keys? How the hell do you get waylaid between Newark and West Orange?"

As I stared at the city skyline, one that included a peek at Lady Liberty herself, I muttered, "MaryCat had a plan."

"MaryCat had a plan."

I rubbed my eyes. "Are you going to repeat everything I say?"

"Maybe. When it feels like you're speaking words that make sense. What kind of plan did your two-day bride have?"

"One that'd stop us losing our heads to the Irish."

"We could take them." He pshawed.

"Could we though?" I inserted softly. "Without losing *any* brothers?"

Rex was one of the most intelligent men I'd ever come across. Not only that, he *cared*. Under his rule, fewer men had gone to jail and had lost their lives while serving the Sinners, and I knew that was because of our Prez who reasoned first and acted second.

"What was her plan?"

"Well, I told you that the Points have an issue with their lower ranks."

"The rape issue." He grunted, and I heard the sound of him cracking his knuckles in the background. "I remember. I have to say, that doesn't sound like O'Donnelly Sr. He's a headcase, sure. Crucifies those he hates, but otherwise, he leaves women out of his business. You know what happened to his wife changed him."

"Made him crazier," I muttered.

"Yeah, with enemies. Not with their women. Never heard of enemies' women being mistreated by the Points."

"No," I agreed, because I hadn't either.

"You're saying O'Donnelly Sr. doesn't know about any of this?"

"MaryCat didn't think so. She thought he'd stop it if he knew."

"And that was her plan? To go to him and to tell him how his house of cards is built on women's misery?"

"More like she was going to tell his wife. But shit derailed. When I dropped her off at the compound, she met with Conor O'Donnelly."

"The computer guy."

"Yeah. Him. He got his brothers involved. Mostly, they're just happy that she's safe, but they were stunned to hear what MaryCat had to say. They want to help."

There was silence on the other end of the line. Then... "I'm listening."

"How do you feel about going into business with the Five Points?"

Rex scoffed. "Yeah, I can see that happening."

"They have something in mind. They ain't said what, but I can see it. And," I admitted, "I told you last month about their business with the Rabid Wolves. They're filtering drugs through Canada."

"You did," he concurred. "You think it's related to that?"

"I think so. Those fuckers aren't reliable anyway. You and I both know that. Getting their gear up to the border could be something we take over, and we have better distribution routes too. So long as the Wolves deal with the border crossing, our risk is minimal."

"What makes you think Senior would be interested?"

"Ain't me who thinks so. His sons do." I thought it was wise not to mention Conor O'Donnelly's belief that the Points would beat us in a war...

"This is all supposition until it's not. You want to put O'Donnelly Sr. and me in a room to talk business then I'll do it."

"You still got Points outside the gates?"

"No. I wouldn't have told you to come home otherwise. Her father's here though. Parked outside. He ain't left."

"I told her to leave her gear at the compound. MaryCat thinks the fucker had a tracking device on her."

"That's messed up, Digger. Getting into bed with these fuckers—"

"Would be a smart business opportunity," I tacked on before he could finish. "And if the head doesn't know what the hands and feet are doing—"

"Or dicks."

"—or dicks," I muttered, "then we can't judge until we give them the chance to make amends."

Rex snorted. "You're taking their faith into account, I presume?"

"Well, it's what Catholics do, ain't it?"

"The O'Donnellys aren't like any Catholics I've come across. You know anyone else, never mind a devout follower, who crucifies people?"

"Not since Roman times."

"Exactly." Rex sniffed. "It's a weak leader who doesn't know what his men are doing."

"Maybe. Not sure you know what the Prospects are up to at all times though."

"I'm pretty sure—"

"How about the fact that Mickey's got a weed habit?" I added.

"Motherfucker. Why didn't you tell me that sooner?"

I shrugged. "Ain't a snitch and it's not a problem. Yet."

"'Yet' being the operative word."

"*But*, also, according to the O'Donnellys, their mom is sick. When she's sick, their dad goes ape."

"Aper than usual?"

"Apparently."

My statement was met with silence, then, "I'll speak with him. Me and him. No guns, no fucking guards. Ya hear me?"

That'd be a tough request but... "I'll see what I can do."

Rex released a soft chuckle. "You're more invested in this relationship than someone who only walked down the aisle to save a brother's sister."

I rubbed the back of my neck. "She's different."

He fell silent, then he rasped, "If she is, then hold onto her, Digger. Not many of those come around, and when they do, they flitter through your fingers so fucking fast that they could be a mirage."

"Yeah. I'm thinking so." I cleared my throat. "It's too fast for any serious talk. Don't mean I don't want it to get there, but I don't intend on freaking her out."

"Some shit just makes sense right from the beginning," Rex disagreed, and seeing as I knew of his past with the club's lawyer, I wondered, and not for the first time, what the hell had gone wrong between them.

Because he knew of my proclivities with secrets, I was well aware that Rex had gone out of his way to hide the reasons behind their breakup.

I sighed. "She's young, Rex."

"So? You're not ancient."

"Might as well be. Plus, I'm a—"

"Would you stop going on about being a fucking felon? Jesus Christ, Digger, her dad probably has a bigger rap sheet than you do."

I grinned to myself. "She said that too."

"So she's got a head on her goddamn shoulders. That's something. Plus, this entire situation has been directed by her, so she isn't dumb.

"You want her, keep her. What are you? A sinner or a saint?"

Though I groaned at his joke, I retorted, "Rex, shut up. This whole situation came about out of desperation. I'm not saying I don't want her. I fucking do. But she's had her choices stolen from her every step of the way. The moment she's safe and she can lead her life how she wants, she'll want to go back to—"

"To, what? A household where her father rules the roost and with an iron fist at that? Her mom ain't exactly good people; we know that from Sin. Hell, she's a bitch of biblical proportions, so there's no protection there.

"That ring on her finger doesn't save her from his fists, Digger," Rex warned. "Senior might punish her ass of a sperm donor, but that won't keep her safe long-term. It's not like he's going to end the bastard's life over this."

The warning had me stiffening with tension.

No one, not her father, not Aidan goddamn O'Donnelly Sr., would *ever* hurt her.

Not on my watch.

"You know what you have to do," Rex rumbled.

He was right—I did.

I'd wait to see how O'Donnelly Sr. punished the asshole, then I'd make my move.

31

DIGGER
DUALITY - SLIPKNOT

MARYCAT WAS NERVOUS.

She kept playing with her fingers, so I grabbed her hand. Her palm was sweaty, but I clasped it firmly with mine. Of course, that left her other hand free, and she kept on tugging on her hair, twining it around a finger. In turn, that led to her biting her nails.

Everything about our location had her on red alert. We were in one of the Points' infamous cement factories—where fuck knew what went down with fuck knew who.

It was telling that even she, someone sheltered from the truth of their world, knew of this place and its significance to the Five Points.

Rumor had it that Senior, though he did not need to get his hands dirty, regularly soaked them in blood in one of several cement factories the family maintained as a front.

I knew Aidan, Finn, and Conor O'Donnelly were inside the back office. We hadn't heard any shouting yet, so we were in the dark as to the state of play.

"God, I regret eating that Reuben," she mumbled then started jiggling her foot.

I knew that if she developed another tick, she'd be doing an Irish jig on her seat.

So I went on the offensive.

"You think I'm not going to keep you safe?" I asked softly.

Startled, she shot me a look. "I-I didn't think—"

"Well, you should. You're safe with me, MC. There's no need to be so anxious."

She released a breath. "I'm scared for you. Not me. It wouldn't be the first time I—"

"You what?" I queried when she fell silent, but I knew what she'd been about to say and more of that rage from earlier rushed through me.

"Doesn't matter," she denied. "I just want this over with."

"You'll meet with Senior first. Your father won't be there. He's at the compound," I assured her, watching her shoulders slump with relief.

"R-Really?"

"I told you earlier, baby." I turned in my seat and cupped her chin. "Weren't you listening?"

She swallowed. "I-I must have misheard you."

My brain caught on fast. "You thought he *would* be here?"

MC nodded. "Sorry."

"You don't have to say sorry," I chided, gently squeezing the soft pad of her chin. "Everything's going to be okay. He'll never hurt you again, MC. I swear to you."

Shooting me a brave smile, she nodded—but it was clear that she didn't believe me.

It made me say something I shouldn't say, encouraged me to utter words that'd get me into shit later.

"No matter what, MaryCat, he'll never lay a hand on you again. I'll see to that."

Her eyes caught onto mine, then they rounded. "Y-You—" Then she whipped her head to the side. "No! You can't do that. If you do that, then you might go to prison. Second offense," she rasped, more to herself than to me. "I'm not going to let you—"

"Ain't no letting me do nothing. He hurts so much as a strand of your hair and he'll pay."

She swallowed. "But I don't want you to fight him. I don't want to see him—ever again."

"You don't have to. We can move you out. Today, if you want. I can help set you up at Sin's place until you find your feet. I know your life's in Manhattan, but West Orange is nearby—"

"Can't I move in with you?" she whispered, her fingers clamping down on mine.

"I live in the clubhouse."

"We could move into Sin's together? I-I like you, Digger."

"I like you, MC," I informed her calmly, pushing my forehead against hers. "But until you stop thinking like a rabbit who's running away from a fox, I'm not going to pressure you—"

Her already-rounded eyes widened even more. Then, she let loose a shriek and shoved me away. "A rabbit running away from a fox? You jackass." Her hand slapped my shoulder. "This situation has nothing to do with how I feel for you. I already know what I want. I've wanted you since I was sixteen! I don't care if it was a crush or not. I don't care if it was me trying to rebel.

"You're a better man than anyone I've met in twenty-one godfor-saken years, Digger. In less than a week, you've shown me who *you* are. Why wouldn't I want that? If you don't want me, then stop messing around with my feelings, dammit—"

"Not want you," I snapped, aware that my cell buzzed but ignoring it to retort, "Of course I want you. You think I'd have jumped into goddamn bed with you if I didn't? You think I make a habit out of taking something that doesn't belong to me?

"I'm thinking of you, MC. Above my own wishes, above my own desires. It's fucking killing me trying to protect you from myself when all I goddamn want is to snatch you away and keep you safe. But I ain't a Five Pointer—"

"No, you're not a Pointer," someone rumbled, making both of us freeze in place. "And I'm not sure I appreciate the implication that a filthy biker thinks he's better than one of my men."

Head whipping to the side, my gaze collided with none other than the man himself.

The head of the Irish Mob.

Aidan O'Donnelly Sr.

Even as I was wondering where the hell he'd come from, I tipped my chin forward as I got to my feet, snarling, "Sinners don't rape their women to tie them into a marriage."

Senior frowned but flicked a look at Mary Catherine. "It's good to see you, child. You've had us... *concerned* about your whereabouts."

"Don't fucking talk to her. You're the head of the Irish Mob but you don't know what your lower ranks are doing," I spat, uncaring that I'd fought down Rex's logic and defended him to my Prez earlier. "You're the damn reason she had to run away to the Sinners for help—because her brother was there and she knew he'd save her from what her father had planned."

"When I want to speak with you," Senior ground out, "I'll address you. Until then, shut your goddamn trap."

I stormed forward, but with surprising strength, MC snagged a hold of my hand and dragged me back.

"Digger, you're making it worse." I shot her a bewildered look that had her huffing out a breath. "Don't, Digger. It's okay. Let me deal with this." To O'Donnelly, she whispered, "It's true, Uncle Aidan. Father left me with no choice."

The older man angled his head to the side. "According to him, you were excited about the match. It's the only reason I didn't outright reject the notion. I was going to speak with you at church this week, but you disappeared before I could."

"So, he did get your sanction on this?" I demanded.

My cell buzzed again.

Pissed at the interruption, I was about to ignore it when another notification set my phone vibrating.

> Rex: MaryCat's father's AWOL.
>
> Rex: You hear me?

> Rex: He's left the compound. The fucking Prospect on the gates didn't think to tell me. It was only when Cruz took over that he looped me in. Maverick checked the CCTV and he's been gone around ninety minutes.

Fuck.

> Me: Beat his ass for me?

> Rex: I'll leave him for Sin. You know what he's like when his blood's pumping.

"I know my father too well."

MC's soft words had me settling a hand on her lower back and shoving my phone into my pocket.

If O'Donnelly *had* called her father here, I'd have to tear him a fucking new one.

O'Donnelly frowned at MC. "Meaning?"

"If I'd shown him how I really felt, he'd have locked me in my room and would have kept me there until I agreed to anything he wanted just to get out." She sucked in a breath. "It isn't the first time he's done it, sir.

"I appreciate knowing that you would have spoken with me, b-but h-he has me under his thumb." She exhaled roughly. "I-I'd have been too scared to say no."

"What twenty-one-year-old wants to marry an old, fat fuck like Bill Murphy anyway? Why would you agree to it in the first place?" I demanded.

"Not everyone marries for love, Digger," Senior said calmly. "There's such a thing as hierarchy. I'm sure, even in your anarchic society, you know what that means. Murphy's served me well over the years—"

"He's a rapist," I said flatly.

I saw the anger flash over Senior's expression before he pinned MC with a look. "He touched you?"

"No," MC admitted. "I left before I had to meet with him. Digger is Bill's son, sir. His mother was…"

My jaw clenched. "He took her by force and I was born of that union."

"I know you," Senior murmured, clicking his fingers. "Five or so years back, Bill was attacked."

"My greatest shame is that I didn't kill him."

They often said that the eyes were the window to a person's soul, but until I'd met O'Donnelly Sr., I'd thought that was nothing more than bullshit.

I could see lightning-fast thoughts forming and flickering away as he stared at me, watching me, studying me. Pinning me in place like a cobra just waiting to strike.

I'd served time with some mean motherfuckers, and little scared me anymore, but it was for that exact reason that I knew *which* men to avoid.

Aidan O'Donnelly Sr. was one such beast.

Unfortunately for him, I had a princess I needed to protect, and I didn't mind if he bit my face off in the process.

"That's why you married her? Retaliation?"

Of all the questions to ask, that one surprised me the most.

"*That* is what matters to you?"

"Answer me," he growled.

"Fine. *No.* Why the hell would I need to retaliate against that bastard by marrying a woman he doesn't deserve in the first place? I was saving her from someone I *know* is scum, O'Donnelly. Sparing her when no one thought to spare my mom."

MC's hand clutched at mine. "He was being kind, Uncle Aidan. A true gentleman. I was looking for my brother at the Sinners' compound but he'd left on business. Digger helped me when I had no one to turn to."

Senior's eyes narrowed upon us both, then he jerked his chin. "Come with me."

MC and I shared a look and it was only because her eyes were loaded with desperation that I obeyed his directive. It went against everything in my being to comply with the order of someone who wasn't my Prez or on the council, but sensing that mutiny would only freak her out even more, I held her hand as we followed him.

He strode forward toward a different door than the one his sons were behind, but he paused with his hand on the handle.

Turning to stare at MaryCat, O'Donnelly soothed, "You won't be hurt again, Mary Catherine. Do you understand me?"

Rex's text suddenly made sense. "You asswipe. You brought him here!"

"He's in there?"

The fear in her voice, sweet fuck, it wormed a venomous path inside me.

Senior's brow furrowed. "He is. But he won't harm you. I promise you."

"This is ridiculous," I grated out. "You can't put her in the same room as her abuser!"

Even as MC was gulping, Senior settled his gaze on me. "In my territory, I am the judge, jury, and executioner—"

"Much good that's done her."

Senior's hand shot out at that. One second, I was standing there, and the next, he had me pinned to the wall by my throat. "You need to learn respect, boy, and when to keep your fucking mouth shut," he snarled, thumbs flexing around my windpipe.

Before I could retaliate, however, O'Donnelly Sr. tensed.

"I-I can't l-let y-you d-do that, U-Uncle Aidan."

My gaze darted to MC's, and that was when I saw she had my Glock buried in the other man's stomach and her hand was shaking like she was in the middle of an earthquake.

I didn't know if the emotion coursing through me was pride or absolute fucking terror.

MC had just pulled a goddamn gun on the most dangerous *and* insane man on the fucking East Coast.

"Now, don't be silly, girl," he warned, but his hold around my throat lessened.

She sucked in a breath. "He's my husband. I-I won't let you hurt him."

Her words were stronger this time, the hold she had on the weapon firmer.

Now, pride started to whisper through me.

My husband.

Damn, I was starting to like how that sounded coming from her lips.

"It's okay, MaryCat," I crooned. "He won't hurt me. Will you, O'Donnelly?"

The older man's top lip curved into a sneer. "No, I won't. If you don't keep on pissing me off, that is."

"Put the gun down, MC," I gently ordered.

She swallowed. "I won't let him hurt you."

Back my woman into a corner and she had guts—*got it.*

"I know. You're such a good girl. Thank you. But you don't need to do this." I held out my hand. "Give it to me, sweetheart."

Her bottom lip trembled but, nodding, she carefully moved it away from Senior and placed it on my palm. As my fingers tightened around the gun, Aidan's head whipped to the side to glower at her.

"What did you think you were doing, Mary Catherine?" he chided. "Don't you know you shouldn't pull a gun on a man without knowing how to shoot? If you're going to annoy a predator, you make sure you kill it."

She blinked. "I didn't want to kill you. I just wanted you not to hurt Digger."

He squinted at her then at me. Which was when I realized his sons had told him *everything.* "You keeping her?"

Taken aback, I didn't even have a chance to think before I was nodding. You didn't do shit like that in front of a man like him, not without meaning it. Not without it having repercussions that'd send shockwaves through a city.

As she released a startled exhalation, Aidan was grunting. "Then you teach her how to shoot properly."

"I showed her the right moves earlier."

"That's not enough." He sniffed. "Her father's obviously a worthless piece of shit so I doubt he's given her the means to protect herself from him.

"It's come to my attention, Mary Catherine, that you don't have my number." He opened his jacket and carefully plucked something out of his pocket. "There." He passed her his card. "If this jackass hurts you, you come directly to the source. No more running off, you hear me?"

Gulping, she nodded. "Yes, sir."

He harrumphed. "Now then, if you're old enough to wed, you're old enough to appreciate this." His look was a warning as he retreated a step then ordered, "Come with me."

I turned to look at MC, who had stars in her eyes.

"You told Uncle Aidan…" Her whisper faded.

"O'Donnelly's right." Took getting slammed in the wall by a madman and then having that madman held up by your wife to put the fear of God into a person. This could have ended with her… Jesus, she could have died. My voice was hoarse as I said, "You're old enough to make your own decisions and you're smart enough to know what you want and when. I'm a dumbass. So, are *you* keeping *me*?"

"You know I want to. I-I mean, if we hate each other, then there's always divorce?" She whispered that last part so O'Donnelly couldn't hear, I assumed.

I knew there was a twinkle in my eye as I rumbled, "No divorce when you're Catholic." At her widening eyes, I pinched her chin. "We'll take this slow, MC. You hear me? There's no rush. We got chemistry and that's half the battle, and so is communication. You want me, you can have me. As fucked up as I am—"

"You think I'm not fucked up?" She bit her lip as she slid her fingers around my wrist. "Can't we be fucked up together?"

"We can. But there's no reason we can't build something beautiful together too, no?"

She beamed a smile at me, one that started to seal the jagged parts of my heart that were ruptured from the crap I'd been through over the years.

"We can take it real slow and—"

"I don't have all goddamn day."

Both of us jolted in surprise at that, but we turned and saw O'Don-nelly glaring at us.

My grin was sheepish as I turned to her. "You ready?"

"Probably not," she muttered. "Knowing Uncle Aidan, I mean, anything could be behind that door."

I slid my hand into hers. "We'll face it together, though, won't we? No need to be frightened. Not when you're with me."

Her eyes caught mine and she smiled again. "Together."

I winked and *together*, we walked toward her insane uncle, and only the fuck knew what would happen once we were behind that door.

32

MARYCAT

MARYCAT

I WAS LUCKY.

Uncle Aidan could have done only God knew what to me in retaliation, but even as I'd pushed the gun into his stomach, I knew I was safe.

The O'Donnellys didn't hurt women. If anything, women were their weakness—I knew that.

Everyone knew that.

That didn't mean he'd appreciated being held at gunpoint…

But whatever amnesty women were under, Digger was *not*. So I'd had to protect him. I'd had to.

And now, I had more certainty about us than ten minutes ago, and we were walking toward my uncle and whatever he considered me to be old enough to handle.

My lip was raw from biting it as we entered the room, and I groaned under my breath as I bit down harder than ever, blood dripping into my mouth from where my tooth punctured the tender flesh when my gaze collided with my father's.

Seated behind a board table, the moment he caught sight of me, he jumped to his feet, snarling, "Mary Catherine! Where the fuck have you—"

"Sit. Down," Uncle Aidan barked.

But I was deaf to that.

All I could see was the loathing on his face.

The absolute hatred.

When had that happened?

Why had it?

I just didn't understand how someone could turn so totally against their child because that child's mother was Jezebel reborn.

Digger's hand tightened around mine. It made me jump but it enabled me to break the chokehold Father had on me and let me look at my husband.

His gaze was calm even if his expression was stony.

I tried to allow that calm to filter through me too.

Then, I noticed he was breathing differently and I started to follow him—deep inhalations through the nose and long exhalations through the mouth.

The motion was soothing.

That was when I realized everyone was watching me.

Even Uncle Aidan.

Blushing, I turned to the other men and frowned when I saw Anthony, Sarah's husband, as well as Bill Murphy sitting there.

My blush instantly faded.

"What's going on, Senior?" Bill complained after several moments of silence that, I was pretty certain, Uncle Aidan let fall just to ramp up the tension.

It worked on me—my heart, even with the breathing technique, felt as if it could explode.

"I'm going to ask each of you a question. How you answer will decide your fate."

Bill frowned, and my father continued staring me down with a sneer curving his lips that I never wanted to see again—I didn't think he'd even *heard* Uncle Aidan's warning. As for Anthony, he just looked plain bewildered.

But then, he'd never been the sharpest knife in the drawer—Sarah deserved so much freakin' better than him.

"I've recently learned that there's a subsection of my men who think they can force their daughters into marriage by setting them up with a suitor who'll rob them of their free will by stealing their virginity."

It was Bill's turn to tug on his collar.

"How accurate would you say that is, Anthony?"

"I-I ain't never heard nothing—"

But Uncle Aidan didn't let him finish.

"Furthermore, Anthony, it's come to my attention that," Uncle Aidan stated calmly, "when you met your now-wife for the first time, you were one such man and you forced her into marriage—"

Anthony scowled. "I did no such thing."

"—by," Uncle Aidan continued as if he hadn't spoken, "raping her. Is this true?"

"Where the hell did you hear that?" Anthony demanded, bristling.

"Answer the question."

Anthony's Adam apple bobbed. "Of course, I didn't."

My fingers clutched at Digger's.

Liar.

"You're aware of the penalty of lying to me, I presume?"

Anthony gulped. "Of course."

"And you still claim you didn't force her?"

"Why would I have to force her?" he ground out, clearly deciding that the safest defense was offense. "She was as eager as—"

"Liar," I snapped, unable to listen to him besmirch Sarah's reputation. "I was the one who had to deal with her in the aftermath of your first meeting. You hurt her! She was bleeding."

Anthony's nostrils flared. "You're the liar. I didn't do nothing she didn't ask for."

The cocking of a gun sounded in the room.

Anthony froze, his gaze darting to Uncle Aidan, who'd turned the weapon on him.

"You're not only a liar, you're a fucking rapist. Neither is welcome in my faction.

"Arranged marriage is a part of the life, but that doesn't mean you get to rape your bride, you fucking animal."

He pulled the trigger.

As Anthony's brains splattered the wall behind him, I released a horrified shriek as Digger drew me into his chest and cupped the back of my head. He whispered soft words at me, but I didn't hear him. All I could see was the hole where Anthony's face had been.

"I think that'll ram the message home to the Five Points, don't you, Bill?"

"I think you're right, Aidan," he said uneasily. "It'll definitely send a message to the men."

As Digger smoothed his fingers through my hair, my father rasped, "Get your dirty hands off my daughter, asshole."

Digger didn't so much as pause in his gentle stroking.

But his words had Uncle Aidan musing, "It's funny you should talk about dirty hands. Mary Catherine told me that you were going to force her to marry Bill here."

"It was a good match, sir. You can't disagree," Father retorted. "And arranged marriages are the way we work, as you said.

"Your Eoghan's doing as he's told. Mary Catherine's shamed the family by running away with this heathen."

"Eoghan *is* doing as he's told, but he's a man. A man never wants to settle down," Uncle Aidan dismissed. "And that's different—"

"Respectfully, sir, how is it? Bill's a high-ranking Pointer. It was a good match for Mary Catherine, not that he'll have her anymore," Father growled. "Not after what she's done."

"Eoghan's going to be bridging the divide between the Irish and the Russians. Inessa Vasov won't be marrying a man nearly four decades older than her, and I can guarantee that Eoghan won't force Inessa Vasov into *anything*.

"Mary Catherine seemed to believe that you'd imprison her in her room if she didn't comply."

"A father knows what's best for his daughter," was all he said. "Respectfully, sir, you don't have any girls. They need a firm hand."

"Firmer than a boy?" Uncle Aidan asked mildly.

"They're little sluts if you don't control them. She'd have run around if she could. I already stopped her from whoring herself out once. She's just like her mother—"

"That's enough," Digger grated out.

"It is," I agreed, choking on the words. "I dated one boy. *One.* Kris was a good man. You killed him. You didn't have to do that. I'd have stopped seeing him if you'd have just said—"

"I needed to make sure you learned a lesson," Father answered flatly before repeating, "You're just like your mother. Would spread your legs for anything with a dick." He sneered. "Look at who you turned to."

"What's this?"

Uncle Aidan's tone was like ice. It had me shivering as I replied, "You heard me, sir. He killed a boy from school that was interested in me."

He tipped his head to the side. "You killed someone out of the life? Unsanctioned?"

For the first time, Father appeared nervous. His shoulders hunched higher around his ears as he muttered, "I had to make sure she knew to stay away from outsiders."

"By killing a teenage boy?" Uncle Aidan twisted his neck until it cracked. "It's clear to me that I've grown lax with my lower ranks if this is how you think you can behave. Hold out your hands."

Father swallowed. "What? Why?"

"Hold. Out. Your. Hands."

Though he was scowling, he obeyed, then he watched with wide eyes as Uncle Aidan tucked his gun away then retrieved a knife from a second holster beneath his sports jacket.

"You're right that I've treated my boys no better than you've treated Mary Catherine. I'm many things, but a hypocrite ain't one.

"However, you *can* be punished for this unsanctioned death."

As he rounded the table, my father shouted, "You can't be serious, sir."

"Oh, but I am. Deadly serious. And for thinking you can question me, that's another finger you'll lose.

"Now, take this like a man and I won't cut off any more than are necessary."

Father blurted out, "No! Stop!"

But Uncle Aidan was already there.

At his side.

His knife slicing…

I closed my eyes as Father yelled.

Digger's arm clamped around my waist again.

He pressed my face into his cut.

Another shriek.

Another.

Another.

I heard the sickening sound of blood spurting and *things*, his fingers, landing against a solid surface.

Then:

"Go and get that cleaned up." He tutted. "Leave the fingers there, man. I've got some guard dogs who've earned a treat."

I heard a chair scrape as Father shoved his back, and though he was whimpering as he moved, he still managed to hiss at me, "You'll pay for this, girl."

I shrunk into Digger's hold, but my husband snarled, "You touch her and you'll wish I was only cutting off your fingers."

"You retaliate against her," Uncle Aidan agreed, his voice louder than Digger's, "and you'll earn the same fate as Anthony."

I didn't retreat from Digger's hold until I heard the door slam to a close.

"Now then, Bill. You're my final problem of the day."

"I'm not a problem, Aidan. I bring you solutions, don't I?" was the older man's jovial tone, but even though I didn't know him well, I could hear his anxiety.

"You know me quite well. What would you say I hate more than liars?"

Bill weakly joked, "Russians?"

"I hate them, sure. Ain't too fond of the Italians either. But more than that, more than even the fucking Aryans, I hate rapists," he hissed. "It took me a minute when I met Mary Catherine's husband to figure out where I'd seen him before.

"Now, you said that the asshole who assaulted you years ago was just a random mugger. You'll never guess what he told me today."

"Who's 'he?'" was Bill's perplexed retort.

"Mary Catherine's husband."

"I don't understand what he has to do with my mugging."

Digger's tension transmitted itself to me, and I clung to him, not seeking comfort but offering it—he was vibrating with emotion.

I couldn't even begin to imagine what he was thinking or feeling.

The man who'd hurt his mom, who'd ruined her life, was here.

His *father* was just a few feet away.

"Don't you recognize him?" Uncle Aidan demanded. "He's the man who attacked you. Except, he's saying that it goes deeper than that. He's saying that you're his father. That you're a dirty, fucking rapist. Just like Anthony—"

"No! Of course, he ain't my son! I've never seen him before in my life!"

"Liar," Digger spat.

"I'm not a liar! I don't know you. Who the fuck do you think you are, spreading this kind of slander about me?"

"He thinks he's your son," was my uncle's calm retort. "He thinks you attacked his mother."

"I know he did. My mom *never* forgot and neither have I. You're fucking lucky you survived that day. It's my biggest regret that I didn't wash the earth of your hide."

"I've never met you," Bill repeated frantically.

"What a strange thing to lie about when he served time for attacking you," I whispered, peering at him over my shoulder. "It's easy to prove."

Bill cleared his throat. "I-I was injured and don't remember much about the attack. You should shut your trap, Mary Catherine. This ain't your place. This is men's talk."

"*Men's talk.* I see one man here," Digger sniped. "Aidan O'Donnelly. Not you. You're not a man. You're a fucking cockroach and my mom wasn't the only one you hurt. You think I don't know what secrets you've got buried away?

"You don't even want to know how I earned my road name. *Digging* for secrets is what I do best.

"You're a fucking animal. A piece of shit who shouldn't have been within two feet of MaryCat, never mind be her prospective bridegroom!"

Bill slammed to his feet and from one second to the next, the mask of confusion faded and was replaced with vitriolic hatred as he glowered at Digger. "I won't have you disrespecting me, you piece of shit.

"You talk about your mother like she was a fucking saint. She was a dirty slut who was begging for it. Then she thought she could get me to pay for *you.*

"As if I even knew who you belonged to. As if I'd pay for something that could have been anybody's spawn—"

Digger squeezed my arms and carefully moved me aside. Even in the middle of this, he considered me first. But in the blink of an eye, he was halfway over the table, his hands around Bill's neck.

As he choked my ex-fiancé, the older man cried out with pain as he scrabbled against Digger's grip, but that didn't stop my husband.

Instead, he kicked things up a notch.

Switching his hold, he slammed Bill's head into the table. Over and over he repeated the move until Bill had stopped flailing and was sobbing softly.

I watched on in despair, uncertain of what to do, unsure of whether I should try to stop this or not.

When Uncle Aidan urged, "Stop now, son. Stop," relief hit me. Then, he turned to me, directing, "I want you to wait outside, Mary Catherine."

My eyes widened. "No!"

"Mary Catherine," he repeated, tone sterner. "Leave the room. We'll be out in a moment."

"D-Digger?" I squeaked.

"Do as he says, MC," Digger answered, his breathing still heavy from exertion as he pinned Bill's bruised and bleeding face to the wooden surface.

Mouth quivering, I backed away, but as the door closed, I heard Aidan say, "Retribution tastes sweet when it's this long in coming."

I staggered over to the seating area and plunked my ass down.

It didn't take a mind reader to figure out what was happening in there, to realize what my uncle had spared me from seeing.

Funny how he didn't spare me from Anthony's fate.

Was that because his execution was a promise that Uncle Aidan would fix things?

I hoped so.

And maybe, just maybe, he was giving Digger and me permission to be together.

Why else wouldn't he want me to see whatever Digger did to his sperm donor?

On edge, I sat on my hands as my feet fidgeted against the floor. I couldn't hear anything out here, and the isolation in a place like this quickly got to me.

Five minutes later, the doors burst open. Aidan appeared first, then Digger who…

I blinked.

He looked lighter.

The tension beside his eyes wasn't as pronounced.

The downward curve to his lips, at the sides, wasn't as prevalent.

I noticed all that as I shot toward him, not stopping until I was tunneling into his arms.

He didn't shove me away, just held me as tightly as I needed him to.

The scent of alcohol was strong—not on his breath, but on his arms.

God.

That was when I forced myself to tune into what Uncle Aidan was saying. "…you can have his property once it's been cleansed. You're certain there's a body hidden there?"

"As certain as I can be without digging it up myself."

My uncle grunted. "Mary Catherine, I'm grateful to you for bringing this situation to my attention. I'll make sure it doesn't happen again."

Anxiously, I tilted my head to the side so I could study him. "You can't promise that."

His smile was cold, *chilling*. "I think you'll find that I can. Word will spread about Anthony's fate. That's enough for a start. I'll get Father Doyle involved so we can see who else was forced into marriage this way." He moved over to me, carefully untangled me from Digger's hold, then pressed a kiss to my cheek. "Congratulations on your wedding. I wish you a happy future together."

"T-Thank you, Uncle Aidan," I muttered in surprise, but I heard the warning buried within the blessing, and I knew Digger had too.

Uncle Aidan would make sure that my future was happy, or Digger would pay the price.

He hummed. "I'll have Lena send you a gift." To Digger, he drawled, "I'll be in touch with your Prez to arrange a meeting. Warn him that I don't regret setting Five Pointers around your compound—"

Holy hell, they'd barricaded the Sinners in?

"—and I'd do it again in a heartbeat—Mary Catherine's family. But I have no desire to go to war with your MC."

Digger bowed his head. "I'll tell him."

His tone was remarkably level—either he'd known about his brothers being barricaded or he was just very zen after the altercation with his father.

Somehow, I thought it was the latter rather than the former.

He flicked a look between us then compounded his earlier warning with, "Treat her well or I'll make certain you do."

When he turned away, heading toward the office where we'd left his sons earlier, I bit my lip then stared shyly at my husband. "Should I say thank you to Conor, Aidan, and Finn?"

"If you need to," he answered easily, wriggling his neck from side to side.

The move had the joint popping.

He sighed. Deeply. Except it seemed to come from his very soul. As if he could breathe easier now that the load on his shoulders was lighter.

"You killed him, didn't you?"

His gaze was measured as it met mine. "Would you hate me if I said yes?"

"No. I'd just prefer to know, that's all. I mean, I do know. Uncle Aidan wouldn't have said…" I heaved a sigh. "I'd like to hear it from you."

"I killed him. It's a burden I knew I was carrying, but one I didn't know was so heavy."

"You look happier," I agreed, hesitantly pressing a hand to his abs.

"You scared of me now?" he asked, obviously having noticed my hesitation.

"Of course, I'm not. You're my protector," I gently cajoled, not wanting to see any darkness mar the buoyancy of his mood.

"I'm glad he told you to get out. You didn't need to see me like that."

"Even if I had, it wouldn't change my feelings for you," I assured him.

"Better not to test it."

I rolled my eyes, but… "You know in the future?"

"I don't know it well," he teased, his tone light. Lighter than I'd heard it before. Lighter than his mood. *Good.* Our conversation hadn't changed that. "Seeing as it hasn't happened yet."

I huffed. "You know what I mean."

"Not sure that I do, actually," he joked, but he chucked me under the chin. "What about the future?"

"I don't want you to go to jail again."

If the words came out in a rush, then so be it.

He tilted his head to the side. "You might be glad to get rid of me. One day."

As I looked deep into his eyes, slowly, I shook my head, reminding him, "Some things don't have to make sense to work, Digger. I think we're one such thing."

His lips twitched as he cupped my cheek. "A Five Pointer and a Sinner? That's definitely something that doesn't make sense."

"Until it does," I prodded.

He let loose a laugh, agreeing, "Until it does."

33

MARYCAT
NEXT EXIT - INTERPOL

MARYCAT

THREE HOURS LATER

REX STARED at my hand before he slipped his palm against mine and gingerly shook it. I wasn't so *ginger.*

"Pleasure to meet you, Mary Catherine."

I cleared my throat, correcting, "MaryCat."

A minuscule smile broke the stern man's staunch expression. "I'm Rex, *MaryCat.*"

Digger slung his arm around me. "You can let go now, MC."

Rex snorted as I ceased pumping his hand up and down in greeting. "So, you're sticking around, huh?"

"She is."

Rex nodded. "She can't stay here."

Before hurt could lodge itself inside me, Digger snickered. "No way. I figured we'd bed down at Sin's place until he got back. You have the key, don't you?"

"Good thinking." He rubbed his jaw as he rounded his desk and sank into his chair. "The key's in the safe. I'll get it for you before you leave."

"Why can't I stay here?" I queried. "I don't want to put you out, Digger."

"Should probably have thought twice about marrying the man, then."

Digger glowered at Rex. "Shut up, Prez. I made the suggestion. She was just crazy enough to go along with it."

"Precisely what I need," he grouched, but his gaze was soft as it landed on me. Some of his sternness faded as he studied me. "You can't stay here, MaryCat, because the clubwhores will eat you for breakfast."

Confused, I queried, "Do you mean that literally or sexually?"

His brows lifted. "I don't even know."

"I can handle myself." To Digger, I assured him, "I really can. You haven't gone to Sunday service with a bunch of catty Five Pointer daughters who are worse than any characters from a show on E!."

He didn't need to know that I spent most of my time in the restroom with Sarah at those events. I wasn't about to have him leave his home just because I'd turned everything upside down.

But Digger was shaking his head. "You're too good for this place, baby girl. We'll set up somewhere better. Start as we mean to go on."

I could feel something solid settle in my chest again. Something that leaked warmth into my bones and filled me with that dangerous chemical—hope.

"If you're sure," I said softly.

He winked at me. "I'm sure. We're only here so I can grab the key." To Rex, he demanded, "O'Donnelly said he barricaded the compound."

Rex cracked his knuckles. "I don't like that man." I guessed that was as much of a confirmation as Digger was going to get with me in the office.

"Few do," I inserted wryly before I mumbled, "I'm sorry for all the problems I've brought to your door."

"I'm used to it." He flicked a look at Digger. "While I've got you, Storm wanted to speak to you. He's having one of his sober moments," Rex groused. "You can leave MaryCat here. I won't bite."

Digger rolled his eyes but, to me, said, "I'll be back ASAP, MC. Don't leave the office without me. Rex is good people. I wouldn't leave you with him otherwise."

Though I nodded, I was frowning as he departed.

"If you make him choose between this life and the one you build together, you'll lose him."

My eyes flared wide at that statement as I turned to study Digger's Prez. "I have no intention of making him choose anything. I already asked a lot of him in a short space of time, and you heard me. I was willing to stay here—"

"Nah, that's not the way to go about this either." Rex leaned forward and plunked his elbows on the desk. "I know my men. Better than they think I do.

"Digger's one of the best. Solid worker, trustworthy, loyal. Fuck, he's worthy enough to sit on my council, but it's full and I got men who are like my siblings on there.

"He's also got a streak a mile long for picking up waifs and strays, so you fit the bill.

"If he's claiming you as his own, then you're a lucky broad because one of a dozen clubwhores just wish he'd claim them for longer than a night. But he wants you. Wants to leave the clubhouse *for* you." He scratched his chin. "You make him keep his life separate, you'll lose him.

"Already got one brother going through that shit right now. If he'd introed his woman into the life, things would have gone a lot smoother for him, but the stubborn ass wouldn't listen and she's not the kind of chick who'd pull a gun on the craziest man in Manhattan."

"He told you about that," I said flatly.

"He did."

My mouth tightened. "I've read the books—"

"What books?"

"The MC romance—"

He frowned. "The what?"

"Books about women who fall for bikers."

His eyes widened. "That's a thing?"

"It's a thing," I confirmed, amused by his bewilderment. "I know that clubwhores are bitches and that they want a biker to claim them. I know that bikers don't want them because they give it away on tap. It's how the books always go—"

"This isn't a book, MaryCat," Rex pointed out, still bewildered.

"No, but it's still people. People want what they can't have." I stared him down. "I appreciate the warning, and I want you to know that I won't pull Digger away from the club.

"Like you said, I've already messed around with his world. I want to fit in, Rex. I want to find a place for me."

"Why?" Rex tilted his head to the side. "You're designer purses and houses in the suburbs. Not leather jackets and parties in the back-yard around an open fire."

"Can't I be all those things?"

"People rarely are. You want a bit of rough? That it?"

"Is this you protecting his honor?"

"Maybe. Or it could be me trying to stop a guy I respect from breaking his fool heart." He pursed his lips. "Don't get me wrong, I advised him to keep a hold on you if he wants you, but I'm just checking in that you're worthy of him."

Though he was pissing me off, I was glad that Digger had someone who'd guard his back.

With that being the case, I decided that honesty was the best policy.

"We don't love each other. Yet." Hands balling into fists, I repeated, "I want to fit in. I *will* fit in."

"Why?"

"Isn't it enough that I want to?" His expression told me it wasn't. "Because I'd love to be a part of a family. Because Digger's got one and I crave that sense of belonging.

"Because Manhattan never sat right with me. Because I need more than the confines of life as a mob wife." I sucked in a breath. "That ride down to Vegas sucked. It hurt my ass, my entire body ached, and I felt like my teeth were vibrating hours after I got into bed, but it was *wild.*" I didn't know that my eyes were gleaming. "It was freedom. It was me and him, running from my truth, heading toward a better one. One that was of my own making. It was independence.

"No seat belts tethering you in place, just my arms around his waist. Hair in the wind, me and him on the road, nothing holding us back.

"I don't ever want to have to ride that far again in such a short space of time, but it changed me."

Rex scoffed. "No, it didn't."

"It did," I snapped, starting to get pissed at him again. "My life was studies and Sunday church. It was a strict routine and yoga after dinner. It was hiding things in my toilet tank because I knew my father searched my room. It was cameras in places where they shouldn't be and eyes on me at all times. My phone was tracked, guards watching me whenever I left the house." I shuddered. "It was a prison. It was cuffs. It was *chains*. Digger is the opposite of that. He's," I finished softly, "freedom."

He drummed his fingers against the desk. "He gonna brand you?"

"I don't think so. Not yet. I think he believes, like you do, that I'm not made for this world, but I'll prove to him otherwise."

Rex hummed. "I never said that."

"Never said what?"

"That I think you ain't made for this world. This world," he repeated, "MaryCat, is made for anyone with the balls to claim it for themselves. No rules, no laws, just the open road and brothers who've got your back." He nodded, more to himself than to me, then grumbled, "You'll do for him. Just don't break his fucking heart by changing your mind years down the line.

"If you *are* going to go, do it soon. Bikers might have tough shells but when we love, we love deep."

Because that was the last thing I expected a rough and ready MC Prez to be saying, I blinked at him. "That sounds like the voice of experience."

His lips twisted. "Trust me, it is."

He grunted as he got to his feet then rounded the table and walked behind me. Figuring that he was going to grab the key to Padraig's house from his safe, I kept my eyes on my knees. I heard the squeak of a heavy door, then it slammed closed, and finally, something was dropped on my lap.

"Sin won't mind you staying there, but he'll have a problem with Digger hooking up with you. Watch out for a fight, don't be shocked if it gets physical fast, and if you can break it up, do. They're close and Sin's a mean motherfucker when he loses his temper."

I peered at him. "Thank you for the warning."

He gifted me with another grunt. "You going back to school? Digger mentioned that you were still studying."

"Yes."

"What's the endgame?"

I hitched a shoulder. "Genuinely, I don't know. But it seems a shame not to graduate. I-I never really thought I'd get to put my degree to much use. I knew I'd be married sooner rather than later, and after that, you don't really do anything other than be a housewife."

"What is this? 1950?" he argued. "How backward are the Five Points?"

"Very." But then I thought of that look in Uncle Aidan's eye and mused, "But maybe a change is in the wind." I shot him a pointed look. "Uncle Aidan respects strength and smarts. Don't talk down to him or give him smack. Deal with him like it's a corporate business meeting and you'll get ahead.

"I don't have to know much about the mob to know that the Irish are one of the most powerful factions on the East Coast—"

Rex dismissed that with a waft of his hand. "It's not about how I talk to him. It's about how *he* talks to *me*."

"You advised me on how to handle Sin when he meets Digger. I'm giving you the same in return.

"Uncle Aidan has warped morals, but they're there all the same. Honor is important to you; otherwise, you wouldn't appreciate loyalty so much. He's the same. Just wears a suit."

He narrowed his eyes at me. "I appreciate the insight."

I shrugged. "Do with it what you will."

For a moment, silence passed between us, then he rumbled, "He seems lighter."

"Digger?" At Rex's nod, I sighed. "He killed his father. With Uncle Aidan's approval."

"He's more like Nyx than he knows."

Ah, the makeup brand brother.

I didn't have a chance to reply because the door opened and Digger walked in. "How is it possible he's worse sober than he was high?"

Rex hitched a shoulder. "You know what he's like without Keira."

Suddenly, Rex's warning made more sense.

An Old Lady had left a brother, and the brother was reeling. Enough that he was using.

"A fucking mess," Digger agreed, swiping a hand over his face.

A pensive expression drifted over Rex's features. "Whatever's going on between them, he won't tell me."

Digger grimaced. "Fuck." He turned his focus on me, and there was a softness to his eyes, a warmth, a need. Hope and desire and excitement—they were all, somehow, wrapped into one tender look. I felt the mirror of those emotions in my being. "Let's get you out of here, MC."

"She's got the key." Rex pointed at him. "Get her used to riding. She likes the wind in her hair."

My cheeks blushed, but Digger hooted. "You going poetical on me, Prez?"

Rex, unashamed, smirked. "I'm just good at listening to women. Unlike some asswipes in my club. Now, fuck off. I got shit to do."

Digger, still chuckling, grabbed my hand and tugged me to my feet. That was when I saw he had a satchel in his hand—the stuff I'd left behind before our epic journey had begun.

I snagged it and then pulled out my phone. "What's your email so I can forward you the URL of the blog where I found the clubhouse's address, Rex?"

The Prez wafted a hand. "Maverick's deleted it already."

"Maverick?" I inquired.

"Resident hacker."

"Neat."

Digger plucked my satchel from my grasp as if it were too much for me to carry while informing Rex, "Aidan O'Donnelly said he'd be in touch, by the way."

The Prez shot me, not my husband, a calm look then opened the lid on his laptop. "I'll believe it when pigs fly over West Orange."

34

TEXT CHAT

Mary Catherine: Took me a lifetime to get my phone back, Sarah.

Mary Catherine: I'm not dead! Yay!

Sarah: OMGGGGggggg!!

Sarah: Best news ever.

Mary Catherine: Well, just wait…

Sarah: What?

Mary Catherine: Never mind. ;)

Sarah: Stop being secretive!

Mary Catherine: Guess who got approval to be married to be a biker?

Sarah: :O :O :O

Sarah: No fucking way!

Mary Catherine: Yes way.

Sarah: Your father?

Mary Catherine: Ha! No. Uncle Aidan.

Sarah: Holy shit!

Mary Catherine: Right? Gave me his blessing AND cut off some of Father's fingers for Kris too.

Sarah: Wow. That's HhhuuuGe.

Mary Catherine: I am so fucking happy right now.

Mary Catherine: I wish there were more justice for Kris but...

Sarah: Yeah. This life sucks.

Mary Catherine: It does, but it sucks a little less today.

Mary Catherine: Anyway, I have the worst period pains of my life so I'm going to sleep.

Mary Catherine: With my husband.

Mary Catherine: PINCH ME NOW.

Sarah: LOL.

Sarah: It took you months to stop talking about him...

Sarah: Funny how life turns out.

Mary Catherine: Yeah. <3 TTYL?

Sarah: Always.

35

TEXT CHAT
THE FOLLOWING DAY

Mary Catherine: Thank you <3 SO MUCH. For all your help.

Conor: Da told us what happened. He's fucking crazier than usual. You must have been scared shitless.

Mary Catherine: A little bit, but it doesn't matter. Thank you for helping us.

Conor: You don't have to thank me. Hell, we're family.

Mary Catherine: You could have still pushed me to the curb.

Conor: And miss out on a free chauffeur service? Complete with biker guard?

Mary Catherine: LOL. Anyway, I better get going.

Conor: You tell that man of yours that if he hurts you, I know what to do with a cattle prod.

Mary Catherine: Prod cattle?

Conor: Hmm. And other things.

Conor: Take care of yourself, Mary Catherine. Don't be a stranger, okay?

Mary Catherine: You too, and I won't be <3

36

TEXT CHAT

MARYCAT

Sarah: YOU!!

Sarah: YOU KNEW!

Sarah: OMMGGGGG.

Sarah: Aidan O'Donnelly Sr. just came to see me.

Sarah: I'm freaking out.

Sarah: Anthony's dead. Mary Catherine, Anthony is fucking dead, and you totally knew and you kept it from me and I don't care! I don't fucking care.

Sarah: Because I never have to have his hands on me again. OMG. I'm going to pass out. I know I am.

Mary Catherine: I had a feeling Uncle Aidan would tell you. I didn't want to spoil the surprise.

Sarah: You were there?

Mary Catherine: I was.

Sarah: Did it hurt?

Mary Catherine: It was too fast to hurt, I think. It wasn't pretty.

Sarah: Yay!

Sarah: He's dead and it was gloriously gory.

Sarah: Is it bad that I want to dance?

Mary Catherine: Can I call?

Sarah: No. His mom's here. I rang her after Aidan Sr. left.

Sarah: Christ, I hate her too. I hate her so much. More than I ever told you.

Mary Catherine: Thank God she's not your mother-in-law anymore.

Sarah: More like thank God that I managed to get an IUD implanted before he could get me pregnant.

Sarah: Mary Catherine, I never have to touch him again. Oh, I want to laugh! I want to sing! But she'd give me shit for it.

Mary Catherine: So? I repeat—she's not your MIL anymore! You can laugh and sing and fucking dance if you want to!

Mary Catherine: Go for it.

Sarah: You know what? I WILL.

Sarah: I'm FREEEEEEEEEEEEEEEEEEEEE.

Mary Catherine: You are!!

Sarah: I know this is down to you. The next time I see you, I'm going to give you the biggest chocolate cake this side of Hell's Kitchen.

Mary Catherine: You don't need to give me anything. I mean it. I'm just glad you're free.

Sarah: Love you, Mary Catherine.

Mary Catherine: I love you too, honey. Enjoy your freedom and if you can, take a picture when you shove two fingers in your MIL's face.

Sarah: <3 <3 <3

37

DIGGER

LOVESTAIN - JOSÉ GONZÁLEZ

TWO WEEKS LATER

"MARYCAT, I need you in the kitchen, please!"

At my holler, I heard the stomping of footsteps from across the house as well as, "I know, Sarah. I know. But we can't celebrate that he's dead in public. It'd look weird." She snorted. "Yes, we care. You're still a part of the Points! I don't have to care—" A pause. "I do *not* sound smug. I do not!"

"She did."

Hiding a grin, I shot Sin a look. "She did."

MC loved being a Sinner—*got it.*

That was when a sharp gasp sounded from the doorway.

"You let go of him!" MC demanded, racing over to us where Sin had me in a headlock that I wasn't fighting.

Why would I?

He was her brother.

Some shit was sacrosanct.

"Mary Catherine," Sin rumbled. "It's a pleasure to meet you in the flesh."

"Oh. You're… Padraig? I-I didn't recognize you with the beard." I saw her shuffle from one foot to the other. "Can you please let my husband go?" She huffed. "I need to stop saving you from these situations, Digger. I mean, Rex warned me, but—"

"What situations?" Sin grumbled, squeezing me tighter until I was literally choking around his hold.

Unlike with O'Donnelly Sr., MC showed no fear as she slammed her cell on the counter.

One second, Sin was concentrating on squeezing the air out of my lungs, and the next, he was on his knees, cupping his dick.

To me, she clutched at my cut and mumbled, "Are you okay? Did he hurt you?"

I wheezed a little. "I'm fine. I'm fine." I rubbed my throat as I fell on my ass. "He was just showing that he cares, MC." And it was cute as fuck that she thought I needed help defending myself.

Shit, she was fucking cute all-round.

My pocket-sized, ball-busting princess.

She frowned as she crouched in front of me. "Cares about who?"

"You," Sin croaked, slowly rocking forward on his knees until his forehead was against the ground.

Still rubbing my neck, I muttered, "You never thought to treat your dad to this bag of tricks you have up your sleeve?"

Her eyes were big. "No."

"Why not?"

She shrugged. "I don't know."

I brought out her inner Xena—*got it.*

"Want some ice?" I tossed at my brother.

"There are..." He coughed. "...peas..." He groaned. "...in the freezer."

MC was already there, though. Peas in hand, she knelt in front of Sin. "I won't say sorry, Padraig, because you shouldn't have hurt Digger. But it's a pleasure to meet you and I promise I won't do it again." She paused. "Unless you hurt Digger. I won't stand for that."

Sin rolled his forehead on the ground and peered at me. "She..." He moaned. "...for real?"

"She's for real." I hid a smile when I saw she had a frozen bag of chopped onions, smaller than the peas, for my throat. "A surprise though, ain't she?"

"I am here, you know?" She frowned and gasped. "Oh, shit. Sarah!" She picked up her phone from the counter, where I saw she'd put it before, and murmured, "Sorry, Sarah. I was just meeting my brother for the first time. How did it go? About as well as can be expected. What is it with men? Digger saves me from a fate worse than death and Padraig, who wasn't even here, decides to go all *Lethal Weapon* on him!"

"Hey, I..." Sin hissed. "...can hear..." He sputtered. "...you."

MC just sniffed. "Good. You should *thank* Digger, Padraig. I'm going to finish my conversation with my best friend, and by the time I return, I want to restart our first meeting, understood?"

I blinked at her surprisingly bossy tone.

"Under...stood."

My lips twitched as I scrabbled over so that I could lean against the cupboard door at his side.

Watching the sway of her hips as she moved away, I muttered gruffly, "She's happy."

Sin grunted.

"Why were you guys away for so long? You should have been here, man."

"Pedo moved. Chased. Lost. Found again."

"He's dead now?"

"Yeah." Groaning, Sin sagged onto his back, but he kept his knees high, the bag of peas squeezed between them. "Fuck, she got me good."

"Should have seen her point a gun at O'Donnelly Sr. She's got more of a backbone than you'd think at first."

"More like you've been a bad influence," he complained.

My lips quirked into a grin. "You might be right."

He sniffed. "Don't sound so proud."

"Why not? I want to keep her, Sin."

"Keep her?" He pshawed. "She ain't a toy."

"Never said that she was. But I mean it. One day, I'm going to brand her."

Sin jerked upright, bag of peas and his broken dick be damned. "You had better be fucking kidding me."

I ducked away from his incoming fist and grabbed a hold of it between my hands before I jerked his arm to the side to the point where I could have twisted it out of the socket.

With a warning glare, I promised him, "I'm not kidding. It started weird and it's getting weirder, but I'm finding that I like weird. Especially her variety of it."

He stared at my hold on his arm. There was a real threat to the move—he knew I wasn't bullshitting around. "You care about her?"

"At first," I admitted, "it was about you. Then, she was sweet. Kind. Gentle." I grinned then repeated, "She pulled a gun on Aidan fucking O'Donnelly for me, man. What about that isn't there to like?"

Sin frowned but tugged on my hold.

With another warning look, I let go. "She's too good for this world."

"She'd disagree. It's not like I'm going to stop her from going to school," I pointed out, not wanting to admit that he'd insulted me. "It's not like she ain't happy here. You heard her yourself—she's proud to be with me."

Sin's frown deepened. "It'll never work. Just look at how shit went down with my dad and her mom."

"Her mom's your mom too."

"Barely. Egg donor, more like."

"You don't know her, Sin. I know her better than you do." I studied him. "You can't tar her with the same brush as your mother. She isn't her."

Sin surprised me by not arguing further. He just shook his head and offered, "You can stay here until you find somewhere to live. I'll bed down at the clubhouse."

"Thanks, brother," I said, watching as he stiffly clambered to his feet. Before he could leave the kitchen, however, I called out, "Not every woman is like your mom, Sin."

He flipped me the bird over his head.

"MC wanted to invite you to Christmas dinner," I hollered, knowing he was storming toward the front door. "Don't fucking disappoint her, asswipe."

A few minutes later, I heard the rumble of his bike and smirked to myself at the image of him holding the peas to his junk as he rode toward the compound.

That was when MC peeped her head around the corner. "He left?"

Nodding, I beckoned her over, and she dropped to her knees then tucked herself into my side. She was, I'd come to learn, even more of an affectionate little thing than she'd been at the start.

I was surprising myself with how much I enjoyed the way she'd stick fast to me—especially in bed.

"Jerk. I meant it when I said I wanted to restart our first meeting."

I draped my arm over her shoulder. "You didn't have to knee him in the balls, MC."

She arched a brow at me. "He was choking you."

"You're his sister."

"He didn't like me."

"You'd just kneed him in the balls."

"No. I could tell. In his eyes."

"He was in pain. And you'd just kneed him in the balls."

She huffed. "*Before* I did that. I saw it."

"Sin's weird around women. Your mom saw to that."

That had her grimacing. "I can't blame him, then. She's a piece of work."

I hummed. "Thank you for defending my honor. Again."

Her grin was mischievous. "You're welcome. Again." Her eyes twinkled. "I think you like that I pulled a gun on Uncle Aidan."

"Oh, I do."

"Are you going to tell everyone at the clubhouse that I kneed Sin in the junk too?"

"Nah. He'll tell everyone that."

"He will?"

I nodded. "'Course. Shows you've got guts."

"I don't think I do. Not really. I just don't like to see people hurting you."

What was that? A fucking football, right in my throat?

I sucked in a breath, refusing to be unmanned by my tiny wife. "No one ever cared about me before."

"Same could be said about me. Well, apart from Sarah." She huddled closer, then her hand moved to my throat. Her fingers traced where I knew bruises were starting to form. "Is this your mom?"

Tilting my head back against the bar, I sighed. "When she was younger. Before I wrecked everything for her."

"You could never wreck anything for the women in your life, James," she chided, then she pressed a kiss to my cheek. "We have to protect each other, don't we? Even from ourselves."

Because I knew where she was coming from, I reached over and cupped her chin. "We do. Even from ourselves."

Her happy smile told me she liked my concession. "Did he say if he'd come to Christmas dinner? Or did you tell him I can't cook?"

I drew her deeper into my hold, assuring her, "I'll make sure he's here for your burned offerings, baby. Don't you worry."

38

DIGGER
COUNT ON ME - BRUNO MARS

THIRTEEN WEEKS LATER

WITH A YAWN, I opened my eyes. Spying the first edition copy of *Lord of the Flies* that MC had given me for my birthday on the night-stand, I smiled then rocked my head to the side when I realized she was awake as she drowsily tickled a lock of hair over one of the tattoos on my throat.

"I wish you were ticklish."

That had me snorting. "You say strange shit first thing in the morning."

Drowsily, but with a semi-serious tone, she countered, "I say strange shit all the time."

"Not all the time. Mostly before coffee or after a long day of studying or work." I rolled my eyes. "I still can't believe you got a job. It's not like you're not busy enough with school—"

"I like having a job." Her smile was happy. "Plus, I never thought I'd get to use my degree. I just thought it would be a piece of paper I got to frame.

"Now, I can help out Mr. Banks, and after I graduate, he said I can carry on working there while I get my masters in urban planning and can experience the issues civil engineers have on the ground."

She sighed, and that sound was also happy, and that was when I knew I was a sap because fuck, her happiness was all I really wanted anymore.

When she smiled like that and sighed like that and said shit like that, it amplified my day. Brightened my mood.

I'd never understood until her how someone else's joy could mean more than my own, but now I did.

Reaching over, I pulled open the nightstand drawer and retrieved the small box from within.

Flicking it open with my thumb, I stared at the contents, hoping she'd like it, before I dumped the box back in the drawer and returned to her side.

With a questioning look, she smiled at me. "Everything okay?"

"Would you wear something for me?" I asked softly.

"Of course." Her eyes flared. "Did you get me that silk lingerie?"

I snorted. "Not yet. But here." I shoved it at her.

She stared at it.

Her mouth rounded.

Then, she whispered, "Is this what I think it is?"

I cleared my throat. "It is. Would you wear it?"

A part of me wasn't sure if it was good enough for her. It might have cost a small fucking fortune, but it wasn't Harry Winston—

"I love it," she cried, sliding the ring on her finger and oohing and aahing as she turned her hand so the light hit the princess-cut diamond. "Thank you! Thank you! Thank you!" she declared as she hurled herself at me, dotting my face with kisses.

I'd never tire of her exuberance. It was still so alien to me, but I fucking loved it and never wanted her to change.

That was why I had to say it. I just had to. The words refused to stick fast, but why did I need to hold them back anyway?

Why couldn't I say them, and with pride, too?

"I love you."

Her hold on me loosened.

A soft breath whooshed in the air.

I thought she'd analyze it to death.

But all she did was say:

"I love you too."

The words meant everything, but it was the look in her eyes that mattered even more.

Unable to stop myself, I shifted onto her, humming with satisfaction when she spread her legs and immediately clasped my hips.

She had her period so I knew I couldn't take this anywhere, mostly because I hadn't corrupted her enough for period sex—I was working on it because she had wicked pains every month and I knew orgasms could help with that—but it didn't matter that this couldn't end in sex.

In fact, it made it better.

Sex muddied the waters.

I wanted nothing muddying *this*.

Pressing my lips to hers, I gently kissed her before peppering more kisses along her jawline. She tilted her head so that she could whisper in my ear, "Is it as easy as that?"

I couldn't stop myself from teasing her. "Nothing about you is easy, MC."

"It's the first time we said it though," she whispered, her thighs tightening their clasp around me.

I grunted. "We were patient."

"Too patient. I felt it months back."

My lips twisted. "Me too."

Her head rocked forward. "Why didn't you say something sooner?"

I hitched a shoulder. "Don't know. Why didn't you?"

She blinked. "Don't know. And I thought we were getting better at communicating."

Tightening my hold on her thigh, I snickered. "We are. Every day is an improvement."

Harrumphing, she frowned at me. "You didn't think…"

"Don't make me lose my buzz," I warned.

She stilled. "You did! You thought I'd change my mind."

"I didn't, actually." I arched a brow at her. "Sin thought you might, but I didn't."

"He has trust issues," she grumbled.

"Hella trust issues," I concurred.

Then, she shot me a shy smile. "You didn't doubt me? Really?"

"Not once. Just didn't think we were ready to say the words," I admitted, and I wasn't lying.

Since her first meeting with Sin, I'd known she was in it for the long haul.

Some shit, you just knew in your gut, and MC's constancy was one such thing.

"This is the best day ever."

I shot her a sheepish grin. "Nah, that was the day you decided to get a taxi to the compound."

MC let loose a joyous laugh as she hugged me to her, smushing my face in the tits that refused to stay cocooned in the tank top she only wore when she had her period.

"I fucking love you, Digger," she crowed, making me chuckle.

"And I fucking love you, MaryCat. I know I'm doing everything ass-backward, but..." My lips twitched as I asked, "How do you feel about heading out to get branded today?"

Her squeal, I figured, was the only answer I needed.

39

MARYCAT
VIDEO GAMES - LANA DEL REY

TWENTY WEEKS LATER

PIGS HAD FLOWN over West Orange.

It had taken longer than anticipated, but Uncle Aidan had visited the compound today, Finn and Aidan Jr. with him, as well as a slew of guards, and a deal had been struck.

The Sinners were, officially, transporting who knew what for the Five Points.

Hence the party tonight.

"Are you ever going to dance with me?" I complained to my husband who, unsurprisingly, didn't like dancing.

Digger frowned. "I don't dance."

"You have to dance. I'm your wife." I peeped a huge smile up at him. "You have to make me happy."

"You sounded plenty happy this morning—"

My hand clapped over his mouth before he could finish that sentence. "James!" I chided.

"Ooh, you brought out the 'James.'" A twinkle sparked in his eye. "That's when I really know I'm in the doghouse." Before I could do more than shriek, he leaned into me and, a moment later, tossed me over his shoulder. With one hand on my ass, he strolled me away from the riotous music in the disgusting room the Sinners called a bar and took me outside. "You can't dance to rock. You don't have it in you."

Upside down, I huffed and was about to speak, but there were a few catcalls from his brothers which culminated in Sin striding toward us, demanding, "What the hell are you doing?"

"What does it look like I'm doing?"

"Hi, Padraig," I greeted, twisting up to look at my brother. "I didn't see you earlier."

He frowned at me. "I was busy."

"Sleeping around?" I tutted. "You're such a manwhore."

Sin was a hard man to get to know. Digger said he had PTSD, but I just thought he was unhappy. Really, deeply, truly unhappy.

And for some reason, he thought happiness was found between a woman's legs.

Now, if that were true, I had to reason that women would never have to take antidepressants if we had the mother lode of joy in our cooches.

But heck, what did I know?

I wasn't a veteran, and as shitty as Mother had been to me, the things Digger had shared about Sin and her... I'd been fortunate. Crazy though, it seemed.

Digger chuckled. "She has you there."

"What's going on?"

Sin's posturing had me grunting. "I don't particularly enjoy being upside down, Padraig. *However*, I don't need my big brother to wade into the fray to get Digger to put me the right way up. In fact, I hope he's taking me somewhere he'll dance with me."

"Digger? Dance?" Sin barked out a laugh. "You have about as much chance of that as the moon being made out of cheese."

"Digger never had a wife before," I chirped.

"That's true. Digger never did," was Digger's reply, but he was snickering as he clapped me on the ass. "Come on, idiot. You know I'd never hurt MC. Ain't you figured that out by now?"

"I'd flash you my brand, but my position won't allow it."

"I've seen that goddamn thing so many times by now that it's imprinted on my retinas," Sin complained. "And don't show me your engagement ring either. It sparkles. I get it."

I smirked when Digger crowed, "She's proud to be mine."

Pinching his ass, I retorted, "And you're not happy to be mine too?"

"That goes without saying," Digger countered, then he nudged Sin in the shoulder. "Look at it. Her brand. All over my arm. So fuck off. She's mine."

"I'm her brother," Sin argued. "I have to watch out for her."

"She's got me to do that for her," Digger said, but his tone was milder. "She's safe, man. She's always safe with me."

"Even if I'm upside down," I remarked.

Sin huffed. "I'm going to find Kendra."

My nose crinkled. "Ugh. You need to get better taste. Kendra's a horrible, *horrible* person."

"Ain't fucking her for her personality."

When he strode off, I muttered to Digger, "We need to find him a nice girl."

"We really don't."

"We do! He's not going to find any peace with the likes of Kendra."

"Your brother's got a lot of issues."

"No. You *don't* say," I mocked. "Seems to me that everyone in the Sinners has issues."

"That's probably why we get along so well," he teased.

Maybe it was.

Each brother, I'd come to learn, had their quirks. Some were kind behind the brutish looks, and others were grumps to their core, but that didn't mean they weren't worth getting to know.

Just like my husband, still waters ran deep.

Digger's art skills, for example, continued to blow my mind. And whenever I watched him retrieve a simple notepad and a number two pencil, something sighed inside me because he was comfortable enough around me to work on his art. To show me when he'd completed a magnificent piece that he'd created with middle-school materials.

I smiled at nothing, accepting that I was the lucky woman who got to see beneath the cut.

"But you're right. Kendra's a bitch."

"Damn straight she is." She was the worst of all of them.

"She hasn't tried anything with you?"

Confused, I asked, "Tried anything?"

"To fight you?"

My eyes widened. "To fight me? No." Sheesh.

Before I could pepper him with more questions, because this conversation could only mean that I hadn't heard the gossip about a catfight, Link cuffed Digger on the arm. "She has legs, you know."

"Trust me, I'm aware. Maverick won't come down?"

Link scoffed. "No."

"I was hoping one of the whores would convince him."

"Whores aren't convincing," I inserted. "Honestly, you guys think you know so much but you don't."

"Little bit," Link teased, "we know plenty."

"Yeah, but not about *that*." I harrumphed.

"Why you carrying MC?"

I rolled my eyes at Steel's inquiry. "Because he wants all the blood to rush to my head."

"Why? Does that make for better orgasms?"

Digger chuckled. "I dunno. I'll leave it to you to run those experiments, Steel."

"You can kill a person by hanging them upside down like that."

"Nyx, cheerful as always," I greeted.

"What's going on?"

"In general? Or with MC?" Digger asked him.

"General."

"Digger wants to know why a clubwhore can't convince Maverick to come downstairs when the man wants to be left alone."

"It's fucking weird how you know so much about everyone, Mary-Cat," Link mused. "Especially when you don't hang out here often."

"I listen," I pointed out. "Plus, I have a job and studies—"

"Hell, that ain't a complaint. Can you imagine how much you'd know if you *did* hang out here?" Link whistled. "Steel'd lose his job."

Steel offered, "You can be Secretary, MC. No one else I'd trust with the position."

"That's quite all right," I said primly. "If you want to resign, though, Digger would look great on the council."

"MC!" Digger chided.

"What?" I swung up to see him better—it didn't work. "You'd be so good on the council. You're wasted doing what you do."

"She has a point. You really are," Nyx rumbled. "You should talk to Storm about him giving you more opportunities. I figure you don't want to go on as many runs?"

I didn't pipe up then, knowing this was technically 'MC' (and not me) business, but I squirmed on his shoulder, hoping he'd agree.

"Yeah. You know how I work. I'm more about the gathering of intel than anything else. I'll speak with Storm."

Nyx grunted.

He was an odd duck.

It was like he cared about nothing, but he cared about everything.

Men were strange. I was lucky that Digger was semi-normal.

"You taking her to the field beyond Rachel's?" Steel asked Digger.

"Yeah."

"You old romantic you," Link joked, shoving him again, which, of course, jostled me in turn. "Never thought I'd see the day that Digger got all mushy over some broad."

"Hey! I'm not some broad. I'm his wife." My tone turned smug. "*And* his Old Lady."

"DON'T SHOW US YOUR BRAND AGAIN."

My cheeks flushed when all three men declared that at the same time. "Shut up. I don't show everyone."

"You really fucking do." Nyx took a sip of his beer. "You need to get her to stop flashing it, Digger."

My man just chuckled and tapped me on the butt. "She's cute. What's a Sinner to do?"

I didn't have to look at Nyx to know he was rolling his eyes. It was practically audible. "Go and be romantic, dipshit."

Link cackled. "Your way with words is improving, Nyx."

"*You*," Nyx growled, "shouldn't even be here. You're supposed to fix my fucking bike—"

As the three men ambled away, Link and Nyx bitching at one another about Nyx's hog, I asked Digger, "Which field beyond Rachel's?"

"Behind her house."

"Why would you take me there?"

"To see the sunset."

"Oh." I didn't know if it was the blood rushing to my head or that he was so crazy thoughtful, but tears pricked my eyes. "That sounds lovely."

"Knew you'd like it."

"You know, if you carry me over your shoulder the whole way, I might puke."

He snorted at my serious tone. "I'm being a gentleman."

I chuckled. "Who said I wanted a gentleman?"

That had him freezing in place, then he bent over and helped me stand. Just as I found my feet, he hauled me back into him, but this time, my knees were on either side of his hips and he had a hold of my ass.

"There, that's better," I muttered, though I pressed my forehead to his for some stability. "Man, I'm dizzy now."

"And they said the magic would die."

It was my turn to snort. "Who said that?"

"Everyone." He started walking again. "Brothers, hell, even Sarah did, didn't she? After she called you crazy and then sobbed on the phone with relief that that ass was dead when her mother-in-law left her alone the first time?"

"Yeah, but what does everyone know?" I nuzzled my nose against his. "Some stuff can *never* make sense and still be perfect."

"You ever read about chaos theory?" he mocked, but he pressed a kiss to my lips—to shut me up, I thought. "I never said I agreed, just that people have a habit of running their mouths about us."

I couldn't argue about that.

The clubwhores all looked at me as if I were dirt on *their* shoes, which I found highly ironic as I was one of the few Old Ladies who treated them with any decency.

Most of his brothers acted as if I'd sprouted fully formed from a meteor landing and was an extra-terrestrial lifeform sent to plague them.

I thought Storm liked me, but Storm was… well, *Storm.*

I'd never met a man who'd fucked up so badly and who lived with the guilt as if it were a septic wound.

And hell, I'd been raised Catholic!

Storm was the most repentant Sinner of them all. I was almost convinced that Keira, his wife, was a real bitch, but I didn't think he'd have loved her so hard if she were.

The thought had my brow furrowing. "Do you think they thought we were like Keira and Storm?"

Digger grimaced. "I mean, probably? But they've been together a hell of a lot longer than us. Plus, Keira's father is a deacon—"

I chuckled. "Father's many things, but not that." Still, I whistled under my breath. "Fuck, that must have been a culture shock for her."

"Just a little." He nuzzled his nose against my jawline. "Rex is very happy with you."

"Hardly. More like he's happy with you."

"Well, it's a dual thing. If he's happy with me, he's happy with you. O'Donnelly only came because of you."

"I think he was waiting us out. Seeing if I'd run." I harrumphed. "You're right. Everyone thought the 'magic would die,' didn't they?"

He grinned at me. "You know, I love your optimistic nature. You only just figured that out. That's too fucking cute."

I sniffed. "They're the negative Nancies."

"Anyway," he drawled, "the club is going to be rolling in it. If it continues for as long as the Five Points have planned, we're going to have to come up with a way of laundering millions."

"Ask Storm."

"One, it's not down to me. Two, he's VP. Of course, Rex will ask him for his opinion."

"No, he goes quiet. Haven't you noticed? He does it in private, so I can't imagine he's much better at a council meeting."

"He's losing hope," Digger concurred. "Poor bastard."

I bit my lip. "I wish I knew Keira."

"She wouldn't thank you for reaching out. She's never integrated with the club."

"I don't either."

"By comparison, you do. You're here, ain't you? Keira's never attended a BBQ, a family potluck, or a party."

"That's sad."

It also made me understand more of Rex's 'welcome speech.'

"Yeah," he agreed. "But with how the clubwhores have been treating you, I'm not sure I judge her how I used to. They're getting too big for their goddamn boots."

"I can handle them."

"You shouldn't fucking have to. In fact, I don't think you should come around here without me."

"I don't need a chaperone," I groused indignantly.

"No, you need a keeper." Though I huffed, he demanded, "You like him, don't you?"

"Who?"

"Storm."

I shrugged. "He's a good guy, just lost."

"Very lost." He heaved a sigh. "We're here."

Blinking, I tipped my head back and stared up at the sky. My grin was wide as I saw the multiple shades streaking overhead, purples and reds, golds and oranges.

"It's beautiful," I murmured.

"Just like you."

"You say the sweetest things," I teased.

He huffed. "I'm trying."

My humor faded. "You do more than try, Digger. I hope you know you make me very happy."

He shot me a dopey grin. "Really?"

"Really." I studied him. "No regrets?"

"None."

And that was that.

40

DIGGER

SOMEWHERE ONLY WE KNOW - KEANE

THIRTY WEEKS LATER

"I CAN'T BELIEVE I'm doing this," I ground out under my breath.

As always, my reckless wife just curved her arms around my neck and laughed with abandon.

The day had been a good one—if long.

She'd graduated. *Summa cum laude.* None of her family had attended other than Sin, but the O'Donnellys had, as well as most of the council and a few other brothers that she'd collected as friends over her time in West Orange.

A bunch of rough bikers sitting down in the hall had caused some raised eyebrows, and Sarah, her BFF, had ducked down in her seat a couple times, but when we'd whooped and cheered for her, MC had bounced on her heels and had fist-pumped the air in a way that she'd never have done a year back.

Though each day was a lesson in MaryCat, a part of me wasn't sure if she'd like the two halves of her world colliding, but when she'd seen the bikers, even grump Nyx, in the audience, she'd beamed happily at me.

Proud.

That was what she'd been.

Proud.

And she kept on showing me that pride. In turn, it made me want to give her the fucking universe.

That was why we were out here in our backyard before I showed her the mirror I'd had Jackson and Cruz install on the ceiling above our bed.

The bribe to keep their traps shut had cost more than the mirror.

Fuckers.

"I'm not pulling my dick out," I retorted. "You have to do it."

Snickering, she reached between us, her heels digging into my ass as she forced herself upright so that she could settle on my lap.

When my dick was swinging in the breeze, she crooned, "You've got an erection."

I huffed. "You're wearing your graduation gear, a skirt with no panties underneath, and you're on my lap. What else is it going to be other than hard as fuck?"

Her grin was loaded with her delight—she loved it when I said shit like that. That was the thing though—it wasn't *shit.*

MC brought out a side of me that I didn't even know I possessed.

She made me softer in some regards, tougher in others.

I was the reason her mom hadn't attended the graduation ceremony today, for example.

Sin and I had paid the bitch a visit because we weren't about to allow her to spoil MC's day.

As for soft—well, the mirror and the bribes said it all, didn't they?

With her hand stroking my cock, she nuzzled her nose against mine, bringing me back to more important matters. "Digger?"

I hummed.

"I love you."

"I love you too," I rasped as I clutched at her ass and drew her deeper into me.

When my dick collided with her hot, slick pussy, I hissed and *felt* how bare she was.

I'd known this would get her hot, but with zero foreplay, she was drenched.

She whimpered, hair falling over her shoulders as her head rocked backward. Her hair was longer than ever, and I fucking loved it. All that strawberry blonde silk was a siren song I never wanted to stop listening to.

She leaned forward and pressed a kiss to my lips. "I love you," she whispered again.

I smirked. "I love you too, baby. Now, be a good girl and sit on my dick so that I can fuck you on my bike around the goddamn backyard."

Which was my compromise. As well as a reward for doing so goddamn spectacularly in school.

I felt her grin against my mouth, but with a hum, she wriggled her hips as she slipped me inside her. Both of us moaned as her pussy took its sweet time in taking every inch of me, just like always, and then, with us connected, I carefully leaned forward and started the engine.

"You hold the fuck on, okay? The bike does the moving for us," I warned, but I knew she was already gone. The vibrations from the engine had made her eyes dazed.

"F-Fuck, James," she sobbed as we rolled around the front of our new house.

Having sold off most of Murphy's assets, I'd managed to find us a nice spread in West Orange.

The perk of it was we (now) had a mirror above the bed, a walk-in closet, and a study for her, as well as a big yard.

I hadn't had this particular activity in mind when I'd seen the listing, but...

Who was I kidding?

I wanted to give her everything she craved, and if most of those cravings revolved around me, my dick, and going on runs with me, who was I to argue?

She was the perfect Old Lady.

Perfect.

In every fucking way.

My feet skimmed over the graveled yard as we rounded one corner of the house, and I kept a steady speed, not wanting to jar her when I couldn't really hold onto her like I wanted.

It killed my buzz, worrying about her safety, but my dick was helpless to the ever-tightening clutch of her cunt around me.

MaryCat had more of an exhibitionism kink than expected—*got it.*

When we went over a bump in the driveway, she cried out and her hands loosened around my neck.

"MC," I barked. "Tighten your hold on me or we stop."

"Don't stop!" She squirmed on my lap, hips rocking from side to side as her forehead ground into mine. "Fuck, this feels—"

I gritted my teeth when her pussy started pulling wicked moves around me, moves that she'd learned this year from a magazine and which she'd been tormenting me with ever since.

"Goddammit," I barked, cruising to a halt and planting my boots in the gravel so I could cup her face and kiss her how I fucking needed to.

As my tongue thrust into her mouth, she started to bounce on top of me. The engine was still running and with each 'bounce,' she moaned, telling me wordlessly how good this was making her feel.

"My good girl," I rumbled, pulling back. "*Summa cum laude.* Do you know how proud I am of you?"

Her cheeks, usually bright pink when we were like this, flushed red.

"Such a good fucking girl," I continued, not needing her to answer, just knowing how wild this made her. "When you walked on that stage, I thought to myself, she's mine. That beauty up there, she's all mine. My woman. My wife. My Old Lady. And your speech—everyone was looking at you. *Everyone.* But you flashed your hand around like a good girl, letting every fucker know you were taken." I grabbed said hand and pressed a kiss to her rings. "Who do you belong to, MaryCat?"

She mewled, "You. Always, always, you, James."

Grunting, I took her mouth again, and this time, slower than before, we rode around the driveway.

The vibrations seemed to intensify with how slow we were traveling, and her squirming sped up as she ground into me, fucking herself on me with the help of my hog.

"I-I-I—" She groaned. "I'm gonna c-come, James."

"Give it to me, baby. I want it. Give it to me like the good girl you are."

She released a sharp cry as she imploded. That was when I turned off my engine, and not giving a damn about my hog for the first time in my life, I straightened up, let it drop to the gravel, uncaring about the paint job, then strode toward the house.

She jerked with surprise with each step I took, and it had her orgasm continuing until the constant caress of her cunt around my cock started to drive me insane.

Pinning her to the wall beside the front door, I took what I needed and began fucking her against it.

Sobbing when I started to thrust into her fast, she surged past the first orgasm and slid straight into the second one.

My tongue fucked her mouth at the same time, swallowing those soft cries because they belonged to *me*, not our neighbors, and as I exploded inside her, as she held me in an endless clasp, her fingers tightening in my hair, her arms clutching at my shoulders, her legs clinging to my hips, she pulled away to whisper the golden words...

Words I'd never, ever tire of hearing spill from her lips: "I love you."

Fuck, I could never have known how much better that declaration would make this.

How it would be the cherry on the goddamn sundae to have her tell me that as she milked my dick of everything that I was.

But it was a bliss I'd been enjoying for months now, and one I never intended to be without again.

Sweating, overheated, wrung out, I pushed my forehead to hers. As I came, I growled, "I love you too, MaryCat. Always."

It was the truth.

The complicated, crazy, nonsensical truth.

I was a Sinner, and she was a Five Pointer, but together, we'd forged our own path.

And we always would—*got it?*

AUTHOR NOTE

Dear Reader,

Remember at the beginning when I said that this book had a hope-fulness to it that healed something in my heart?

Fingers crossed, you understand now. <3

Don't forget, in my Diva and Spoilers' groups, there'll be a bonus scene once FILTHY SINNER hits 500 reviews.

You can join both groups here:

www.facebook.com/groups/SerenaAkeroydsDivas

www.facebook.com/groups/SerenaAkeroydsTeaAndSpoilersRoom

Also, if you're looking for the crossover reading order, you can find it here:

FILTHY

FILTHY SINNER

NYX

LINK

FILTHY RICH

SIN

STEEL

FILTHY DARK

CRUZ
MAVERICK
FILTHY SEX
HAWK
FILTHY HOT
STORM
THE DON
THE LADY
FILTHY SECRET
REX
RACHEL
FILTHY KING
REVELATION BOOK ONE
REVELATION BOOK TWO
FILTHY LIES
FILTHY TRUTH

The Five Points' Mob Collection and The Dark & Dirty Sinners' MC series are both complete. As for The Valentini Family, there is one duet remaining that has yet to be announced.

Much love,

Serena

xo

FREE BOOK!

Don't forget to grab your free e-Book!
Secrets & Lies is now free!

Meg's love life was missing a spark until she discovered her need to be dominated. When her fiancé shared the same kink, she thought all her birthdays had come at once, and then she came to learn their relationship was one big fat lie.

Gabe has loved Meg for years, watching her from afar, and always wishing he'd been the one to date her first and not his brother. When he has the chance to have Meg in his bed—even better, tied to it—it's an opportunity he can't refuse.

With disastrous consequences.

Can Gabe make Meg realize she's the one woman he's always wanted? But once secrets and lies have wormed their way into a relationship, is it impossible to establish the firm base of trust needed between lovers, and more importantly, between sub and Sir…?

This story features orgasm control in a BDSM setting.
Secrets & Lies is now free!

CONNECT WITH SERENA

For the latest updates, be sure to check out my website!
But if you'd like to hang out with me and get to know me better, then
I'd love to see you in my Diva reader's group where you can find out
all the gossip on new releases as and when they happen. You can join
here: www.facebook.com/groups/SerenaAkeroydsDivas. Or you can
always PM or email me. I love to hear from you guys: serenaakeroyd@
gmail.com.

ABOUT THE AUTHOR

I'm a romance novelaholic and I won't touch a book unless I know there's a happy ending. This addiction is what made me craft stories that suit my voracious need for raunchy romance. I love twists and unexpected turns, and my novels all contain sexy guys, dark humor, and hot AF love scenes.

I write MF, menage, and reverse harem (also known as why choose romance,) in both contemporary and paranormal. Some of my stories are darker than others, but I can promise you one thing, you will always get the happy ending your heart needs!

—